Where the Garden Begins

J. Suthern Hicks

DEDICATION

Thank you to the heroes throughout
history who have sacrificed to keep us free.

Inquires can be made by contacting the author at
HumbleEntertainment@yahoo.com

Editor: Diane Bryan
Cover Design: Tatiana Minina
A Shophar So Good Book: www.shopharsogood.com

ISBN: 0997077808
ISBN-13: 978-0997077803

ACKNOWLEDGMENTS

A simple acknowledgment may not reveal the depth of my gratitude to all who helped me in this writing adventure, but hopefully the permanency of paper and ink will suffice for now.

Mara Magliarditi
Shauna Hill
John Davis
Gloria Davis
Kevin Forrest
Pastor Wade Mikels
Michele Suh
Diane Bryan

Where the Garden Begins

CONTENTS

CONTENTS

Chapter 1

A Sticky Beginning

One fussy bug's penchant for gossip and his ability to snoop around undetected is what helped set into motion a most unusual series of supernatural events. It began the night that he was summoned by the red fox to a meeting with the Council of Three.

Yes, it all started with a walking stick. Not the common hiking accessory used to assist walkers, but a rather delicate insect found primarily in forests. Its scientific name, a bit hard to pronounce, is derived from the Greek word meaning "apparition." Quite fitting for a bug that many of his neighbors thought to be impossibly nosey. This particular walking stick, who answered to the name Sticky, relished gossip, which caused his antennae to instinctively tilt whenever a juicy bit of news passed his way.

Sticky was considered to be the most persnickety walking stick to have ever inhabited the woods of Garland County. He also happened to look very much like a stick, a most efficient camouflage for eavesdropping. He was reddish brown, just a smidge over five inches long, and very thin. Sticky had no neck, making it rather difficult to detect at which end his head sat. His six long legs resembled those of a giant spider, and were perhaps what made others reluctant to touch him.

Choosing to keep their identities a complete mystery to all the creatures of the woods, the members of the highly respected Council of Three always meet under a new moon when the skies are darkest. They wanted Sticky to spy on the humans in the house beside the giant hickory tree—a bachelor named Henry Fray and his mother Azora. Sticky usually nosed around *despite* the wishes of others. To do it by request was quite new to him.

His assignment, if he chose to accept, was to learn the exact time of Henry's departure in the morning. Because of his fine-tuned antennae, Sticky picked up on vibrations better than most, and so he heard the Council of Three whispering something that they did not intend for him to hear:

"If these humans only had just a little faith there would be no need for Sticky to conduct this covert operation. None of us condone spying, but considerable energy has been expended to spark these supernatural events. It is paramount that we help cultivate faith among the unbelieving humans. The others are already in position, and there is no time to think of another plan. We need this insect's skills."

Sticky had never been popular with the other inhabitants of the woods, but that had more to do with his nocturnal nature than his prudish personality and gossipy temperament, or so he reasoned. He hoped that the Council's plan to use him would boost his likability factor with the locals. So, right there in front of the three most revered members of the community, he danced a six-legged jig and gleefully accepted their assignment.

Sticky wasted no time getting to the house and attaching himself to one of the window screens overlooking the living room. He was concentrating on his mission when he heard someone behind him trying to get his attention.

"Psst. Psst. Psst!"

Although he had obviously heard the voice, Sticky refused to take his eyes off the house. No, not for one second.

"Psst! Hey, Sticky, it's me," said a bug flying within a smidge of Sticky's head.

"Hush and be mute, Dauber. I don't want to miss anything," said Sticky with a pretentious British accent. His insistence on always speaking with an accent annoyed many of his neighbors. Very few around these parts, Sticky being no exception, had ever been out of the woods, let alone to another country. But because Sticky spent so much time near Henry and Azora's house, he overheard lots of television, and some of his favorite shows were of the British variety.

"Are they up yet? I don't see any lights on. Are they up? Are they up? Are they up?" asked Dauber as he repeatedly dive-bombed the dutiful eavesdropper.

"Stop buzzing around and pick a spot, will you?"

"Oh, fine," said Dauber.

No dirt dauber in the woods could hold a candle to Dauber's striking physique. He had a dark body, almost black, that could also appear to be the purest of reds in just the right amount of light. His blue wings, perhaps his most magnificent feature, were almost translucent.

If you gave him only a superficial glance, he could be mistaken for a common wasp. Upon closer inspection, however, his whole body resembled that of a sci-fi jet fighter. He had six sleek legs with race car yellow stripes; all were attached to his front end. He had a separate bulbous compartment in the rear that held his infamous weaponry.

Dauber had the look of a real life superhero.

Unfortunately for Dauber's social calendar, Sticky and the rest of the insects figured him to be more of a super villain than a superhero. Perhaps time would change his neighbors' preconceived notions, but regardless of their negative opinion of Dauber, everyone had volunteered to work together for the greater good.

The critters in the woods had set aside all their differences. They had labored tirelessly to orchestrate a chance encounter between Henry and a young gardener named Jimmy. The Council of Three knew that Jimmy had knowledge to share with Henry's family that could alter the course of many lives for the better. The timing had to be perfect, and therefore they had to know the precise second Henry would leave for his trip.

"Dauber, have you got your beastly part done yet?" asked Sticky.

"Of course I have. In super, phenomenal speed, I might add."

"Fancy that." Sticky rolled his bulging eyes.

"Easy for you to say. Do you know how much work goes into one of my meticulously crafted houses?"

"You mean one of your mud tombs?"

Anyone who has ever spent much time outdoors, where critters constantly struggle to survive, knows that dirt daubers capture their prey and place them into mud casings. Small insects, mostly spiders, are high on the list of dirt dauber delicacies. It's not a purely selfish act as these mud casings also house and nourish their tiny offspring.

"You say tomb, I say womb. Anyway, it takes a lot of work, and I am not even tired. So I thought I would come help you," said Dauber.

No matter what anyone had to say to the contrary, Dauber appreciated all the different personalities in the woods. An appreciation demonstrated by his willingness to lend a helping hand, especially to the needy or wounded. He once had brought Lady Lizard food for an entire week after she lost her tail.

If not for all the negative gossip about Dauber, perhaps the other insects would have known that he only captured the poisonous spiders that caused more harm than good. Dauber had inadvertently saved many lives in the woods, a fact that few would ever know. Unfortunately, they mostly regarded Dauber as a killer and thus avoided him whenever possible. This is why he tried so hard to prove himself loyal and worthy to others. Yes, Dauber's lonely life was most undeserved.

"How, pray tell, do you plan on helping me?" asked Sticky.

"As soon as you get word on the man's departure, I can fly over to let one of the birds know." Dauber flapped his wings just enough to make a buzzing sound.

"Fly, fly, fly! We all know you can blooming fly, Dauber. You're a wicked pilot and a fancy architect. You're great at everything."

"That's very kind of you to say, Sticky. I must admit that I do have exceptional instincts. I was born with them. The ability to do all these phenomenally fantabulous things I do was bestowed upon me by a most benevolent Creator."

"Is it instinctual to be so humble as well?"

"There is no need to be caustic, my fine friend. We are all bonding together here and doing our jobs to make the plan run smoothly. It just so happens that my part is larger than most. I can't help that. I would be more than happy for you to fly over and inform our feathery friends of the human's departure time, but you can't fly, can you?"

Without saying another word, Sticky lifted and tilted his head slightly to the left in order to hear any sounds that might be emanating from the living room. He hoped Dauber would take the hint and fly away.

"Don't you think you should be stationed at the other window?" asked Dauber. "I mean, don't most humans spend the better portion of the morning near their food storage containers?"

Choosing not to answer, Sticky tilted his head ever so slightly down and to the right. One might think him a trained agent for Scotland Yard just by the way he moved his tiny head. Sticky was no fool. The kitchen in this house had no table, and the table in the dining room sat adjacent to the living room. All the sound from the dining room to the living room could be heard from this window, but the same could not be said of the kitchen window.

Dauber, after another five minutes of nonstop chatter and buzzing, finally got the hint and lit quietly on a branch of a nearby boxwood shrub. He decided to groom his legs while waiting on word from Sticky. Grooming is serious business for a dirt dauber. One rarely had the luxury of free time to groom to satisfaction, so Dauber could not have been more pleased to have this opportunity. Unfortunately, Dauber only made it to his third leg before he noticed out of the corner of his compound eye that Sticky was excitedly motioning him over.

"Have you heard? What's the word? What's the word?" asked Dauber with his wings fluttering excitedly.

"Be still already," said Sticky. "All that buzzing around is making me dizzy!" With that, Dauber landed on the window screen only centimeters away from the walking stick.

"Well?" inquired Dauber.

"He has already had his coffee. He will be leaving any minute now. Go, and tell everyone to get ready. Chop chop!" Sticky spoke in the manner of Sir Arthur Wellesley, 1st Duke of Wellington, and arguably the greatest British General ever. The Duke had recently been profiled in a British documentary and quickly became one of Sticky's favorite nineteenth century commanders.

"*Any minute?*" asked a stunned Dauber. "I need more time than that! I need to inform the robin, so she can go tell the rabbit, and I need enough time to make it back to my nest in the tire before the man drives off. What in the woods have you been doing all this time? Why didn't you tell me sooner?" Dauber's antennae flinched repeatedly as if he were being shocked by a current of electricity.

"Well, I began motioning for you to come round when you finished licking your first leg. Then I screamed and hollered until you had finished slobbering all over your second leg. By the time you finished the blooming third, I became croaky and rather exhausted. You would have thought, with all those eyes in your head, you might have noticed me sooner."

"Lucky for us, my friend, I have increased my aerodynamics by at least twenty percent with that cleaning," said Dauber. "So hold on tight, cause I don't want to blow you off this screen when I depart."

"Just go," pleaded Sticky. Dauber flapped his wings and took off with lightning speed.

"Cheerio and Godspeed, ol' chap!" said Sticky, yawning. Only mere seconds passed before Sticky began to creep slowly down the screen onto the ruddy bricks below.

The sun had fully risen, and Sticky wanted to find a dark, quiet place in which to sleep. The last hours had been quite busy and tiring. He would undoubtedly sleep very well while dreaming of all the friends and neighbors who would stop by later that night to congratulate him for the awesome job he had done. Listening.

Chapter 2

A Rabbit's Hop
from Mile Marker 109

Dauber managed to inform the robin of Henry's impending departure in record time. The robin immediately took the shortcut over the trees to relay the information to the cutest little cottontail ever to have graced Garland County. The adorable baby rabbit would use her charms to distract Jimmy, an avid animal lover, and keep him from getting into his truck until the perfect time.

The little cottontail hoped to entertain Jimmy by hopping just out of his reach, teasing her admirer, and then quickly bouncing away. She had even practiced what appeared to be a backwards somersault to really get his attention. With her help, Henry and Jimmy would meet at just the right moment in time. Nothing, it has been said, is by chance.

The difficulty would be for Dauber to get back to the garage and into Henry's Ford pickup truck before it started moving. Dauber, with the assistance of a few of his female relatives (as they are usually the architects of his species), had spent the entire night making a mud casing around the air inlet on the passenger side tire of the truck.

The casing had to be snug enough to keep Dauber from falling out while the tire spun. Any other critter would have been unable to withstand the centrifugal force, but Dauber would use his mud hut to hold him securely as he slowly deflated the tire. The only catch was that he needed to be inside before the truck began moving.

If the truck started moving without Dauber already in position, the whole plan and everyone's hard work would be for naught. Unfortunately, Henry had already backed out of the driveway. Dauber's little heart raced faster than he ever thought possible, but his commitment to completing his role in the operation never wavered.

He was a top athlete, the best in the woods. He had trained his entire life for a day such as this, and he refused to go down without a fight. He flew faster than he ever had before, and yet he felt motionless, frozen in time. Dauber's whole body burned, and he thought there surely must be flames shooting out his backside.

Dauber had to project where the truck would be in the ten seconds it would take him to reach the tire. The trajectory had to be perfect. If he underestimated the speed of the vehicle, any possibility of getting inside the hubcap would be missed. If he overestimated, he could be smashed to bits. Moving vehicles were not very forgiving to his kind.

Dauber put all negativity out of his mind and set the flight pattern the best he could. He closed his eyes and said a prayer as he pushed through the air with all his might. He flapped his wings so fast they disappeared. He looked naked, as if he had no wings at all. With his head down, legs back, and antennae speedily making calculations, he truly resembled a superhero.

Dauber opened his eyes mere milliseconds before the moment of impact. Much to his amazement and gratitude, his antennae were spot on. He turned his body ever so slightly to dodge a spinning spoke on the hubcap and coasted inside. He barely missed latching onto the mud casing, but managed to grab a bit of road tar only inches away on a lug nut.

The force of the rotations wrecked havoc on Dauber's spatial awareness. He would need to crawl the rest of the way to his mud lodgings. There was no possibility of flying or jumping without getting battered by the spokes, or being tossed out of the wheel well altogether. To make matters worse, he could not tell up from down.

As he thought of what to do next, the truck came to a screeching halt. The powerful jolt from the sudden stop caused dust to fly everywhere. Dauber barely managed to keep from being catapulted out of the hubcap, but he did not waste a moment to gather his wits. Within seconds he found the mud casing and crawled safely inside. He took a deep breath and exhaled a sigh of relief.

"Home sweet home," Dauber said aloud. He looked out at the street and noticed something red and furry jump into the woods. The red fox perhaps? How did she know of his predicament? Regardless, Dauber could not have been more thankful for her help. Had she not stopped the pickup truck, he would have failed to accomplish his task.

The wheel began rolling again. Dauber hastily applied pressure on the elm twig he had placed in the air valve the night before. The position of the twig had been perfectly situated so it would not need much pressure; just the slightest push by Dauber. The air escaped easily. Everything had been timed so the tire would become completely flat somewhere between the post office and highway marker 109.

"Whew, that sure smells stale." Dauber's antennae were

blown backwards by the force of the hissing air. Dauber looked like he had just spent two weeks fighting in a war. His right wing had a crimp in it. He had lost several grippers (similar to toes) in the road tar. He had a slight corneal abrasion on his left eye that would more than likely heal in a few days.

But unknown to Dauber at that moment was the sad fact that he would never again be the fastest insect in the woods. His wing would never be perfect again. Many sacrifices must be made in order for destiny to be fulfilled. Sacrifices that only a select few would ever know about.

Dauber would have done it all over again, no doubt, because when the hissing air ceased to flow, the truck rolled to a complete stop not more than a rabbit's hop away from mile marker 109. Dauber did the impossible. Yes, he had a lot of help, but this destiny-changing moment never would have occurred without the heroic efforts of this simple little dirt dauber.

Why was this event so important? Well, if it had not been for that precise moment in history, Jimmy the gardener would never have met Henry, the man in the Ford pickup truck. Jimmy thought he had simply helped a fellow traveler change a tire. But the ramifications of the meeting between the two men would echo throughout eternity.

This supposed "chance encounter," as it would come to be known years later, was the pivotal point in the beginning of a new period of enlightenment. When Seth and Melissa, the nephew and niece of Henry, found themselves on the most profound of supernatural adventures, it would be because of what Sticky and Dauber had accomplished by orchestrating this meeting—just a rabbit's hop away from mile marker 109.

Jimmy himself had spent considerable time on a supernatural journey of sorts. Through his passion for understanding the divine nature of God, he had developed great knowledge concerning the seemingly incongruous relationship between faith and science. His knowledge and passion for this relationship is what eventually helped propel Seth and Melissa on a discovery of their own.

Much respect should be paid to Dauber for his accomplishments that day in the woods. Instead of reacting in fear of being stung by dirt daubers, perhaps folks should appreciate all the diversity nature has to offer. Unlike the common wasp, dirt daubers very rarely pursue and sting. They are solitary creatures that do not answer to kings or queens. They do the jobs they were created to do, and they raise their young well.

Hopefully, history will be kind to the dirt dauber, and all will remember this story in their honor. For had it not been for the courage and strength of one tiny creature with translucent wings, this tale might have never taken place.

Chapter 3

Planting Seeds

The sound of water falling from the sky usually resonated well with Azora's love of nature, but the water coming from the sprinklers sounded like rapid weapons fire as it hit the living room window. Had it not been for this persistent noise assaulting her eardrums, Azora would have undoubtedly slept past her typical thirty-minute catnap.

The fact that her son neglected to reset the sprinkler box timer to a more accommodating schedule irritated Azora. He knew she always took a nap at noon, and he also knew she would have preferred to water the old fashioned way. Henry meant well, she supposed. He simply wanted to give her one less chore to do. The year before, Azora had developed so much pain in her back from pulling the hose around the front and back yards that she could hardly pick the fruits of her labor.

Azora always found plenty to keep her busy. Though unwise and unnecessary to push herself so hard, she insisted on proving to the world that she could outdo folks half her age. She was a young eighty-two, with a sound mind and a fairly cooperative body, but she knew that her remaining years were quickly speeding by, and nothing could stop or slow down the inevitable.

Most of her friends had already passed away. Funerals were as commonplace as a Sunday sermon. Her closest friend, Stella, died of a strange skin disease. She could not remember the name of the malady, but the visual would never leave her memory.

Her favorite sister died of breast cancer at the young age of sixty-five. Her late husband succumbed to a heart attack even younger—at thirty-seven. Azora, however, seldom thought about all the loss she had endured. "Why belabor the images of death when there is so much life to be lived," she often said. But despite her strong exterior, she could get very lonely at times.

Living with Henry, her middle-aged son, worked out well for both of them. Azora felt that she was the one who actually benefited the most from the arrangement. She loved living in the country away from all the crowds and noise, and she would never have been able to afford such a nice home on her own.

Henry traveled a lot, and Azora kept an eye on things for him when he was gone. She also tended the garden, cooked most of the meals, and cleaned. Henry never requested or expected anything from his mother, but she insisted on doing these chores. When she offered, he refused to take any money from her to help pay bills. He knew her funds were quite meager.

Azora was not the best housekeeper, but she kept the small three bedroom, one bath house tidy enough. The kitchen, where she spent many hours each day, took only minutes to clean. Other than not being able to open the fridge and oven at the same time, the tiny kitchen suited Azora's needs just fine.

Henry did not pay too much attention to the interior of his house, preferring instead to focus on the outside. He was quite proud of his latest accomplishment. When the well went dry the past summer, he had successfully connected the city water lines to the house. Both Azora and Henry detested the idea of chlorinated water, so as soon as the well refilled, Henry would be switching the pipes back.

Azora, like her son, also preferred chores that took her outside the house. Her true passion rested a few hundred feet from the back porch—her garden. Azora absolutely cherished anything that would spring up out of the dirt. Her garden brought her the most joy when it created food that she could put in a pan to fry or a pot to boil. She truly loved the entire process of watching and helping things grow.

She insisted that each new growing season be endowed with trusted seeds, preferably from plants she herself had previously harvested. Azora knew that the best tomatoes came from non-hybrid plants. Hybrids are cross-pollinated to reduce the amount of acidity, among other reputed improvements. Lower acidity apparently reduces the probability of people getting canker sores. Canker sores or not, according to Azora, nothing tasted better than an old fashioned home grown "tomater."

Her love of tradition and the past did not stop with tomatoes. Azora relished anything that brought back memories of her youth. This sentiment permeated every aspect of her life, but none more than those things affiliated with the church. The last preacher who tried to convince her to sing modern church songs lost a parishioner. She knew she could not win the battle of the ages, but she refused to abandon the tried and true.

With her catnap over, the yard soaked by the sprinklers, and the house clean enough to meet her standards, what else needed to be done?

"Where is that calendar?" Azora asked, with no one to hear

but the spider hanging in the corner. Even if the spider wanted to answer, he did not know. He was far too busy weaving webs to pay attention to the occupant below.

As she rummaged through the old pine desk, she spotted the calendar. Even though Azora routinely wrote a lot of information on the big squares, like what day she planted the cucumbers, trash day, and when her grandkids were coming to visit, everyone knew she bought the calendars because of the pretty pictures. She had always loved to paste pictures from old calendars into scrapbooks with her grandchildren, and this particular calendar featured dogwood trees. As Azora admired the beautiful trees and their blossoms, she noticed her handwriting on one of the upcoming dates.

"Oh, my Lord, the kids are comin' for a visit on Friday. I forgot all about it! I've got to get out in that garden and plant those tomatoes before they arrive. I can't let the plantin' wait a whole 'nother week...unless I could get them to help me. For land's sake, Azora, you know kids today don't like workin' none." Before she could get to the back door to look for her shovel, the doorbell rang.

"Who on earth could that be?" She briefly considered ignoring the bell, but she knew whomever it was would find their way around to the back yard and interrupt her planting. So, with a sigh, she raised her voice and gave a shout. "I'm a comin'!"

Azora opened the door in a most unwelcoming fashion. Standing before her was a rather tall young man who looked to be in his early twenties. He wore a brown Stetson hat and held a pair of worn leather work gloves.

"Do I know you?" asked Azora.

"No, ma'am. I'm here to take care of your yard. My name is Jimmy." Jimmy extended his arm, but noticed that his hand was not received with the normal southern charm he had come to expect.

"My yard? What do you mean? *I* take care of my yard. I didn't call anyone to do any work. Now if you don't kindly back up and excuse yourself, I'm goin' to call the police, young man. I may look slow, but my gun ain't so far away that I need to prove otherwise."

Trying hard not to laugh, Jimmy backed up a few steps and closed the screen door. "I'm sorry. I thought your son told you I was coming today. Henry hired me to do the mowin' and other yard work. He told me you would let me know what else needs to be done. I didn't mean to startle you."

Azora's scowl softened somewhat and her brow lowered to half-mast. "You didn't startle me. One can't be too careful these days. How do I know this ain't some kind of a scam?"

"If it helps any, I could come back after you talk to your son."

"No, that won't be necessary. When I turned the cable man away last week I thought my son was going to send me to a nursin' home! You would have thought missin' an episode of his favorite TV show was the end of the world." Azora pushed the screen door open. "Come on in. I'll get you a glass of cold water."

Jimmy stood still. "I would love a glass of water, but I shouldn't come inside. Too dirty and sweaty."

"Well, suit yourself." She began to close the screen door. "There's a shovel next to the water spigot. Grab it, and meet me around back in the vegetable garden."

"I don't think your son intended for me to dig a garden, ma'am."

"Are you gettin' paid by the hour?"

"Yes, ma'am."

"Then grab the shovel, and grab a couple more hours, unless you want to see me die of heat stroke attemptin' to turn over that hard dirt. I need to get my tomatoes planted." She closed the door on Jimmy. "Good Lord, have mercy! What does an old woman have to do to get a little help around here?" she mumbled to herself.

Before going into the kitchen, Azora stopped to sneak a peek at Jimmy from the living room window. She watched him shake his head, and then push the lawnmower out of the driveway.

"What a nice young man," she thought. She changed her mind about the water, opting to pour the good stuff for him instead. Her homemade lemonade. After all, she wanted to make a positive first impression. If she played her cards right, she might never have to dig another hole again.

Jimmy had decided to move the lawnmower in case an emergency vehicle needed access to the driveway. The last time he saw someone this old he was at his grandmother's funeral. Jimmy had never spent much time with his grandparents, so older people made him feel a bit awkward.

Jimmy's parents had split up on his first day of third grade. He remembered it well because it was the last time he saw his mother. After his mother left, his father was under great stress because he had to work additional hours to help pay the bills. They barely saw each other, and Jimmy became a very lonely child. Whether he was right or wrong, Jimmy had decided that his father was to blame for his mother leaving, and this caused even more distance in their relationship. He never really felt loved by his earthly parents and that, perhaps more than anything, made him wrestle with his relationship with God at a young age.

Although not religious himself, Jimmy's father often took his son to church, where Jimmy eventually found answers to his basic questions about God. Even though faith came fairly easy to him, he never stopped asking the hard questions.

Jimmy knew that with time, study, and prayer, the God of

the Bible would become the Father he always longed for. More than an abstract impersonal entity up in the sky, God was someone Jimmy could rely on. He trusted the promises of the Bible and lived according to the Word of God as best he could.

Jimmy never hesitated to ask a stranger if they knew about Jesus. Most people seemed not to mind when Jimmy approached them with theological questions. Perhaps it was the non-judgmental manner in which he discussed the subject, or maybe it was the innocent look in his eyes. Either way, people usually responded with grace and candor.

"Well," Jimmy said to himself, "maybe I was put here to introduce this old ornery woman to Jesus. It couldn't hurt to dig a few holes while I'm at it. Hmmm, that doesn't sound so good."

After moving the lawn mower, he quickly located and entered the gate to the rear yard. He took in the vast landscape before him. To the right there were wildflowers under native pines and dogwood trees. Rocks lined numerous flowerbeds. Dirt paths wound around and under majestic oak trees. The more he looked, the more beautiful the surroundings became.

Based on a quick glance, it might appear that the landscape had just evolved into its current state. But upon closer examination, it was evident that someone had worked very hard to create and maintain such a beautiful yard. Everything, as wild as it looked, had its place.

Perhaps the most inviting feature was an old wooden bench resting under the shade of a large weeping willow tree. The bench looked sturdy enough to seat at least two people comfortably. A cushion, which had seen better days, still managed to offer its services, as did a small round wrought iron table. Jimmy could not tell if anyone ever used them.

Around the trunk of the tree were purple, green, and orange coleus plants. The limbs of the willow glimmered in the sun like a green waterfall. They were trimmed just high enough for a man of average height to clear, which meant Jimmy had to bend down a bit.

To the left of the willow tree there was a vegetable garden. The garden had been completely enclosed by chicken wire on the top and sides, which probably kept most of the birds and other varmints out. Though the enclosure did not fit in with the otherwise natural surroundings, it had been crafted well.

As Jimmy continued walking towards the vegetable garden, he realized he had forgotten to grab the shovel. He immediately doubled back toward the house, only to be abruptly stopped by Azora.

"Take a seat there under the tree and we'll discuss the plan."

Jimmy nodded but kept walking. "I'm just going to grab the shovel real quick."

Azora motioned with her hand for him to take a seat on the bench. "The shovel can wait. I need to rest after that long walk from the house."

Jimmy walked back to the bench and sat like a child scolded by his teacher. "Whatever you say."

"Here, I brought you some lemonade. Made it myself. Put a little sprig of mint in there too." She smiled as she handed him the glass and joined him on the bench. "It's nice to make your acquaintance, Jimmy. My name's Azora."

"I know, your son told me. That's quite an unusual name." Jimmy took a drink of the lemonade. He tried his best to conceal a grimace caused by the overly tart flavor. "I don't think I've ever heard that name before."

"That's because I'm probably the only Azora in the whole world. I looked it up once in a book of names, to no avail."

"How did your parents come up with that?"

"Just made it up, or so my mama said. I had a sister named Flossie. She died as a baby. I guess she just made that name up too. Who knows, people didn't go on about such things back then. You don't look like you're from around here."

"I am. Born and raised. But my parents were from Cuba. Thank you for the lemonade...it's very...lemony."

"Cuba! Well, ain't that somethin'. Don't believe I ever met a real live Cuban before."

Jimmy laughed. "Actually, I'm one hundred percent American. My parents were Cuban."

Azora quickly interrupted. "It's all the same difference. You're Cuban and American. Cuban-American, I guess. My people have been around these hills so long there ain't no tellin' where they came from originally. But then, I guess we all really came from the same place, didn't we? Adam and Eve."

"You're a believer?"

"In the Bible? Well, of course I am. All my people believed in the good Lord. It's this new crop I'm worried about."

"New crop?" asked Jimmy.

"The young kids today. My grandkids in particular. They think the Bible is a fairytale."

"Why would they think that, with all the historical and scientific evidence, not to mention the manuscript evidence? It's one thing to say you don't believe, but another entirely to say the Bible is a fairytale."

Azora looked a little perplexed. "Evidence? What's evidence got to do with anything? That's why they call it faith, young man. Maybe more people would believe if everyone wasn't so worried about proof and evidence! Good Lord, have mercy!"

"Do you remember that verse where it says to love God with all your heart, soul, and mind? God doesn't expect us just to have blind faith. I suppose it's fine if we do, but God certainly doesn't command or even suggest such a thing."

"I suppose you are going to sit here and tell me what God wants. I've read the Bible backwards and forwards. I know what

God says in the Bible," said Azora.

Jimmy stood up and looked out over the garden. "Okay, what about understanding what God says in His other book, the book of nature?"

Azora pointed to the back porch. "The shovel is up that away. You might want to go get it before you dig yourself a hole down here with your mouth that you can't get out of. There is only one Holy book, young man. I don't go for no cults or false idols. If you want to worship nature, or be a witch, or a voodoo Cuban man, you go right ahead, but don't go bringin' that garbage here on my land!"

"Ma'am, I agree with you. I only follow Jesus. Just Jesus. No other gods. But if you have indeed read your Bible backwards and forwards, you will recall the verse that says 'The heavens declare the glory of God, and the firmament shows His handiwork.'"

"Firmament? You mean dirt?"

Jimmy smiled. "Yes, the earth itself declares the Glory of God. On it lays the record book of nature—the other revelation God has given that tells us about Him."

"Well, on that note, there's a bunch of firmament that needs to be dug up over there underneath that chicken wire. If you wouldn't mind turning the compost over and tilling the soil a bit, I would be much obliged. And you can call me Azora instead of ma'am. How old do you think I am, anyway?"

"Not a day over fifty, I would guess."

"If you are a Christian, you ain't a good one, lyin' like that!"

"I would be happy to till the soil for you. Would you like me to plant those tomatoes as well?"

Azora slowly rose from the bench. Jimmy stood with her and watched every movement in case she got a little wobbly. She resented Jimmy's obvious caution, but said nothing as she pulled her blouse down over her hips.

She took a few steps towards the house, holding her head high, and then stopped and turned around to look at Jimmy. "No, thank you. I do the planting around here. You just get the soil ready." Azora headed for the house, purposefully quickening her pace. She wanted Jimmy to witness just how much strength and vitality she still had.

Jimmy could not help but be impressed by the speed and agility of the eighty-two year old. He lifted his glass of lemonade in a toast to his new friend. "Here's to you, Azora!" He remained in place for a few moments while contemplating the challenges before him. He did not know what would be harder, the dirt he had to till, or discussing religion with a mind that had been set in its ways for so many years.

Jimmy's concern was actually more about Azora's family. He knew that God honored faith, and Azora seemed to have plenty of it. He just hoped she would consider that God made everyone differently, and some people, like her grandchildren, for instance, had questions that deserved well-reasoned answers. No worry, he thought. He had plenty of time to consider how to converse with the octogenarian while he dug holes for her tomatoes.

Chapter 4

The Family Arrives

At six in the morning Azora could usually be found reading in bed, in-between her catnaps. Since her schedule had always been quite predictable, it startled the critters in the woods to hear her rushing around the house so early. But she could not contain her excitement. She had not seen Seth and Melissa, her two youngest grandchildren, in over a year. Her other family members visited even less.

When any of her grandchildren did manage to visit, whatever the hour or season, she cherished every moment. She related better to children and young people; they were far less judgmental than their older counterparts, and more willing to play games, listen to stories, and explore nature.

Life had offered far too many trials when Azora's kids were young. She had no husband, little money, and even less time to spend doing fun things with them. Consequently, her relationships with most of her children were strained, to say the least.

The grandchildren, unlike their parents, only remembered Azora's better qualities. Catching crawdads in the creek, playing Chinese checkers, and doing crafts together were just a few of their fond memories. Yes, the grandchildren were her chance to create a positive legacy. A legacy that would, hopefully, bring tears of sadness upon her death, rather than complaints about all the things she had done wrong.

"It's already after six, where does the time fly?" said Azora. She could find no real reason to be out of bed so early. Nothing needed to be prepared in advance of her family's arrival, and the house looked tidy enough. They usually ate out, or a simple meal would be fixed at the house, most of which would barely be picked at by the guests.

Azora never seemed to notice that most people did not care for her cooking. She took great pride in experimenting and creating unusual food combinations. The year before, she had made a casserole dish consisting of sauerkraut, hot dog bits, baked beans, and cheddar cheese. The concoction would never be given a name, but it would remain forever etched in the memories of all who had dinner that night.

Azora's notion that she "was not long for this world," as she put it, played a prominent role in her anxiety regarding the spiritual destiny of her grandchildren. With each successive visit from them, Azora became more manipulative in her mission to convert the siblings. "I wonder if I could get those kids to go to church with me tomorrow. Perhaps if I faked a fainting spell they would come along out of guilt," she thought.

When the grandkids were younger they did not mind going to church. As they got older, however, it became a grueling chore to wrangle them up on Sunday morning. Melissa, the seventeen-year-old, would still come along, but only to appease her grandmother. She could not have cared less about God, as evidenced by her hollowed out Bible containing an ever rotating assortment of teen romance novels. But anything was better than nothing, or so Azora thought.

The beautiful spring day resembled a Matisse painting, with warm smears of yellow, pink, and creamy blue filling the sky. White billowy clouds floated above, flowers bloomed below, and the sun added just the right touch of warmth to it all. Even so, Azora thought she might stay inside and read a bit.

After preparing for company, a little slumber in her favorite chair might restore some much-needed vigor. With her latest book open and resting on her chest, she carefully eased back into the worn, cracked leather chair, and closed her eyes.

She began to dream the moment her eyes closed. Not a dream from deep sleep, but a daydream of wishful thinking. Azora imagined being in heaven. She was with her husband again after having been apart for many decades. Her children loved her without any memories of all the wrongs she had done. In the dreamy perfection of God's world there was also a garden for her to tend, just as in her earthly home. It was exquisite, filled with the most brilliant colors she had ever seen. There were no words in the waking world to adequately describe its incredible beauty.

The birds landed on her shoulder while she tied fragrant jasmine to a beautifully carved trellis made of gold. Not a hard, cold gold, but a gold that felt warm to the touch and glowed with the radiance of a thousand angels. There was no need to rest. No need to sit a spell or fan the heat away.

The sun never went down and the garden went on as far as the eye could see. There were so many surprises to be discovered; an endless array of never before seen plants and flowers. There were tiny, adorable creatures busily buzzing among them. Azora smiled faintly as she fell into a deeper sleep where the dreams were even more amazing, but rarely remembered upon awakening.

The three knocks on the front door had not landed very hard, though loud enough to wake Azora. Her brow remained wrinkled until she got her bearings. She pushed herself up by the arms of the old library chair, wiped the spittle from the corners of her mouth, and then absentmindedly pulled her blouse over a waist that had seen its share of extra pounds over the years. Just before opening the door she said a quick prayer that all would go well.

"Hello. Hello. How was the drive? I was just about to put a pot of tea on the stove. Come in. Come in," said Azora.

"Hi, Mom. You look lovely," said Bethany. She was a simple beauty, with a slight figure, and a lovely smile that could not be matched in sincerity and warmth. Her brown hair was naturally highlighted by the sun, and cascaded in lazy waves just below her shoulders. She often hesitated before speaking, just in case someone else had something to say, and her distinctively deep voice possessed a cadence that revealed a vulnerability that made everyone immediately trust her.

She was the youngest of Azora's children and was known as the peacekeeper of the family. But it was Bethany, more so than her siblings, who had legitimate reasons to harbor deep resentment towards their mother. Yet she was the one who stayed in contact with Azora the most.

Azora glanced behind Bethany and asked, "Where are the kids?"

"Oh, they're coming. Seth is parking the car and Melissa is telling him how to do it. Is Henry home this weekend?"

"No, it's just us. He'll be gone for a couple of weeks. He's helping set up a new store out of state, some place in the middle of the country." Henry was often away on long business trips.

Bethany carried a bag of groceries into the kitchen. "The house looks great. I just brought a few things for breakfast and snacks. I thought we could eat out for dinner. No need cooking big meals." Bethany desperately hoped her mom would not insist on making dinner. She could not stomach another culinary experiment.

"I'll tell you what, sweetie, if you and the kids promise to go to church with me Sunday morning, you can have your pick of any restaurant in town."

Bethany briefly hesitated before responding, in order to choose her words carefully. "Mom, that sounds wonderful, but I can't promise that the kids will go. They're young adults now. I can't force them to go if they don't want to."

"Of course you can. They still live under your roof, don't they?"

"Mom, that's not how it works today. I can demand they go to school or do the chores, but they are old enough to make their own spiritual choices."

"Well then, maybe you should have thought of that when they were younger, before they were too old. Children need a foundation."

"Let's not argue about this right off the bat, Mom. I'll tell you what. You feel free to ask the kids whatever you want, and you can deal with how they respond."

"Fine, that's just what I'll do then."

The front door slammed open and Melissa ran straight into the kitchen. Melissa, unlike her older brother, was a poster child for what over-indulgent parenting had done to her generation. She wore clothes that were devoid of any modesty. Black fingernail polish and dark red lipstick were staples in her tiny black purse. Her naturally blonde hair had not been seen in six months. It was covered in the deepest black drugstore hair dye available. However, for reasons unknown even to herself, Melissa always attempted to be the perfect little girl of yesteryear for her grandmother.

Melissa tenderly wrapped her arms around Azora's waist and

kissed her lightly on the cheek. "Grandma, can I have the guest room this time? Seth is an idiot and idiots should sleep on sofas!"

"There is no guest room, sweetie. Your uncle took the bed out and made that room into his office. There's a hide-a-bed in there though, and you kids are welcome to fight over that. And it's not nice to call your brother names."

Melissa pouted, more out of habit than conviction. "A hide-a-bed? That's just like a sofa, only worse."

Bethany turned Melissa toward the overnight bags left at the door. "Pick up the luggage, put them in the office slash guest room, and come back in here and give your grandmother a proper greeting."

"Why do I always have to do the heavy lifting? Why can't Seth do it? Gosh!" Melissa threw her arms up in the air and sashayed over to the bags. She contemplated picking up all three, but opted to just grab two instead, mumbling to herself, "Dingle berry can get his own bag." She dramatically walked down the hallway to the guest room, office, or whatever it had been transformed into.

Along the way she noticed the old familiar portraits on the wall. Her great grandmother, whom she had never met, resided at the top, followed below by at least one picture of each of Melissa's cousins. Melissa always seemed to dwell on the fact that there were more pictures of Aunt Martha's kids than of Seth and her. For many years, she figured that Aunt Martha just sent more pictures. But lately she had the feeling that Grandma simply liked them better. After all, they had never missed a Sunday at church in their lives. She thought they must be more similar to Grandma than she and Seth.

Melissa loved her grandmother more than she would ever be able to express. As a child, when no other adults would take her seriously, Grandma Azora always listened. It was more than just an adult appeasing a child, Azora really respected Melissa's thoughts. She also played games and worked on projects with her granddaughter, something Melissa's own parents rarely found the time to do. Grandma Azora became an oasis in a world of condescending adults too busy to care about a young girl's grandiose hopes and dreams.

Religion, however, would eventually become the one area where grandmother and granddaughter would find division. Melissa did not know if she believed in God, but she would never say so out loud, at least not to her grandmother. When she was younger, she would even go to the little church in town and sit next to Azora and sing the hymns she had heard since childhood. She knew how to play the game and make her grandmother happy.

Melissa had never found a reason to believe. To her, God was an idea developed by men to contain the imagination and freedom of an out of control society. She understood the benefits of encouraging simpletons and would-be criminals to find a higher power, a God that makes people obey rules and regulations, and gives them a purpose to their lives. This undoubtedly helps keep crime rates lower, and makes for better family structures. Melissa, nonetheless, did not take the time to thoroughly contemplate the idea of God. She would much rather think about herself...and boys.

To the chagrin of her parents, Melissa had always been a flirtatious girl. Her first job was as the neighborhood physician, at the age of six. She routinely lined up all the little boys on the playground to feel their foreheads and check their pulses. Her intentions were completely innocent—until middle school, where on the first day of sixth grade she tried to pull Ricky, a cute little red-headed boy, into the janitor's closet for a kiss.

Perhaps Melissa was more bark than bite, but making sure she remained innocent had become a full-time job for her mother and father. They would not allow her to date until high school, and then only with adult supervision, which did not bode well for Melissa's popularity.

"I get the bedroom!" Seth yelled. He rushed through the front door, kicking off his shoes while running past his mother and grandmother. Seth personified the typical college boy, minus the drinking, fraternities, and girls. Unlike his sister, he took school seriously and refused to get distracted by extracurricular activities.

He had just begun his second year of college. His major had not yet been decided, but he wavered between biology and chemistry, a fact that had not gone unnoticed by his sister, who also loved those subjects. At first glance, one might assume he studied accounting or political science. He dressed, as Melissa often put it, like a dentist at a piano recital.

"Stop right there, young man." Bethany put her arms out to block Seth's attempt to lay claim to the guest bedroom. "Give your grandmother a hug."

"Hi, Grandma. It's really good to see you. You're looking great!"

Azora welcomed Seth's embrace. "Well, it's good to see you, too. Your ol' Grandma's not feelin' too well these days though. It would be nice to have a young man to help around the house."

"I'm in college now, Grandma. I don't even help Mom around the house anymore. Right, Mom?"

Bethany rolled her eyes. "Yeah, that's why you don't help around the house. Because you're in college."

"Ah, Mom, please. I helped Dad paint the house last summer. Hey, Grandma, is there water in the creek?"

"I reckon. Rained cats and dogs the other day. The creek should be full of water."

Seth smiled. "Great. I'm going to catch a whole load of

crawdads tomorrow."

"Tomorrow?" Azora scowled. "Tomorrow is the Lord's day, Seth! You're going to church with us, aren't you?"

"Seriously? Gosh, Grandma, what's the point? If I go, it's just to make you happy."

"And what is so bad about making your Grandma happy?" asked Bethany.

"More importantly, who gets the bed?" answered Seth.

Bethany tugged his ear. "No one. There is no spare bed. It's the sofa. Or a hide-a-bed in the guest room which is now an office."

"Seriously? I don't think Uncle Henry likes visitors very much. But, that's fine, I'll take the sofa. Melissa can have the hide-a-bed." Without waiting for a reply, Seth rushed out of the kitchen and down the hall. "Is there still a bathroom?"

Azora yelled after him, "Make sure and put the seat back down when you're finished." Shaking her head in the direction of Bethany, she said, "He always leaves the seat up."

"Well, don't look at me. Is that my fault too?"

Seth, unlike Melissa, actually liked the idea of church and God. But when he started his college science courses and learned that the earth was about 4.5 billion years old, and that the universe was almost fourteen billion years old, he had a hard time wrapping his head around the belief that God created the earth in six days, and that the earth was only about ten thousand years old.

He had heard that some Christians believed in an old universe, like science taught, but then whose interpretation was correct? It seemed to Seth that most people just randomly picked what they thought was literal or just a parable. "Perhaps in another thousand years Christians will figure it all out," Seth thought. Until then, he was content to remain in favor of science and facts, rather than religion and faith.

"Hurry up and get out of there! I gotta go!" Melissa beat on the bathroom door hard enough to crack her black nail polish.

"I'll be finished in a second. Stop pounding on the door. Gosh!" Seth had finished using the bathroom several minutes earlier, but he was not about to let Melissa in without making her suffer as long as possible. Seth knew he was too old to continue with juvenile sibling rivalry, but he also figured there would never be enough opportunities to get back at Melissa for all the trouble she caused him when they were kids. How does one get revenge on a sister that announced to the entire school lunchroom, using the Public Address System, that her eleven-year-old big brother still believed in Santa Claus? Seth would forever be known to his classmates as "Santa's little helper."

When Seth finally opened the bathroom door, Melissa pushed her way through without waiting for him to exit. "Did Grandma already hit you up to go to church?" she asked him.

"Of course, and you owe me ten bucks." There had been an ongoing bet over the years on who Grandma would mention church to first.

"Dang!" Melissa snapped her fingers. Quickly changing the subject she asked, "Are my roots turning?" Her attempts to contort her neck for a better view in the mirror were unsuccessful.

"Yes, they're turning ugly. You really need to stop dipping your head into tar pits."

She pushed Seth away. "Shut up!" She continued to dig around her scalp to assess the damage. "I think Grandma has given up on my salvation. She must think I've gone to the dark side with all this black I'm wearing."

"Haven't you?"

"Very funny! Why should I believe in God? What has He ever done for me?"

Seth laughed. "Assuming there is a God, I would say He has

done everything for you. If you're not going to believe in God or a higher power, you should at least have a reason why, Melissa."

"You should at least have a reason why, Melissa," she repeated, mockingly. "What's *your* reason for not believing? Teach me, brother dear."

Seth opened the bathroom door wider, but before walking out he snidely remarked, "Trust me, your little pea brain wouldn't understand. It involves science."

Melissa began mocking him again. "It involves science...it involves science...How do you involve science? That doesn't make any sense. You involve people and you get involved with cute boys, but you do not ever involve science! Stupid!"

Seth headed down the hall, and Melissa went about the more important things in life—grooming herself.

Seth entered his Uncle Henry's office and locked the door behind him. He plopped down on the sofa, took out his phone, and scrolled through his contact list. He came to the newest number added and smiled as he touched the phone's screen.

"Hi, Audrey? This is Seth from class. Natural History. Yeah, the guy that sits right behind you. Your number? Oh, well, I guess I should apologize, but last week I heard you give your number to the girl next to you, so I put it in my phone just in case there was some emergency or something. You know, in case class was cancelled. I figured I could give you a call and save you the long walk all the way across campus. How did I know you had a long walk? I see you walk sometimes, and I know you have Political Science before Natural History. Creepy? Yeah...I guess you're right."

Seth put the phone down and sighed. Lucky for him there was no cell phone coverage inside his uncle's house, which made it a great place to make pretend phone calls. Whatever time Seth saved by not getting involved with girls, he lost by pretending to be involved with girls. His lack of social interaction had more to do with his insecurities than his focus on his studies. Seth hoped that someday, when the timing was right, he would meet the girl of his dreams, and she would be very happy that he had her phone number.

As Seth contemplated his imaginary girlfriend, everyone else in the house slowly drifted to their own private worlds. Melissa remained in the bathroom, where she would undoubtedly spend the better part of the evening, contemplating her roots. Bethany unpacked her suitcase, thankful for something to keep her busy, and appreciating a temporary reprieve from her mother's barrage of questions.

Bethany loved Azora, but it always took her a few hours to adjust to being in the same house with her. Therefore, she took her time unpacking. Neither she nor her mother cared much about the latest fashions, so though small, her mother's closet had plenty of space for Bethany to hang her own clothing. Bethany detested shopping and remained content with just the basics. Azora felt similarly—as long as she had enough clothes to last a week before having to do laundry, she was satisfied with the size of her wardrobe.

Azora went out to water the plants on the back patio, but got distracted and found herself all the way down by the creek looking at dogwood blooms. She picked a flower off a low hanging branch as she recalled the legend of the dogwood.

The legend holds that in Jesus' time its timbers were chosen for the cross and Christ made a promise that still holds true:

"Never again shall the dogwood grow strong enough to be used. Slender and twisted, it shall grow blossoms like the cross. With blood stained blossoms marked in brown, the center represents a thorny crown. All who see will remember Me, crucified on a cross from the dogwood tree."

She said a prayer for her grandchildren and gave thanks to God for all the good things in her life. No matter how routine this visit seemed at the moment, none of them were prepared for the events that were about to take place. The prayers of the righteous availeth much, but God's plans are often much different than man's. Or even a grandmother's.

Chapter 5

Lights Out

Azora knew young folks enjoyed sleeping late, and this fact rarely bothered her. But this morning she felt extremely annoyed. She was quite certain that everyone was hiding in bed in order to avoid church. Even Bethany could still be found curled up in a ball under the covers.

The clock approached eight, and the church service commenced at ten sharp. The downright obviousness of the ploy to avoid church was eating Azora to the bone. Not knowing what else to do, she decided to make breakfast. She had no idea when anyone would get out of bed, but the smell of food would undoubtedly speed up the process. Although it was well known that Azora lacked ordinary culinary skills, she could always manage to scramble up a tasty batch of biscuits and gravy.

She filled an iron skillet with bacon. After the strips of pork belly released enough fat to equal about two tablespoons, she poured it into another pan, and quickly stirred in a little flour.

She slowly whisked in enough milk to turn the mixture into a thick gravy. If no one was looking, she liked to add a little butter.

The aromatic offering had more impact than an alarm clock, and would wake the soundest of sleepers. Unlike her other meals, no white lies were necessary when it came to complimenting Azora's biscuits and gravy.

Azora had no clue what anyone thought of her cooking. She enjoyed her homemade meals and figured everyone else felt the same. This misconception did not arise out of ignorance on Azora's part, but out of naïveté. During her childhood, most people were grateful for whatever food was placed in front of them.

Azora's kinfolk were so poor that at one point, during the Great Depression, the only place they could find to set up residence was at the cost of displacing a bunch of hens from their coop. With the sawdust and manure shoveled out, and a few additional boards nailed up in the right places, the hen house became a home. The coop was not exactly draft free, but it kept the rain out and the kids in. If Azora's parents were ashamed of their newly acquired accommodations, she would never have noticed. Truly, the thought of someone not appreciating every single blessing placed in front of them was beyond Azora's comprehension.

While stirring the gravy, she thought of ways to wheedle the kids into going to church without causing too much hullabaloo. She had tried guilt in the past, but by far her most successful ploy had been to elicit sympathy. The year she alluded to the possibility that she might have cancer brought her much success. Her doctor really did want her to come in for an exam, so she did not exactly lie. She really could have had cancer. At any rate, her manipulations worked. Everyone went to church that April morning. But it was never wise to use the same tactic twice. There must be some trickery she could use that she had not considered before.

She had to think of something foolproof because this morning's sermon should not be missed. The pastor was going to preach on hell. Yes, hell. If past sermons on love, faith, and salvation had not won these three over, surely a good old fashioned sermon on the pit of misery and anguish would wake them out of the depths of their denial.

Bethany was the first guest to rise and shine. Perhaps shine was a bit optimistic, but she gave her mother a hug, and made the morning coffee. "The biscuits and gravy smell so good Mom, but you shouldn't have gone to the trouble."

"No trouble at all," Azora said as she continued stirring. "Do you reckon the children might be gettin' up out of bed anytime soon?"

"I suppose I could go wrangle them up. Weekends are the only time they get to sleep late."

"Who are you kiddin'?" Azora said wryly.

Bethany yelled down the hall, "Seth, Melissa...wake up, get up...breakfast is almost ready." She turned toward her mom and asked, "So, have you figured out a way to get them to go to church this morning?"

"No. I gave up. They can do as they will. They've come all the way down to visit their grandmother, but if they'd rather sleep late and not participate in traditional family outings—then so be it!"

Seth entered the kitchen, yawned, and wiped the sleep from his eyes. "Good morning. What's for breakfast, Grandma?"

"Biscuits and gravy. Is your sister up yet?"

"She's taking a shower. She'll be out in a few minutes. I don't remember her missing a home cooked breakfast...ever." Seth attempted to open the oven door to look in on the biscuits, but Bethany closed it before he could get the door all the way down.

"Go set the table," said Bethany. She handed him four plates and then gave him a gentle push towards the dining room table. After setting the plates down, Seth went back for utensils and napkins.

Azora took the biscuits out of the oven and placed them on the counter while Bethany finished up with her mother's gravy. Azora lovingly placed the biscuits in a bowl, and then put a clean dish towel over the top to keep them warm. Bethany poured the gravy into an orange Pyrex dish while Azora finished frying the rest of the bacon. All the while, Azora tried to think up a last ditch effort to get the kids to Sunday service. She would never give up, despite what she might say to the contrary.

Seth finished setting the table, and Melissa, true to his prediction, had already seated herself, eagerly waiting to be served breakfast. Azora placed the bacon on the table and joined Melissa. Bethany attempted to set the biscuits and gravy down, but she couldn't maneuver the dishes in her hands. She glanced at Melissa for help, but Melissa, as usual, was in her own world.

Bethany turned to Seth with a look of exasperation. "Seth! Could I get some help here?" He quickly came to her rescue, averting a messy accident.

Bethany stood there for a moment looking at her children. Maybe she should have forced them to go to church more often, she thought. She knew they were decent kids, but perhaps they would have become less self-absorbed.

Azora motioned for Bethany to sit. She grabbed her daughter's hand and said, "Let's give thanks." The four of them bowed their heads as Azora continued, "Dear Lord, thank you for this food we are about to receive. Thank you for all the blessings of food, shelter, family, and health. May we all give you the attention and time you deserve by whatever means possible. All the praise and glory to You. Amen."

Melissa quickly reached out for the biscuits, barely beating Seth's attempt to score first. "Aren't there any eggs?" asked Melissa.

"Yes, ma'am, they're in the refrigerator. The pan is still on the stove. Help yourself," Bethany answered.

"Yeah, right." Melissa rolled her eyes as she broke her biscuits into small pieces.

Azora abruptly got up from the table. "Please excuse me, I need to go to the restroom." She made her way to the bathroom door, and when she was sure no one was paying attention, she continued quickly down the hall to the circuit breaker box. She had come up with the idea the night before, but because it had inherent weaknesses, she decided to only go with it if she could not think of anything better. Needless to say, she had not thought of anything better.

She quietly removed the picture that hung over the fuse box, and slowly opened the grey metal door, not making a sound. Inside she found the main breaker and pushed it down, trying hard to avoid any loud clicks. The hall went dark, but just enough light seeped in from the bedroom windows to allow her to close the breaker box and re-hang the picture. She knew the loss of electrical power would not immediately cause alarm because there would be plenty of light coming in from the windows.

"Well, it happened again," Azora said as she walked back into the dining room.

"What's that, Mom?" asked Bethany.

"We've lost all our electricity. It happens from time to time out here in the country."

"Should we call the department of power services?" asked Seth.

Azora casually sat down and answered matter-of-factly, "It won't do any good, they won't come out on a Sunday unless it's an emergency, and it usually comes back on in a few hours anyway. Besides, the phones won't work either."

Melissa interrupted, "Oh, my gosh. I forgot to charge my phone last night. I won't be able to play any games. What am I supposed to do until the power comes back on?"

"Just watch TV," answered Seth sarcastically.

"But they don't have cable out here!" Melissa glared at Seth.

"Oh, right. Because cable works without electricity. You're so brilliant." Seth looked at his mom with a hint of desperation. "I really needed to get going on my term paper, but the battery on my computer will only last about an hour."

Azora rose from the table and stated rather diplomatically, "Well, the three of you can wander around here in the darkness while I attend Sunday services, or perhaps you might want to come with me and get truly enlightened."

Seth ran both hands through his hair. "It's almost like divine intervention. If there is a God, this looks like something He would have done to get me to go to church with you."

"That's not a bad idea. There won't be anything else to do around here until the electricity comes back on. You two might as well come along with us," said Bethany.

Seth responded, throwing up his arms. "Alright, alright, I'll go to church. Mission accomplished everybody...but you may not like the end result."

Melissa chimed in, "Yeah, sometimes God's greatest gifts are unanswered prayers."

Bethany was astonished. "Wow, I didn't realize how painful this would be for the two of you. It's just church for Pete's sake!"

Seth glanced at his grandmother and then back to his mother. "Mom, do you realize what a laughing stock I would be as a biology major believing in a book that says the earth was created in only seven days?"

"Six. He rested on the seventh," Azora added.

"That's right. It's six. I forgot. But that's even worse, Grandma. *Six days*? That's a joke in the scientific community, and I don't want to be a hypocrite sitting in church all the while thinking what a crock it all is."

Melissa picked up her plate and headed towards the sink. "Why couldn't it be a miracle? If God is real, and He was smart enough to create people and animals and dirt and all that stuff, then why couldn't He create a planet in six or seven days?"

Bethany interrupted, "Besides, not all the Bible is literal, Seth. Maybe you need to take some literature courses with all your science classes. Isn't that what a university is supposed to do, make you well-rounded?"

"Mom, Christians like Grandma say that God created the universe in six days. But then why would God make it look like the earth is over four billion years old? It doesn't make any sense."

Azora responded. "Melissa hit the nail on the head...it was a miracle, plain and simple. God created the universe in six days and on the seventh he rested. That's today. So let's give it a rest and stop arguing. Put on what you're going to wear. We're leavin' in thirty minutes."

"Well, there you have it," said Seth.

Melissa found the whole idea of going to church under these circumstances a bit more palatable. Seth was more or less being forced to do something he hated, and Melissa would be there to witness the torture. She also had the added benefit of watching the cute church boys stumble over her.

Seth, on the other hand, dreaded the whole day. Attending church with a grandparent was a concept he could understand and theoretically enjoy, but Azora was not a typical grandparent. Bethany could surely attest to the times Azora would not allow her to leave the table for hours unless she ate her Brussels sprouts, which to this day still made her gag. Azora always took extreme measures to make her case.

The problem was not just that Azora expected everyone to go to church; she expected them to believe every word the pastor spoke. And their leaving the sanctuary believing everything the pastor said was still not enough for Azora. She passively demanded that everyone discuss the finer points of the sermon on the drive home or at dinner. And God forbid that anyone should have a discouraging word. The proposition proved impossible.

Nonetheless, despite the manipulative paths Azora often took in order to get her way, she could be fun and loving. After all, the kids came to see their grandmother by their own choice. They may have been tricked into attending a Sunday sermon, but no one had to twist their arms to get them to Grandma's house. At any rate, Azora was getting her way. Everyone was going to church. Her prayers were answered. Sort of.

Chapter 6

Dinner, Fire and Brimstone

Getting everyone to agree on the same restaurant was almost, not quite, as hard as getting them to go to church. In Azora's infinite wisdom, she let the restaurant wars remain between the kids. After a little back and forth, they ended up agreeing on Mexican food, but then spent ten more minutes arguing about which Mexican restaurant had the best cheese dip. Azora could not have cared less, as long as chiles rellenos were on the menu (mild peppers battered with egg, stuffed with cheese, and lightly fried).

Jose's won their patronage after Bethany gave the deciding vote. Once seated, the conversation quickly became an awkward combination of silence and triviality. It was obvious to all, including Azora, that no one wanted to talk about the sermon they had been tricked into attending that morning.

Seth had to be very selective with his words because he knew that one wrong move could give his grandmother an opening to start her own sermon. So, as far as he was concerned, silence was golden.

Melissa picked up on Seth's avoidance tactic during the chips and salsa, and although she preferred not to discuss such a boring topic as religion, she relished hearing her brother try to worm his way out of confrontation. She smiled as she thought about how to instigate an argument without giving herself away as a purposeful initiator.

"Grandma, I have to say, it was really special to spend the day with you," said Melissa.

"Well, thank you, sweetie. It warms my soul to hear you say that."

Bethany raised an eyebrow at Melissa's sweet tone of voice, suspicious of her sincerity. She turned to Azora. "Mom, Henry was telling me he was thinking about hiring someone to do the yard work. Did he find anyone?"

"As a matter of fact, a young man came by the other day, very nice Cuban fellow. I kept him so busy with the garden that he didn't have any time left for the yard, so he's comin' back again tomorrow."

"Cuban? Really?" asked Melissa.

"You better tell him to keep his shirt on, Grandma. With Melissa and her hormones running around the house, someone might get hurt," said Seth.

Melissa quickly shot back. "So, Grandma, I absolutely loved the sermon this morning. I think the concept of hell is so important to understand. Don't you, Seth?"

Seth glared at Melissa, then glanced at his mom for help.

Bethany tried her best to divert the conversation back to safer topics. "How are your green chilies, Mom? I'm so glad they were in season. We all know how much you love your chiles rellenos." Bethany shot a look over to Melissa, but Melissa did not acknowledge her mother as she continued on her mission to divide and conquer.

"Yes, hell is certainly a hard topic to cover, but I think as hell goes, the pastor did a hell of a job getting his point across," said Melissa.

"And what would that point have been, dear sister?" Seth asked, unable to stop himself. No matter how much smarter Seth thought he was, his sister would always know how to push his buttons.

Being the youngest in the family was hard for Melissa, especially because she felt the need to be so outspoken. She constantly struggled to get attention and always felt as if no one understood her.

"I, for one, think that a good God would not have a place like hell, but rather would simply make evil people nonexistent upon their death," Melissa said.

Azora responded, "Of course there is a hell. The Bible talks more about hell than heaven."

"How can you prove it either way? There may be a hell and there may be nothing after we die. The point is, we won't really know until we die," said Seth.

"Hogwash!" said Azora.

Yet again trying to save the dinner conversation, Bethany chimed in, "Perhaps you are *all* correct."

Azora quickly responded. "What kind of God would that be? Just lettin' people pick and choose the afterlife willy-nilly? Why in the world would He have ever had the Good Book written in the first place if it didn't mean what it said?"

"Exactly. Why? There are so many contradictions in the Bible, especially with the creation account," said Seth.

"What do you mean?" asked Bethany.

"It's like I said before. A lot of Christians believe the planet is only about ten thousand years old. I can't go any farther into the Bible until that question is resolved. Exactly how old is the earth and what was the timeline for everything like plants and animals? If you can't give solid reasoning and answers for God's own description of the creation of the universe then why should I believe anything else the Bible has to say about hell and the afterlife?"

"There are no contradictions in the Bible," Melissa said. She was obviously trying to gain bonus points from her grandmother, while at the same time pushing Seth's buttons.

Seth responded, "Of course there are. Take Genesis Chapter One for example. It talks about there being light, but then later on talks about the sun being created. That is a contradiction. How can you have light on a planet before the sun even exists? It makes no sense."

Azora, flustered, responded abruptly, "Well then, you have obviously never heard of God's second book."

"God's second book?" asked Bethany, a little stunned.

"Of course. It's called the record book of nature."

"What are you talking about, Grandma? I've never heard of that book," said Seth.

"Well, it's not written down, silly boy! Every good Christian knows about God's other revelation." Azora nervously knocked over her glass of tea.

Everyone at the table became very uncomfortable, except for Melissa who could not have hoped for more. Bethany and Seth exchanged looks as they soaked up the spill with napkins. Bethany tried to change the subject, but Azora was so upset she just stared at her plate with pursed lips and folded arms.

Azora could not believe what had come out of her own mouth. She could not think of anything else to say, so she had just blurted out the first thing that came to mind. Of course, she did not have the slightest clue about God's "other book," or how it fit into the discussion, but she remembered Jimmy had mentioned it the day before.

"Like I said, every good Christian should know about God's

other revelation. But I for one am too exhausted to continue on with young know-it-alls. My heart might just stop beatin' right here at this table. In fact, I can feel the palpitations. I'm palpitatin'!"

"I'm sorry, Grandma, I didn't mean to get you upset," said Seth.

"Oh, I'm not upset. I just don't have the energy to explain such a complicated subject, but I know someone who does."

"The pastor?" asked Bethany.

"No, no, no...Pastors can't be bothered with such things. They have the sick to tend to, and young lovers to marry."

"Then who, Grandma?" asked Melissa.

"The new lawn man, that's who. He knows all about the Bible and he'll be over tomorrow to contend with all of you doubtin' Thomases."

"Uh, I've got to work on my term paper tomorrow and..."

Azora interrupted Seth. "You will sit down and ask every one of your blasphemous questions, and then you will report back to me with what you learned."

Melissa beamed. She was absolutely overjoyed with the result of the conversation, and could not help but let out a giggle.

Azora stared Melissa straight in the eyes and said, "I hope you have a couple of free hours too, Missy, because you'll be listenin' in, and you'll be as quiet as a mouse peein' on cotton!"

As the dinner progressed to dessert, the conversation turned to more neutral topics. They discussed gardening, school, and Bethany's vacation plans with her husband Patrick. Azora did not quite know what had happened. Should she be upset, excited, or just plain confused? She realized, in fact, that she was entrusting her family's Biblical instruction to a man she met only a few days ago—a man that could very well be crazy, or worse, a cult member.

Yes, Azora should have felt very concerned and confused.

However, for some reason, she felt a sense of peace. She, in fact, did not know Jimmy much better than a stranger on the street, but there was something about him that made her feel at ease. Even if what he had to say proved to be wrong, his words could not be any worse than what the kids already believed, or did not believe.

She indeed was taking a chance, but with chance comes hope. Besides, Azora would not leave everything up to Jimmy. She would spend the better part of the night in prayer. As she had for all their lives, she would continue to pray that her grandchildren would discover the truth, no matter what sneaky methods she needed to employ to increase the odds of it happening.

Chapter 7

A Thousand Eyes

Azora's day usually began at six, but she had spent a very restless night thinking about how she would implement her plan, and by five she had given up any hope of getting more sleep. She took a shower, and was fully dressed before the rooster's crow.

In order for her plan to work, she would need to speak to Jimmy in private, away from the children. Unfortunately, she did not know the exact time he would arrive to do the yard work. Because she did not want anyone to think she might be ignorant about something in the Bible, she wanted to clarify a few things with Jimmy first. If the kids found out that their grandmother had no clue concerning all this talk about what nature had to do with God, she would lose her credibility, or so she thought. She had to appear to be knowledgeable about all Jimmy had to say.

Azora had much wisdom, and she knew the Bible, but she needed to get a grasp on this new subject of dual revelation in order to feel more confident. She did not dwell on the possibility that everything Jimmy might say could turn out to be utter nonsense. For the present, she simply hoped he would spark in her grandchildren a curiosity about the Bible. She put their fate into God's hands, and believed everything would turn out for the greater good.

The early hour made it too difficult to work outside in her garden because the sun had not yet fully risen. Azora decided to stay inside and do some light housekeeping. The unusual morning commotion piqued the interest of the critters in the woods. They were all very accustomed to the set schedules of not only themselves, but also the people in the house.

Sticky had already attached himself to the living room window in order to eavesdrop. And Dauber was busily buzzing around reporting Sticky's findings to any and all interested parties.

"What's going on in there?" asked Dauber.

"Not a blooming thing, really," said Sticky. "She's cleaning a bit."

"Cleaning, you say? Well something is certainly awry. Have you ever known the wrinkly one to clean before the sunrise?" Dauber rested on the brick ledge below the window.

"Something is most definitely amiss."

"How very exciting. Most exciting, my friend. Who should we tell first?"

"Who is going to be awake at this hour, Dauber? I'm quite surprised to see you here."

Dauber grimaced slightly, raised his antennae, and pointed towards the front yard. "Sticky, look behind you."

Sticky turned his head cautiously, not knowing what he would find. Behind him were a thousand tiny, glowing, glittering eyeballs. Everyone in the woods must have been staring directly at Sticky and Dauber. There were the frogs, the crickets, the mice, and the raccoon family from over the dale. Birds of every shape and size were perched on tree limbs or fluttering in place, including hummers who rarely ventured out before the sun had a chance to warm the air.

There were grasshoppers, beetles, opossums, and way too many squirrels. Mama squirrel had a brood last year that no one particularly cared for because they took far more than their fair share of pears, peaches, and figs. The lovely honey bees were buzzing all around, the bumble bees were, well, bumbling, and the bunnies were unusually motionless. The sea of watchful eyes went as far as Sticky could see, even past the road and into the woods.

Sticky slowly tilted his head down toward Dauber and whispered in a stern tone, "This extravaganza wouldn't have anything to do with your busybody wings, now would it?"

"Hey, you're the one with your nose up to the glass where it doesn't belong. Besides, this is an important day. Rumors have been going around that the time is near. Hummer the hummingbird told long-legged Sally—the tarantula who lives in the ancient tree off the old road—that the sky above the tree was changing. Not the entire sky, mind you, just the area above the old tree. I'm telling you, Sticky, this is good news, and everyone is excited beyond belief."

"Well, fancy that! I'm happy to hear the news myself, about the sky and all. I've heard tales of old that it all begins with the wind and the sky. But what if one of the humans came out here and witnessed all this?"

"You worry too much, Sticky. Relax and let everyone enjoy the moment. It's not every day that prophesy is fulfilled."

His voice changed. "Dauber, you ought not to speak of such things. We no more know if this is actual prophecy, or just a foreshadowing." Just then, they heard a crash in the house that made everyone in the yard freeze. As they all remained motionless, barely breathing, as quiet as any creature could possibly be, Sticky turned his antennae back to the house.

Azora was much too nervous to be cooking, as evidenced by her fumbling fingers. After she had swept the broken glass into the dust pan and disposed of it, she found a few ripe grapefruits and cut them in half. She put them in green and orange Pyrex bowls, and set them on the dining room table. She made sure to put the sugar out as well. Even though the fruit was as sweet as a honeycomb, she knew the young ones would still want to add sugar.

The kitchen clock read seven, yet Jimmy still had not arrived. Bethany had showered earlier than usual, but the kids were still fast asleep. Azora found herself relieved, for the first time ever, that the younger generation rarely woke up at a reasonable hour.

The table had been set and so had her plan. She put on her garden apron and wide brim hat. She did not intend to do any work outside, of course. The costume simply helped her ruse to nab Jimmy before anyone noticed he had arrived. She placed her Bible in her apron pocket, poured some tea into a traveling mug, and walked out the front door.

Other than one lone bunny hopping across the road, there were no signs of the visitors who had only moments before scattered and scurried like rain drops on a windshield. Azora retrieved a lawn chair from inside the garage. She had no idea when Jimmy might arrive, but assumed he would try to beat the noonday heat.

In the meantime, Azora intended to scour the Bible in search of something that might mention a lost book of the Bible. Before she got past the concordance, however, she fell into a sweet slumber in the morning breeze. Forty-five minutes later she awoke to the sound of a truck pulling into the driveway. Azora quickly pushed the hair out of her face, and wiped any possible drool from her chin.

Jimmy did not notice Azora right away, which she used to her advantage. She preferred he did not know she was waiting for him. That would give him too much power, she thought. Instead, she wanted to casually bring up dual revelation to him, as though it was nothing more than an afterthought to her. She knew that once the conversation began, he would be unstoppable, as most people are when talking about their passions. Azora moved a bit past the garage just in sight of Jimmy's truck, and turned her back, waiting for him to step out.

After locating his work gloves and Stetson, Jimmy exited the truck, slamming the door. Azora let out an overly demonstrative yelp of surprise.

"You scared the livin' tar out of me, Jimmy!" She clasped her hand close to her chest.

"Oh, I'm so sorry, Mrs. Fray. I didn't see you there. I certainly didn't mean to startle you."

"Well, it's not your fault, I guess. I just came out here to see about the fig tree. For some reason it didn't do so well last year. I think the ants got to it."

"I can put some dust around it if you like," said Jimmy.

"Oh, don't you worry about that, I got it covered. What would God think about you killin' his little ants anyway, with you worshippin' nature and all?"

"Excuse me?"

"The last time we spoke you mentioned you studied God's other book. The book of nature. I thought perhaps that book might prohibit you from killin' insects."

"First of all, I wasn't planning on killing anything. I was simply going to put some pepper dust around the tree to discourage the ants from coming around. Secondly, I think you misunderstood me. I don't follow any other book but the Bible itself. The record book of nature is only a way of describing God's other revelation to mankind."

"Other revelation?"

"Yes. You know, there are many verses that talk about God's creation, revealing his Glory."

"There are?"

"Sure. There's Psalm 8, Romans 1:20, and a few others. I'm sure you could come up with a few of your own if you thought about it long enough, or if you looked for them when you read the Bible."

"Really? I'm just a little confused. You know what? I have an idea. My grandson loves to talk about science and nature and perhaps if you told all this to him, he could then explain it better to me."

"Are you kidding? I would love to talk with your grandson. But I don't mind talking with you more, as well. I have all the time in the world."

"That's so sweet of you, but you might as well kill two birds with one stone, right?"

"That's an ironic choice of words considering how this conversation started. Just let me know when your grandson will be here, and I'll be happy to make a special trip back." Jimmy began to unload the mower, but Azora put her hand on his shoulder to slow him down.

"Oh, no need to get the mower out, he's here now. That is, if you don't mind."

"Well, I was supposed to come back today and finish the yard. I'm not sure your son would think too much of me if I didn't get the yard work done."

"You have more important work to do at this moment. The Lord's work. You let *me* worry about the yard." Azora smiled.

Jimmy shrugged his shoulders as he considered what Azora had to say. He already knew that he would not waste an opportunity to share the Gospel, at any cost—even his job. He pushed the mower into the bed of the truck and closed the tailgate. Azora was correct in her assumption that sharing the Word of God was Jimmy's primary passion. He lived to tell the Good News and nothing gave him more joy.

Heavenly pursuits had only become a priority a few years ago. Before that, Jimmy had seen his share of trials and tribulations. He had been arrested two times by age seventeen for breaking into houses. Jimmy's father pretty much gave up on him after his second arrest. And then just before his eighteenth birthday he disappeared for two days. The entire town thought he had run away from home. When they found him, he claimed not to remember anything.

Fortunately, his life began to turn around soon after that. When he became a Christian. But no matter how many good things he did as a Christian, he knew people would never forget about his past. Only time and evidence of change would heal those wounds.

Chapter 8

The Record Book of Nature

Azora led Jimmy into the house and poured him a cup of coffee from the fresh pot that Bethany had just made. The kids had already showered and were in the process of getting ready for the day. The plan looked like it just might work. Azora only had to shuffle the kids in Jimmy's direction, spark a bit of controversy, and the rest would be history.

But what would be controversial enough to entice Seth to give up a day of homework to discuss religion? Azora could not help but once again question the wisdom of her plan. She started to feel dizzy from all the doubts flooding her mind. What if Jimmy was in fact a member of a cult? What if Seth believed Jimmy, then decided to drop out of school, move to Wyoming, and become a follower of some crazy, gun-toting army of zealots?

"Oh, what am I doing?" mumbled Azora.

But there was no turning back now. Things were in motion, and besides, Seth did not believe anything about the Bible at this point anyway. Perhaps the conversation would give him an incentive to study the Bible, and question his lack of faith in it.

Azora knew that some of the greatest men of the Bible struggled with belief. Saul, later known as Paul, once killed Christians, but later became a believer. Thomas, also known as "doubting Thomas," did not fully believe until he actually witnessed the resurrected Christ. Even Peter, a disciple of Christ and founder of the church, had doubts. But all these men had the benefit of actually seeing evidence with their own eyes. Seth would probably not be so fortunate.

There is a verse in Romans that refers to faith coming from hearing the Good News about Christ. Since Azora did not think Seth would actually see an angel or the resurrected Lord, she hoped something he heard from Jimmy might spark an interest. If only Seth would keep inquiring, the answers would surely come. This might be her last chance to bring Seth, and perhaps Melissa, into a better understanding of God.

Bethany brought a tiny ceramic creamer in the shape of a razorback pig over to Jimmy who had seated himself on the sofa near the entry. "I thought you might want some milk for your coffee." She placed the cream on the coffee table in front of Jimmy. "So...have you actually ever been to Cuba?"

"No, my father would not approve. Castro was very unkind to his family."

Azora shouted from the kitchen, "Cuba shmuba. Who cares about Cuba. Jimmy is as American as apple pie, Bethany."

"Mom, I was just interested in finding out about where Jimmy is from."

"He's from America, Beth." Azora walked back into the living room. She waved Bethany away from Jimmy with her free hand. "I'm so sorry, Jimmy. My family has not been around the world much."

"Mom, what are you talking about?"

Bethany was interrupted by Melissa, who instantly eyed Jimmy and made an entrance worthy of someone receiving an Academy Award.

"Hi! My name is Melissa. And you are?"

"I'm Jimmy, nice to meet you." Jimmy extended his hand.

"Don't be so formal. We're all family here," said Melissa. She leaned over and gave him a polite hug that lasted a little longer than anyone in the room was comfortable with, especially Jimmy.

"My mother's correct. We haven't been around the world much," Bethany said, shaking her head.

Seth came into the living room lugging his homework. His hair was still wet from showering. "Oh, excuse me, I didn't know you had company, Grandma. I was just going to do a little studying. I'll go sit in the office and do it."

"Seth, this is Jimmy. He's a scientist," said Azora. Jimmy looked confused, but he did not have time to make a correction before Seth responded.

"Cool. I'm studying biology myself. What's your area of expertise?"

"Actually, I'm not a scientist. I've been taking some college courses..."

Azora quickly interrupted before Jimmy had a chance to further diminish his qualifications. "You don't have to hold a degree to be scientific. I bet you that Jimmy here knows more about the earth than any professor you have at that college you attend."

"I doubt that, Mrs. Fray, but you're very kind," said Jimmy.

"Who cares about science and all that crap. Let's find out more about our guest," said Melissa.

"Watch that foul mouth of yours, young lady! Tell them what you study, Jimmy," said Azora.

"Well, I've been taking courses related to astronomy."

"Astronomy. See there, Seth. That's a complicated subject, astronomy," said Azora.

"I'm not an astronomer by any means. But I have been studying for a couple of years," added Jimmy.

Bethany asked, "What got you interested in astronomy, Jimmy?"

Azora could not have hoped for anything more. The race was on. She need not say another word, but of course she would. She could not help herself. But this time she had enough insight not to interrupt until all the doubting Thomases were thoroughly hooked. Azora crossed over to the recliner and sat down with a sense of victory and relief. She had done her part. The rest would be up to the good Lord above.

Jimmy continued. "You might find it odd, but I got interested in astronomy because of the Bible."

"The Bible!" Melissa's eyes opened wide, and her mouth dropped open.

"Melissa, let the man get a complete sentence out of his mouth before you commence to gyrating into the conversation," said Bethany. "Jimmy, please continue."

"Yes, the Bible. I had all sorts of questions about the age of the universe and how long people have been on planet earth, but the Bible seemed to raise more questions than answers—or so I thought."

"Exactly," said Seth.

"Ironically, I found that good science actually affirmed what the Bible has been saying for thousands of years. And it all starts with the Big Bang."

"You mean you agree with the Big Bang Theory?" asked Seth.

"Yes, but it's more fact than theory at this point. And the Bible was the first and only religious book to mention it. In Genesis it says 'In the beginning.'"

"In the beginning *what?*" asked Melissa.

"It goes on to say much more. The important thing is that the Bible states there was a beginning. A beginning of everything: space, matter, energy, and even time. You see, until very recently, most scientists believed that the universe was eternal, that there was no beginning. Secular scholars once laughed at the Bible because it stated there was a beginning. However, now we know the Bible was correct. The Big Bang theory actually agrees with the Bible in the assertion that everything had a beginning."

"I don't get why that's even important. I mean, who cares?" said Melissa.

"It's important because if the Bible and science don't agree, we have a problem. If we have a correct interpretation of the Bible and a correct interpretation of nature, both should agree. After all, all truth comes from God," Jimmy said.

"Wow, you are so smart." Melissa did not bother to hide her sudden infatuation for this young man she had just met.

"I agree," said Seth. "If the Bible is scientifically inaccurate then it's pretty much bogus. But Christians try to say the planet is only thousands of years old—and that's just crazy."

"Spirituality is based on faith, and faith includes miracles and divine intervention," said Bethany. "We can't possibly expect to understand everything in the Bible in scientific terms."

"But Mom, why would God make the earth look like it's billions of years old if it were only thousands? There's so much evidence that the earth has been here for billions of years. Yet we're told we're just supposed to ignore this, and believe that God performed a miracle to make scientists think the world is billions of years old, when it's actually only a fraction of that. It feels more like a lie to me."

"Oooh, Seth called God a liar!" Melissa glanced over at her grandmother, but did not get a reaction.

Surprisingly, Azora had not yet uttered a sound. Even more surprising, no one had noticed her unusually quiet demeanor. She wanted to speak up for the God that she knew, but this time she felt the need to simply listen. This time she would consider another perspective. Maybe later, after some serious contemplation, she might offer her own insight, but until then, her mouth would remain tightly closed, and her ears wide open. She could see that Seth, Melissa, and Bethany were very interested in what Jimmy had to say. Well, maybe Melissa had more interest in Jimmy's appearance than his intellect, Azora thought, but at least she was listening to him. That was an excellent start.

Jimmy continued. "Perhaps Seth would be right if in fact the earth was only thousands of years old, but nowhere in the Bible does it say that. In fact, it wasn't until about three hundred years ago that some in the church began teaching a young earth perspective. Before that, the age of the earth wasn't really an issue."

"Why would the church teach that the earth was so young if the Bible never said it?" asked Bethany.

Jimmy answered, "We have to remember that the Bible is not a scientific journal, or a book meant to teach every aspect of human existence. The Bible is, after all, a book with a divine purpose of revealing aspects about our Creator and His creation. This historical book tells of God's plan for us, and the means by which that plan was and will be carried out. But that's for future discussion. What I think Seth has a problem with is how people interpret and teach what the Bible reveals about the natural causation of things."

"Exactly!" Seth agreed. "If I find the Bible credible concerning the basics, then maybe I can consider the rest of what it has to say. But if the Bible can't even get the creation of the universe and a planet correct, how can I trust the rest of what it has to say?"

"That's a valid point," said Jimmy.

"Jimmy, I didn't think we are supposed to question God. Aren't we just supposed to take the Bible literally?" asked Bethany.

"Yes, I believe we should take the Bible literally with the understanding that there are certain things that are parables, other text that is poetic, and some is meant to be figurative. But that's a small percentage. Most of what the Bible has to say is meant to be taken literally. And when we understand the pre and post text..."

"What? Pre? Post?" Melissa asked, staring blankly at Jimmy.

"Not taking a verse or passage out of context. We need to understand the pretext, or what comes before, and the post text, that which comes after. An understanding of Greek and Hebrew is also helpful, but there is nothing wrong with relying on Biblical scholars who have studied these other languages, and who offer explanations of the text in question. The point is that the Bible never said the earth was thousands of years old. Some scholars make interpretations based on their methods of biblical studies, but what I'm going to share deals primarily with the text at hand. God's record book of nature and science as we understand it."

"Record book of nature?" asked Seth.

"Yes. The Bible states that the Heavens declare the glory and truth of God's handiwork. The Bible also says man is without excuse because of this declaration. Therefore, I, like Seth, don't think God would make His declaration look like something it's not. The earth, as revealed through science, is billions of years old. The universe is somewhere around 13.7 billion years old. The universe, according to both science and the Bible, had a beginning. The Big Bang—call it what you like—but God spoke the universe into existence. I have learned in my studies that both science and the Bible teach that the universe has been expanding since the beginning, and that the universe is wearing out. God also took billions of years to make our planet ready for human life."

"Why would He need to take that long? Even a magic Genie wouldn't have to take that long," added Melissa.

"He could have done it in a minute, a second, or He could have taken a trillion years. Nothing is impossible for God. But using the laws of physics that God Himself set up, the universe has taken billions of years to get to this point in time. In Genesis, it goes on to describe the method God used to develop our universe and our planet. He chose to be hands on."

"Regardless of how old it is, we know God did it in six days," Bethany said.

"Days? Well, the Hebrew word for day is *yom*. As you may know, ancient Hebrew only had a few thousand words. In contrast, the English language has over one hundred fifty thousand. So the word *yom* had different meanings. It could mean a twelve hour period, a twenty-four hour period, or a long period of time."

"So you are saying that the days in Genesis are long periods of time," said Seth.

"Kinda like this conversation right now. Long!" said Melissa. The last thing Melissa wanted to do on spring break was talk about religion. The weather outside was beautiful, and it would be relaxing to paint her fingernails while taking a stroll along her favorite trail. However, there was something about Jimmy she could not resist.

She knew her mother would say that she had the beginnings of a schoolgirl crush. But Melissa realized it was a crush that could go nowhere because Jimmy was too old for a girl who was still in high school. But she felt a genuine attraction to the passion Jimmy displayed. The way he talked about science. The conviction behind his words. It captivated the usually superficial teenager, and she felt as if she could sit and listen to him all *yom*.

"Yes," Jimmy continued. "I'll go so far as to say each of the days in Genesis are millions to billions of years long, based not only on the usage of the word *yom* in the Bible, but also because the things that transpired during those six days simply would take more time than 24 hours."

"Okay. Let's agree that the Bible says there was a beginning, and that the earth is billions of years old. Genesis still puts the creation days in the wrong order," said Seth.

"Order?" asked Bethany.

"Yes. Order. The Bible seems to think you can have a planet and life before you have a sun. That's just simply stupid," said Seth.

Jimmy responded. "Yes, it would be stupid if that's what the Book says, but I think you are not paying close enough attention to the actual words and their meanings."

"Let me quote." Seth picked up his grandmother's Bible and began to read. "This is in Genesis Chapter One, verses one through three. 'In the beginning God created the heavens and the earth and the earth was waste and void, and darkness was upon the face of the deep, and the Spirit of God moved upon the face of the waters. And God said, let there be light, and there was light.' It talks about light in those three verses, but later on in day four it says that God created the sun, moon, and the stars at a later time. You see, any competent scientist knows you don't have a planet before the sun. What would the planet orbit around?"

Jimmy answered, "You gotta be careful on two accounts when reading those verses. First, you must have the right point of view. In verse one, the point of view of the writer is from space looking down on the earth. In verse two, the writer's point of view changes to the surface of the planet looking towards space."

"What about verse one where there's all this *hovering* going on, yet the earth was all dark?" Seth asked sarcastically. Seth felt somewhat empowered because although he did not know the Bible well, having never read it, he had at least read the first few chapters of Genesis. His biology professor had even talked about the first chapter of Genesis in class once.

"We know that in the earliest stages of the earth that light could not penetrate to the surface because the atmosphere was too thick with debris and gasses. In verse two, where the point of view changes to the surface, it was first dark because light couldn't penetrate to the surface. Next, when the Bible says there was 'light' it is referring to the light that eventually penetrated through the thinning atmosphere. The atmosphere of earth was once opaque, but eventually became translucent, kind of like a cloudy day. Plus, in day one the Bible says there was day and night. That means half of the world was in day, and half was in night—since it is a sphere. So you see, the sun had to exist in Genesis at that time."

Jimmy paused to think. "Oh, and by the way, the expression 'heavens and the earth' are used together in the Bible to mean the universe and all that is in it. Meaning the sun, moon, stars, planets, etcetera. So, in day one of Genesis, the sun had to have been created before the earth. I just learned that the other day from a study bible that gives the original Hebrew meaning."

"Wow, you speak a foreign language? That is so sexy," said Melissa.

"Okay, one last comment and then I need to get going on my real studies." Seth opened his grandmother's Bible again and pointed to verse four of Genesis. "What about on day four where it says the sun was created?"

"The verse does not say God created the sun. It says 'Let there be...' Meaning—let the sun, moon, and stars appear.

Remember what I said about the atmosphere becoming more translucent? Thus, allowing the light to shine through. Later in day four, the Bible summarizes that God made—or *asah* in Hebrew—the sun, moon, and stars. That Hebrew word *asah* is in the past tense, which would refer back to the events prior to day four, or in this case, the events of day one, like we talked about earlier."

"I totally get it," said Melissa.

"Sure you do, Melissa. You understand what he just said about as much as you understand Algebra," quipped Seth. Seth was actually grateful that his lovesick sister provided a distraction because he had no well-thought-out argument for Jimmy. His knowledge of science and the Bible could not withstand a worthy rebuttal from a more advanced adversary. Seth, much like his grandmother, hated to admit that he might not know something.

Even worse, Jimmy put doubts into Seth's head about his perception of Biblical fallacies. "Could the Bible actually be credible and in harmony with science?" thought Seth. This trip to Grandma's house proved to be one major headache. Seth had enough to think about with his college studies, he certainly did not want to add a major paradigm shift to his already busy academic life.

Seth, unable to come up with facts of his own, attempted one last tactic in order to cast doubt on Jimmy's conclusions. "I don't know. It seems very convenient to say it's all a matter of interpretation or nuances of the Hebrew language. Who's to say the translations weren't changed. I mean, we have so many different translations, and they were all written by men."

Azora finally chimed in. "The Bible was written by the Holy Spirit." She did not fully understand everything they were talking about, and she had never really cared about the age of the universe, or how many days God took to create everything.

To Azora, only one thing proved important, and that centered on salvation through Jesus Christ.

However, she did not find anything Jimmy said to be against the Bible. She might not ever know about the Big Bang Theory or the record book of nature, but she was starting to believe that she and Jimmy shared a love for the same creator—God of the Bible.

"Yes," Jimmy said, "every Word of the Bible was inspired by the Holy Spirit. It's true that men wrote down the words, but they received the words from the Holy Spirit. How else could Moses have known the correct order of a planet's development? Most people today don't even come close to having the knowledge that Moses had thousands of years ago—when science was much less advanced than it is now."

"Yes, and the Book of Mormon was inspired by a spirit, as was the Koran, and probably every other holy book in the world," said Seth.

"Perhaps you just need to have faith and not doubt so much," said Bethany.

"Actually, Seth is on the right path. The Bible is the only religious book that tells its readers, both believers and skeptics alike, to test all things and hold onto that which is true. The true God has nothing to fear as His Word will pass every test. So keep asking your questions, Seth, but do yourself a favor and spend some real quality time trying to find the answers. Mark my words, if you do test the Word of God, He might just test you back. Think about this for a moment...All the religions of the world could be wrong. However, all the religions of the world cannot be true because by their very own words they negate one another. If the God I am talking about is real, and the Bible is true, would you admit it worth your while to investigate?"

As the conversation continued, Azora found herself

pondering something Jimmy had said. That it was okay to test the Word of God. She had never considered such a profound concept. She had been raised to never question or doubt the Word of God. It's true she would have modest questions from time to time, but nothing major.

She would sometimes wonder why God refused to answer simple prayers in the affirmative. Would it really throw off God's cosmic plan to give her the biggest watermelon at the county fair? Or would it hurt the divine order to resurrect a tomato plant when the frost came a little late in the season?

Regardless of her questions, Azora always came back to the reality that she would never fully understand the ways of God. She might wonder, but she would never really doubt Him. She also had faith that her grandchildren would eventually know they were also children of God. Drifting away in her own private thoughts, barely hearing the conversation around her, she sank into a peaceful slumber.

"Grandma! Grandma! Are you awake?" shouted Melissa.

"Good Lord! Have mercy, child. I could have been visiting Lazarus and I would have heard you!" said Azora, rubbing her eyes.

"Sorry, but when Seth's obnoxiously loud arguing didn't wake you, I got a little worried."

Azora looked around and did not see anyone but Melissa. "Where did they go?"

"Seth retreated in utter frustration to the office, Mom's taking a nap, and Jimmy went to work in the yard."

"What happened?"

"What happened? Ha! Seth finally came up against a wall he couldn't knock down. But I think he just retreated to gather up some ammunition. That Jimmy is so powerful...and mighty!" Melissa opened the back door holding a pitcher of lemonade and two glasses.

"Where are you going?"

"To learn more about God, Grandma."

"Oh, sweet Jesus!"

"Him too. Mom wanted me to wake her up in about fifteen minutes. Would you mind?" Melissa did not wait for an answer from her grandmother, and the back door slammed shut behind her.

"Well, whatever it takes," Ažora mumbled to herself.

Chapter 9

Test All Things

Seth was not at all happy with the way things were going on his latest visit to his grandmother's house. Being forced to eat sauerkraut casseroles might cause mild heartburn, but consuming all this new information on science and Biblical interpretation would most assuredly agitate his entire constitution. "Who is this Jimmy, and who cares what he has to say," thought Seth. Nevertheless, he could not help himself. He did care. He had to prove Jimmy and the Bible wrong.

Seth questioned if the Christian Bible really gave approval to doubt and test. Most Christians he knew just believed people had to have faith. Period. Now he had just been told something totally foreign to his previous understanding—that he could challenge and ask questions, and perhaps maybe even relate actual science to the Bible. Ugh! Real science homework waited for him, and he had a sister to pester too. Who had time to think about God?

Yet, he found it intriguing to explore the possibility of a

supreme being, with science as a variable. He just needed to find evidence one way or the other. His personality never allowed him to accept conclusions based on blind faith. He always had to have reasons why he believed in something. Whether it be the proper level to inflate a bicycle tire, or that a day decreases by one second every ten years. There had to be a reasonable explanation, and some proof to back it up.

One day when Seth was ten, he and his best friend Bobby were playing in a field near their houses, as they often did after school. The restaurant at the far end of the field had dumped hot coals behind their garbage bins. Seth and Bobby wondered whether or not the coals were hot enough to burn their feet. Despite what they had been told so many times before about the dangers of playing with fire, Seth and Bobby decided to dip their toes into the grey ashes. Their toes did not burn, and in fact the ashes were soft and cool to the touch.

Both kids jumped in and scattered the ashes around with their bare feet. In a matter of seconds, they discovered that the coals at the bottom of the pile were as hot as fire. Their feet burned and blistered. The heat had seared their skin, and the pain would remain for days. The experience taught Seth an important lesson. He would never again jump feet first into anything. Not without a bunch of evidence to lead the way.

After shutting the door of his uncle's office and closing the blinds to stop any potential glare on his computer, Seth placed a soft pillow on his uncle's favorite leather office chair and sat down. He turned on the computer and entered the password *IHATESANTA*. "Here we go," he mumbled.

After an hour of researching what different scholars had to say about the Bible and the Big Bang, he realized the immensity of the task before him. He also considered, briefly, that perhaps, just perhaps, he should read the entire book of Genesis for himself first. After all, who had actually read the Bible all the way through?

"How long would it take to read something as boring as the Bible?" Seth said aloud. "But I don't have the time or the energy to waste on that. Besides, there must be plenty of information I can get from the internet from smarter people than me who have read the Bible and ripped it to shreds." He typed "test all things" into the navigation bar. This seemed as good a place to start as any.

Seth had more or less accepted the notion that a believer testing the Bible is paramount to calling God a liar. However, it made more sense to him that a supposedly all-knowing and all-powerful being would have no problem encouraging mere mortals to question, challenge, and test. He assumed most people were lazy like him and would not take the time to seriously conduct research that did not result in an immediate reward. If he was getting paid, or better yet, earning college credit, he would have no problem spending hours researching the Bible.

The words "test all things," like any internet search, turned up a myriad of results. First, he had to find out exactly what the Bible said on the subject. Then he would research how various scholars interpreted the text. After forty-five minutes of bouncing around internet sites, Seth finally came up with an answer he could accept. In Thessalonians the Bible did indeed state, "Test all things and hold onto that which is true." But it was made clear by the commentaries that this verse did not mean to test God Himself, but rather test the truthfulness of His Word.

Seth thought that if his sister were to apply this verse to her life, she might test God by jumping off a fifteen-story building, and while falling quickly to her death she would surmise that God did not exist. Seth clearly understood by his research that the God of this book had no fear of His Word failing any test.

The Bible seemed to encourage people to find proof and evidence for what was being communicated in the text. "Well, great," thought Seth, "this could take a lifetime."

"But wait," Seth said to his computer screen. "All I have to do is find one incorrect statement or contradiction and I'm done. If there is one thing that proves false, then why should anyone believe any of it?" The possibility that he was about to save himself a lot of time and frustration reenergized Seth. "I mean, really, how long could it take to find just one contradiction?" he thought.

The next internet search in his pursuit of truth might take longer than forty-five minutes, but Seth had confidence it would be the last search he would ever need to do on the subject of God. He continued to think, in spite of the evidence presented by Jimmy, that the Bible could not support Big Bang cosmology. The Bible would clearly state the earth to be only thousands of years old—or so he thought.

After this research, Seth promised himself, he would begin to focus on his more important university studies. But first, he decided he was in need of a nap. He picked up the soft pillow and tossed it on the sofa, where he quickly followed. He laid there with a big smile on his face. Victory awaited him; the moment when he could silence the ignorant and the uneducated with solid factual science. If they wanted to believe the coals were cool, more power to them, but he was not going to get burned. No one would convince him that the Bible had any scientific worthiness whatsoever.

Chapter 10

Mother and Daughter

The short car ride to the grocery store with her mother to pick up a few necessities served as a rather unpleasant reminder to Bethany of why she only visited Azora once or twice a year. Her mother had always been a marathon talker. And old age was not slowing her down.

Bethany's husband, Patrick, refused to stay more than three days in a row with his mother-in-law, and never more than once a year. The now infamous hamburger patty incident did not help either. Azora had felt compelled to hit him directly on the nose with a hamburger patty after he had tried to suggest, discreetly, that she talked too much.

"Mom, I'm going to go see if the bakery has any fresh bread. Have a seat here and I'll be back in a bit. There's no need for you to bother going all the way to the back of the store with me."

Bethany was hoping she could avoid a routine ten minute grocery store visit from turning into an hour long snail's stroll through the aisles of necessities. Her mother's insistence on talking about everything within reach did more to drive Bethany crazy than to inspire a closer relationship between mother and daughter.

"Don't be silly," said Azora. "It's no bother at all. I love coming to the grocery store. There's always something different on sale, and if you look hard enough, sometimes you can find things on clearance. You know, when they want to get rid of an item because it's no longer sellin' so well, or because the manufacturer has changed the packaging, or because the store decides to no longer carry the item, or because something better has come along. Did you know that one time I bought fifteen cans of kidney beans for ten cents a can just because the date on the cans was already past? Well, we all know a kidney bean is still a kidney bean no matter if it's a few days past its prime or not. So what should I do, spend eighty more cents to get a younger can a' beans when a perfectly good can a' beans is sellin' for less? I tell you what, people today don't know a decent bargain when they see it, or they never had to work a hard day in their life, or they're just too lazy to try and save a little money!"

Bethany had already begun grinding her teeth, but her years of learning to be patient with her mother kept her from losing control. "I just love your sense of adventure, Mom. Here. Take the cart and you can lean on it while we walk." But before Bethany had even finished her sentence, Azora was heading down an aisle, in the opposite direction of the bakery. Bethany smiled to herself, looked up and whispered, "Dear Lord, help me. Please help me."

Azora glanced back in Bethany's direction and shouted, "Well, get a move on, Beth. We'll be here all day if you keep lollygaggin' like that." Bethany smiled again, albeit with eyebrows raised, and joined her mother.

"Why don't you pick out what you need and I'll pay for it," Bethany said.

"Thank you, dear one. But I don't really need all that much."

Knowing that she would be stuck in the store for much longer than she had hoped, Bethany decided to revert back to her original plan and make the best of the time she had with her mom. Better to ask interesting questions than listen to her mom chatter endlessly about the price of beans. "So tell me, Mom, I was thinking about you and the kids and the whole church thing. I honestly don't remember you being such a staunch church goer when I was a kid. I know we went to church, but it certainly wasn't every Sunday. What's the urgency to get Seth and Melissa to go?"

Azora hesitated before responding. She weighed her words carefully. When it came to questions about faith, her intent was to answer as lovingly as she could muster. "When you were a child more people believed in God, whether or not they went to church every Sunday. There was a sense of reverence for the majesty of Jesus. But now...it seems to me, kids don't give God a second thought. They couldn't care less about church, heaven, hell, eternity, salvation..."

"But isn't it *their* journey to take?"

"Yes, of course, dear, but why should they take it alone? We are their teachers. Right or wrong, they can decide that later. But it's up to us to give them the foundation and sense of importance about religion." Azora picked up a jar of pickled okra and exclaimed with much disdain, "Look at the price on these! I mean, okra is the easiest thing on earth to grow. That's highway robbery, if you ask me!"

"So, do you blame me for not making them go to church, or for not talking to them more about God?"

"No, of course not. Well, maybe a little. I mostly blame the world we live in though, Beth. Since when did it become offensive to talk about God in schools or around the dinner table?"

"I just think people get worn out from all the quarreling and hostility about who is right and who is wrong," said Bethany.

"But that's just it, dear daughter. Someone out there is right and there's a bunch of someones out there who are wrong. And if we were talkin' about a horse race where the odds are about losin' or makin' a few measly bucks, then so be it, don't squabble. But we are talkin' about souls. We are contemplatin' where we will spend the afterlife. And I figure that has a lot to do with your earlier question. The older I've gotten, the closer I get to eternity. I'm not goin' to be around much longer, and I want to be sure of where I'm goin' after I die. Perhaps when you're young you think you have plenty of time to figure it out. The truth is, there is never enough time."

Bethany stopped walking and gave her mother a hug. "Do you really think you have it all figured out? Do you know with one hundred percent conviction that your God of the Bible is the right one to follow?"

Azora raised her hands and gently caressed her daughter's cheeks. "I do, Bethany. I believe with all my heart and soul that my God is the one true God."

"I wonder why it's so hard for the rest of us to be so sure."

"I don't know. I think people today are more clever in some ways, and there's a lot of information out there to sort through. People want evidence now...I didn't need answers to so many things when I was makin' my way in the world. But today, it seems that science is the new religion and people want proof, as if it all were a scientific experiment."

"Well, if you are right and God is real, I hope He's up to the test."

Azora walked a few feet over to the produce section, picked up a peach, and placed it under Bethany's nose. "Smell that.

Amazing, ain't it? This thing is a miracle, the taste, the smell, the beauty of its color, its soft fuzzy skin. God made this peach for us. He made everything here for us. If He can do all this, He can pass any experiment, or any test man can put before Him. But what's important is if *we* pass the test. Because there is a hell for those that refuse to believe in God. The only other logical place to be without Him is wherever He isn't, and that place, my dear, is what they call hell. We are all runnin' a race. Some will win a prize that'll last forever, and others run for temporary crowns. My last dyin' breath will be spent making sure my family finishes the race with me." Azora picked up an odd shaped vegetable and shook it. "What in the world do you do with this thing?"

"I have no idea, Mom. It looks like some kind of squash."

"Well, let's take a few home and cook 'em up, shall we?"

"But we don't even know what they are."

"That's alright. We'll stick 'em in some boiling water and mash 'em up with some salt, pepper, and butter. There's hardly nothin' at all that can't be eaten once you put butter and salt on it, sweetheart. Or we could try fryin' 'em." Azora looked down the next aisle. "Where to now?" she asked.

Bethany gently rubbed her stomach. "I need to make a quick stop at the pharmacy."

Chapter 11

Where the Garden Begins

Seth never objected to visiting his grandmother because he loved spending time in the country, and his uncle's house sat about as far out in the country as any place he knew. There were neighbors, but they were spread apart much further than in the city. He had grown up wandering around the sloping hills of Garland County with all the critters and trees.

He missed nature immensely, but thought that the city better suited his overall sensibilities. He often imagined he would retire in the country after he made his money and had a family of his own. For now, however, short visits to see his grandmother would have to satisfy his need to commune with nature.

Seth often snuck out of his uncle's house and disappeared into the countryside for hours at a time. Just a short walk past the creek and he entered into a world that time forgot. No noise to bother him, other than that which nature produced. No buildings or houses to be seen for miles. The trees and brush were too thick to allow much visibility. Even if he were to go to the top of a ridge, very few homes would be noticeable.

He loved the remoteness. He could relax and be himself. He never worried about someone watching him, or invading his privacy. In fact, he could run for miles in just his birthday suit without fear of ever being seen by anyone, other than an animal or two. Yes, there were things like ticks and chiggers to avoid, but modern chemical companies had created sprays to escape being eaten alive.

Unfortunately, it had been about twenty minutes after Seth passed the creek before he realized he forgot to bring bug repellant. The last time he walked this far without protection he got chigger bites all around his waistline. Anyone who has never had a chigger bite should count his or her blessings. It is much like a mosquito bite, multiplied a hundred times.

Chiggers are tiny red baby bugs, almost invisible to the human eye. They are so small and tender that they need soft places to dig into, soft places that never see the light of day. After biting their host, chiggers leave a nasty secretion that causes the surrounding skin cells to die. The result is an irritation that can last from a few days to a few weeks. The need to scratch is intolerable, and like any itch, the more one scratches, the more it itches.

"Well, it's a good thing I'm wearing long pants and socks. That should make it a little harder for the bugs to crawl in," said Seth. Talking to himself, with no one around to think him crazy, also made the woods an enjoyable place to visit.

"What about your arms?" a voice from somewhere near asked.

"Yeah, but I didn't bring any long sleeved shirts with me...Hey, who said that? Is someone here?" He got no immediate response. "Wow, I must be hearing voices. That's pretty cool."

"What's cool about hearing voices? You're a complete

weirdo." The voice spoke rapidly and in a high pitch, reminding Seth of a smug freshman boy he once knew on his high school debate team.

"Who's there? I come out here to be alone, and I really don't feel like being anybody's entertainment this afternoon," said Seth with a touch of false bravado.

"Yeah, well, good luck with that. You've been entertaining us for years."

"Seriously, come out and show yourself. You sound like some punk kid that needs an attitude adjustment."

"Kid? Hah! I'm almost sixty-seven years old. A lot you know."

"No sixty-seven year old sounds like that. Just come out in the open and show yourself."

"I am out. If I were in, you wouldn't be able to hear me, knucklehead!" The voice was not very loud, but whoever it was must have been close.

"Alright, well, suit yourself. Feel free to keep hiding and following me. I'm not really doing anything interesting. But whatever melts your butter."

"Whatever melts *your* butter," mocked the voice.

"Whatever." Seth continued walking until he heard something rustling in the leaves. "I can hear you," he said.

"So, I can hear you too."

"Well, if you're trying to be incognito, you're doing a very bad job of it."

"Who said I was trying to be incognito? You're just too dumb to see me. It's not like I'm trying to hide. Look down here, dummy!"

"Where?" asked Seth.

"Down HERE!"

Seth looked down and all around, but he did not see anything out of the ordinary.

"Okay," said the voice. "I see I'm not dealing with the brightest star in the sky. Look at your feet." Seth looked at his feet. "Now look a foot to the right of your right foot." Seth complied. "Good boy. Now you see the stump?"

"Yes, I see the stump. You better hope you can run fast because if I get my hands on you..."

"Now, from the stump, go due north..."

Seth interrupted, "Which way is north?"

"Oh, brother! It's amazing you can even find your own burrow. From the stump go up to the small rock and then a foot to the left."

"Oh, cool, there's a turtle. Did you see this turtle?"

"Seriously? *Turtle*? I'm a terrapene, dumb knuckle!"

Actually, truth be told, this species of terrapene is also known as an American box turtle, but this little guy preferred the more scientific classification. As Seth stared at the box turtle, he thought how it seemed to be looking directly into his eyes. He watched the turtle's little head move ever so gently, as if in conversation.

Seth laughed. "This is so funny. Oh, my gosh! Melissa, did you do this? A talking turtle? And it looks so amazingly real! Wow. I'm impressed." Seth bent down and picked up the gentle reptile. He looked directly into the small face which protruded out of a shell the size of a large cereal bowl.

"Wow, make it talk again." But instead of talking, the turtle peed all over Seth's hand. "Yuck! That's disgusting!"

Seth dropped the turtle on a small pile of leaves and after smelling his hand, wiped it on a nearby tree.

"Well, that hurt a whole bunch! You big ol' pecker head!" said the turtle on his back, legs grasping futilely at the air. "Turn me over right this instant or you'll pay big time. I promise you that!"

At this point, Seth became utterly confused, but also very

amused. He was game for whatever might come next. No one appreciated a clever practical joke as much as Seth, and this one was worthy of playing along with for as long as possible.

"I love turtles, and I would never leave one to struggle on his back," said Seth. He gently picked up the turtle and placed him right side up, after dusting the dirt off the top of his shell.

Once back on the ground, the turtle instantly did a one-hundred-eighty degree turn, unusually fast for an animal with such short legs. He stretched his neck up and out as far as it would go. "Look me in the eyes, you big bully."

Seth, accommodating the request, dropped to his knees and placed his elbows on the ground to prop up his head. He gazed directly into the soft, round eyes of the hard-shelled creature before him. "Wow, I've never seen anything look so real in all my life."

"I am real. I just peed on your cold, clammy hand, dumb knuckle. If you don't believe I'm real, lick it. Lick your hand, I dare you."

Seth looked very closely at the turtle's mouth and saw that it moved quite organically. Unless one of the greatest puppet masters in the entire world emerged from behind a tree, the odds of this thing being mechanical were next to impossible. "Wow," said Seth.

"Would you stop saying 'wow' already? Now let's get down to business."

"Wow," stammered Seth again. Seth could not help but be mesmerized by the beauty of the talking turtle. Most terrapenes are recognized primarily for their shells, but this one had other outstanding features as well.

Seth had seen many box turtles in his lifetime, but none as spectacular as this one. Speckles of bright orange adorned his head, his legs had spots of pure yellow, and his tiny bulging eyes were tawny in color. Of course, Seth had no way of knowing if it was a male, but regardless of its sex, this pesky reptile had the most kind and gentle turtle face one could ever hope to see.

"You know, this is why I like to get the younger ones. Why He makes me talk to the old ones is beyond me," said the turtle.

"I'm not that old."

"In years, maybe not, but in the ability to see miracles you are very old, tired, and almost nearly dead!"

"What are you talking about?"

"I have been following along behind you for about an hour now, shouting at the top of my lungs, and you are absolutely oblivious. You, my friend, are almost a lost cause."

"Are you really a talking turtle?"

"Yes, dagnabbit. I mean, no, dagnabbit...I am a talking terrapene!"

"Alrighty then. Let's just go with it. Assuming I am awake, have not lost my mind, and this isn't the most expensive elaborate practical joke ever, let's chat. What is it that you want from me?"

"Oh, brother. Are you for real?"

"What? You're asking me if *I'm* for real. Seriously?"

"I don't have time for this. Spring is almost over and I have stuff to do before the heat of summer gets here. Follow me," demanded the turtle.

"Before I follow you, who exactly are you?"

"You mean my name? I don't think you could pronounce what my friends call me."

"Give it a try. I'm pretty good with languages."

The terrapene took his back right leg and scratched the dirt.

"Well, what is it?" asked Seth impatiently.

"I just told you." He took his back leg and scratched the dirt again.

"You mean that's your name?" Seth took his finger and attempted to scratch the dirt in the same way the turtle did.

"No." Irritated, the turtle repeated the same motion with his foot once again.

"That's what I just did." Seth repeated the motion.

"See, I told you that you would not be able to pronounce it."

Exasperated, Seth exclaimed, "Oh, this is insane!"

"Names are unimportant anyway," said the turtle. "I have a lot to share with you, so let's get a move on." Before Seth could get his bearings, the turtle had quickly scuttled about twenty feet in front of him, through the underbrush. "Hurry up!"

Seth mumbled to himself while he looked around for anyone who might be watching...or filming. "No turtle moves that fast."

"Terrapene! Move it!"

Seth followed along, trying to keep the turtle in constant view, while also maintaining enough distance to avoid stepping on him. The creature moved about as fast as a remote controlled toy car, and at times all Seth could see were leaves flying up over his shell. Seth had a hard time pushing branches out of his face and slapping the occasional horsefly away—distractions the turtle did not have to contend with.

It did occur to Seth that he could be going mad, but everything was moving too fast to try to stop and analyze what was happening. For now, he would just go along for the ride. He would sit down to contemplate the rest later.

After what seemed like a solid hour, the awkward hike ended at the foot of a beautiful, old oak tree. "Okay, what now?" asked Seth.

"Start climbing. You see that big hole in there?"

"In the tree? Sure. Climb and then what?"

"Are you that boring that you want a blow-by-blow account of everything that's going to happen to you before it happens? Be adventurous for the first time in your life. Take a chance...step inside and climb."

Seth stared at the determined creature before him, shook his head in disbelief, and after a moment of contemplation, stepped inside the hole in the tree and began to climb. Within a few minutes, Seth realized that yes, he was climbing, but he was going down, not up. He also realized that he was alone.

He called to the turtle, "Hey, aren't you coming with me?"

"Yeah, right, whiz kid. How is a terrapene supposed to climb a tree? Mind figuring that one out for me? You got a tiny jet pack tucked away somewhere in those britches of yours? I mean, seriously?"

"How far do I need to go?" he shouted.

The turtle yelled down, "Keep going. You will know, without a doubt, when you arrive."

So Seth kept climbing. Down, and down, and down.

Chapter 12

The Old Road

It was normal for Melissa to crawl out of bed last when she was on vacation, but she pushed the envelope even further this morning. As the wild bird clock on the living room wall tweeted noon, she was still lounging around in her fire engine red flannel pajamas. If not for the hope of seeing Jimmy again, she might not have gotten out of bed at all.

Much like her brother, Melissa loved visiting the country and exploring nature, but these days, the motivation to do much of anything escaped her. She had a hard time putting her finger on why she often felt depressed. In the past, listening to music gave her a boost of adrenaline, and made her feel better. Writing in her journal also helped. But not so much lately. Thankfully, today, unlike the past several months, she had a reason to greet the world with renewed optimism. It was all because of Jimmy.

Once up, Melissa quickly showered, and then made herself some food. While eating her last spoonful of granola, the thought occurred to her that she did not even know where

Jimmy, the subject of her most recent journal entries, lived. She wanted so much to see him again. He must live in town, somewhere not too terribly difficult to find. If Cupid was on her side, she might just accidentally run into him.

Melissa and Seth rode their bikes into town at least once each time they visited their grandmother, but Melissa had never done it by herself. But she was so determined to find the man of her dreams that she was convinced she could handle the ride alone. The bike ride would also be good exercise. Two birds with one stone, she thought. She had hopes of making this the best vacation ever.

Melissa found Jimmy to be one of the most intriguing young men she had ever met. He was more mature than the boys in her high school, and that alone made the nine-mile trek to see him again worth it. She realized that they were probably not destined to be together. "After all, we are from two entirely different worlds." She spoke aloud as if she were a Shakespearian ingénue. She even waltzed out the front door, all the way to the garage.

As Melissa dusted off the family's old Schwinn bicycle, and checked to see if the tires were properly inflated, her mother and grandmother pulled into the driveway. She felt like a helpless bug stuck to flypaper. Now she was going to be forced to wait patiently and endure a barrage of endless questions from them. She might not make it to town after all.

"Going for a bike ride, sweetheart?" Bethany asked as she stuck her head out the car window. Bethany loved driving Azora's jalopy with the faded yellow paint and missing rims because every time she got inside it, she was reminded of her own youthful indiscretions. Her first date did not have a car, so she had snuck away in this same Plymouth Duster when it was shiny and new.

"Yes, Mom. I thought I would get some exercise and fresh

air."

"Where's Seth?" asked Bethany. "Isn't he going with you?" Bethany exited the car and opened the trunk to retrieve the groceries.

"I don't know where he is. He was already gone when I got up this morning."

Azora slowly stepped out of the passenger side and stood against the car, catching her breath. "Maybe your mom and I will come with you."

"Are you for real?" asked Melissa.

"I certainly am. Why don't you help your mother and me get these groceries in the house and then we'll all go for a stroll."

"A stroll? I was really looking forward to going riding. I'll tell you what, Grandma, why don't we all go for a nice walk after dinner tonight?"

"That sounds like a great idea, Melissa," said Bethany, who knew what would really happen after dinner—everyone would be too tired and full to do anything more than sit in front of the television. Bethany, exhausted after her three-hour grocery store excursion with Azora, was just fine with that.

"Perfect. Well, I'll see y'all later." Melissa hurriedly lifted her leg over the bike seat and jumped up, throwing her full weight into the first pedal rotation.

"Be safe, and don't go too far." Bethany put her arm through the handles of the last grocery bag.

"You worry too much, Mom. I've got my phone. See you later!" Crisis averted. Melissa, free as a bird, excitedly pedaled towards the man of her dreams.

A whole year had passed since she last rode to town with her brother, but she had confidence in her abilities. If she found it too hard, she could always turn around and head back home. But the burning desire to find Jimmy made that possibility less likely.

The weather could not have been more perfect. The fresh spring air felt crisp as it blew against her skin. The tall trees— pine, oak, hickory, and maple—all shaded the road. The sunlight filtered down through the canopy, making beautiful abstract images on the ground. The birds sang love songs as pink mimosa blossoms swirled around in the gentle breeze.

Melissa, like the birds, unconsciously hummed her own love song while she traveled down the asphalt, aimlessly crisscrossing from side to side. The thought occurred to her that Jimmy's truck bed would be plenty big enough to hold a bike for a weary traveler.

The likelihood of anyone younger than her grandmother getting winded on this road, however, was slim to none. Mostly flat, there were only a few rolling hills that might warrant the need for a biker to stand in order to get more power. If any breath was lost, it would quickly be replenished coasting on the downhill side.

Luckily, for the non-motor powered travelers, the road to town had been paved a few years earlier. Before the new blacktop, bikers had to contend with crushed stone. Gravel made an otherwise easy ride a little more exhausting and unpredictable. Flat tires were a lot more common, so the kids would often take a shortcut through the woods on an old dirt trail.

Not too many people used the shortcut anymore now that the main road had been improved. If she could find the trailhead, Melissa wondered if she could then remember the way through the woods. The alternate route would save her at least ten minutes, and she could avoid going by old man Harris' place.

Old man Harris had died years ago, but none of the heirs could agree on what to do with the dilapidated house and overgrown grounds. The ghostly structure had no indoor bathroom, just an old wooden outhouse. Melissa got chills thinking about going outside in the pitch black to use a hole in the ground. The Harris farm gave her the heebie-jeebies.

Her mom would not have been happy if she found out her youngest child was traipsing through the woods alone, and had avoided the main road, but the proposition excited Melissa. She looked even harder for the trailhead. She remembered that there had been vines with purple muscadines draped over the opening of the old trail.

She and Seth would often stop and eat as many of the purple berries as they could reach. During one particularly dry summer, the only berries to be found were too high for them to grab, so Seth convinced Melissa to climb on his shoulders in order to get more. That trip to their grandmother's would forever be known as the vacation when Melissa broke her arm.

Unfortunately, muscadines were not yet in season, so there would be no purple berries highlighting the trail on this visit. Melissa thought she saw some vines as she slid off her bike. She pushed the Schwinn to the edge of the road and held onto it with one hand as she examined the terrain. There seemed to be a trailhead a few feet in front of her. She absentmindedly dropped the bike and walked around looking up into the trees.

Muscadines grow wild and use trees as hosts to support themselves. Upon closer examination, Melissa could see tiny green flowers hanging from the trees. She stood on her toes and stretched as far as possible. The flowers were attached to thin wiry vines. This had to be the trailhead. Her excitement at finding it was slightly diminished by the fact that there were no ripe berries for her to eat.

Now that the old dirt road had been located, Melissa gained more confidence. A shorter trip to town also meant more time left to spend with Jimmy. She took her cell phone out of her pocket and confirmed it had a strong signal. She felt better knowing she could call for help if necessary.

Melissa retrieved her bike and pushed through the vines. Once a few feet in, the trail welcomed her with open arms. Most dirt trails in the area would not be clear enough to easily maneuver a bike, but this one was once the only road to town and all the traffic had packed the dirt down so hard that it would take years before the wild reclaimed it. The new road had been made to go around the low spots that were often washed out with heavy rains.

Melissa, like her brother, enjoyed nature immensely. Being alone in the woods often gave her a sense of peace. But sometimes when she found an area where she had never been before, the anticipation of exploring it made her feel such excitement that her stomach would do somersaults.

She loved the idea that no one could see her through all the trees and foliage. No stuck up girls, like the ones at school, to make fun of her. And best of all, no adults to tell her what to do. She could let out a loud scream, and no one would ever know. She was free to carry on grand conversations with herself.

"I personally think that Jimmy is the perfect match for me," said Melissa as she traversed the trail on her bike. "He is tall, dark, and beautiful for starters. There really is no reason why we couldn't get married. And our children would be the most gorgeous beings on planet earth!" Melissa had become so distracted with her fantasy that she failed to notice a red fox a few yards ahead on the path.

"Our first would be named Francis. I've always loved that name for a boy. And if we had a girl...Well, of course we will have a girl because we will just keep going until we have a girl. Her name would be Lucy. Not Lucille, but Lucy." She abruptly stopped pedaling and looked at her hands. "I think I'll have to stop painting my nails black. I don't think Jimmy is into the darker side of life."

While she contemplated a new color for her nails, the fox crept up closer and whimpered. Melissa looked up and screamed in terror, causing the fox to quickly scamper away. She screamed a second time, dropped her bike, and rushed to climb the first tree within reach. Although she was not the best climber, this magnificent oak had low, thick branches, making Melissa's escape from being eaten alive quite speedy and effortless.

Chapter 13

A Hoot

"Oh, dear God, what am I going to do now?" Melissa asked. She did not really expect an answer, but she got one, nonetheless. She almost fell out of the tree from the force of the response. The ghastly sound was like a foghorn stuck in the throat of a howling wolf being squashed by an elephant.

The only reaction Melissa could muster was an incoherent squeal. She held tightly onto a thick branch as she looked all around to see where the noise came from. Then she heard the horrific sound once again. Not quite as loud this time, it sounded more like a barking dog imitating a train horn. Melissa practically grew up in these woods, yet she had never heard anything like this before. All she could do was thank her lucky stars that she was up in a tree where nothing could get her. Once more the ferocious blast came. She shook uncontrollably.

Melissa began to have an eerie feeling that she was being watched. She slowly looked up, raising an arm to shield her face. She expected something awful, but instead was immediately mesmerized by the most beautiful creature she had ever seen. Her shaking subsided as she froze in admiration of the owl standing on the branch above her. Yes, the huge beast demanded respect, but the angelic radiance the creature exuded completely calmed her fear.

She chuckled, realizing that this might have been the very first time she had heard an owl hoot in the wild. Now that she knew what had made the frightening noises, it became clear to her that they were indeed hoots. Not a hoot one might hear at a zoo or in a movie. These hoots were loud, forceful, and very scary.

Although this giant white owl with its huge round eyes was literally the most exquisite creation she had ever seen, it was also the most imposing. Melissa was afraid to move even an inch. The owl was the size of a small pony, or so it seemed to her. All she could do was stare in awe and hang on for dear life. Her knuckles had become as white as porcelain from gripping the branch so hard. There was something below that might rip her arms off and something above that could pluck her eyes out.

"I thought you didn't believe in God?" A voice from above asked.

"Ex-ex-excuse me?" Melissa stammered. She looked below to see who spoke, only to hear another question from above.

"You just asked God a question, yet you do not even acknowledge there is such a someone. So, who were you talking to?"

"Huh?"

"Or better yet, who would you expect to answer you?"

Melissa saw that the owl's beak was moving. Instead of hoots, words were coming out of it. "Wow, a talking owl. I totally believe in a god now!"

"A god?" The owl retorted.

"Yes. Whatever God it is that gave you the ability to speak English."

"I speak multiple languages, every language really. But who am I to brag? God does indeed get all the glory. But not just any god. *The* God."

"Okay. I'm down with that. *The* God."

"Silly little girl. You see an owl, such as me. You stand on a branch such as the one on which you now reside. You look up and see the stars from afar, yet you truly, in your heart, doubt there is one creator of it all."

"Well, not anymore."

"So, tell me, 'not anymore,' to what god do you now owe your allegiance?"

"*Your* God, obviously."

"Are you that easily persuaded? You hear a talking owl and the paradigm shifts from disregard to total submission?"

Her voice changed. "Submission? What do you mean submission?"

"True belief brings about true behavior and one thinks you would just as quickly climb down from this tree, get on your seat with two wheels, and ride off to marry Jimmy."

"How do you know about Jimmy?"

"I'm not the only loudmouth in these woods. You, my dear, could wake the sleeping sloth atop the forest canopy with your childish banter."

"I am not childish! Anyway, as I said, I absolutely believe in your God. I mean how else could you speak?"

"Even the demons believe, my dear. Belief is only one part of the mystery that is God."

"I don't know what that means."

"Most of your kind are gifted, by the One, in so many wonderful ways, but they are too blind, apathetic, or foolish to see what their gifts are. I, my dear, will let you in on a little secret."

"Yeah? What is that?"

"You have been given one of the greatest gifts of all."

"Really?"

"You, silly girl, were given the gift of faith. You will not struggle to believe. However, belief without knowledge is superficial. You must know something about that which you believe. You must truly seek with all your heart, mind, soul, and strength in order to unlock the full power of this gift."

"Why? If it's a real gift why should I have to do anything to receive it."

"Very wise, my girl. The gift is yours for the taking and you need do nothing to receive that which is free. But a gift unwrapped, unused, or thrown away is not the fault of the giver, now is it?"

"So you're saying I have this gift but I haven't opened it yet?"

"Precisely. You are not as foolish as you seem to be when you are running around performing as a brainless beauty in front of others. Why do you do that anyway?"

"You're a male owl, obviously, or you wouldn't need to ask. Boys like dumb, pretty girls better. Or at least the boys I know."

"You should pay more mind to the boys who value true beauty, the beauty that comes from intelligence and integrity."

"I just have a little fun, that's all."

"A little fun has gotten you to seventeen without learning much wisdom whatsoever. You have just given your allegiance to the one I follow, but you do not even know who that is. True, there is only one creator, but there are many powerful deceivers who would lead you the wrong way."

"So, are you a wolf in owl's feathers?"

"The matter is not who *I* am. The matter is who the *Creator* is. If you truly use all your heart, mind, and strength to seek out the truth, the imposters will be easy to spot. May I show you something?"

"I don't know. Now I'm starting to feel a little strange about all of this. Are you good, bad, or am I hallucinating?"

"Follow me. If at any time you want to turn back, I give you my word, I will not stop you. I promise that after you see what this journey holds, you will return right here to this very spot. I need not tell you that the oath of an owl is perhaps the second greatest promise in the entire universe."

"May I ask what you plan on showing me?"

"The truth. That's all. In order to use your gift, you must have confidence in the gift giver."

"So, what are you saying? You're going to show me God?" The owl hooted loudly in what could perhaps be described as owl laughter.

"No one sees God, not even me. But you will see the evidence. After this experience, you will be without excuse and the decision will still be yours."

"Ouch. That sounds a little scary. No excuse?"

"All are without excuse. So no matter the decision, you will be no worse off than before you left the branch on which you currently sit."

"Well, what do I have to lose then? I have the oath of an owl, after all. Let's go!"

"Follow me, silly girl."

The owl fluttered upwards from branch to branch in what resembled a type of hopping, but with an occasional wing flap. Melissa, using arms and legs, pulled and pushed her way up, with the owl always slightly ahead of her. Melissa had never noticed a tree like this before. It certainly resembled an oak tree, but the branches were perfectly placed for someone of her size to scale without much effort. Melissa still huffed and puffed, but she managed to keep pace with her much better equipped feathery friend.

After a fairly lengthy climb, Melissa sat on an accommodating branch and asked, "How tall is this tree?"

"Why this is not a tree, sweet girl. This is a vine and it goes much farther than even I have been."

"A vine? I've never seen a vine this thick or strong before." Melissa remained seated while she asked another question. "So, what's your name anyway?"

"You can call me Adriel."

"That's a strange name."

"The name suits me fine. Keep climbing."

The two hopped, fluttered, and climbed their way through the vine that looked like a tree, disappearing into the green canopy above. On the ground below, no signs of Adriel or Melissa remained, other than a lonely bicycle on its side in the brush.

It was almost as if such an improbable event never occurred. An owl talking to a girl. And while it may be true that merely believing in the supernatural does not make it real, disbelief certainly does not guarantee otherwise, as Melissa could surely attest.

Chapter 14

A Strange Place to Meet

Adriel had hoped that the climb would be arduous enough to keep Melissa from talking so much, but apparently her lungs were in better shape than he had expected. Not once, on the entire climb, did she shut her mouth for more than ten seconds. No wonder she did not know God, Adriel thought. She never listened.

"Personally, I don't know why all this climbing is necessary. If God can create a talking owl, couldn't he just magically transport me to wherever it is we are going? This is seriously giving me some major doubts about His credibility," said Melissa.

"The climb is nearing an end, my friend," the owl hooted.

"Thank God!"

"There you go again. An arbitrary thanks to an arbitrary entity is received on deaf ears."

"Whatever," said Melissa. "So God has ears?" As Melissa grabbed the next branch she screamed out in pain. Something heavy had landed on her hand. She looked up and saw another person. In any other place and time she would have been startled, but here, she was just annoyed. "Ouch! You're standing on my hand! Would you please move your foot?"

"Sorry. How was I supposed to know someone else would be here, in the tree that never ends?"

"Seth? Is that you?" asked Melissa.

"Are you for real? Melissa? How did you get down here?"

"Down here? You mean up here," said Melissa

"Seriously, what...how did you get here?"

"I just followed the owl. Seth, how did *you* get here?"

"The turtle told me..." The owl screeched, interrupting Seth. "Wow, that thing is loud," said Seth.

"Adriel, meet my brother Seth."

"I know who he is," the owl responded. "Did you think this a chance encounter?"

"I was thinking anything is pretty much possible at this point," said Melissa.

"What are you talking about?" asked Seth.

"I was just explaining to Adriel who you were, but he already knew."

"Who is Adriel?"

"Adriel is the big, beautiful white thing that just flew past you. Isn't he gorgeous? So fluffy. Who knew feathers could look so fluffy? His feathers look amazingly like the hair of Milly, the Persian cat we used to have. Remember Milly, Seth? Who knew owl feathers could look so furry. I love it!"

"You were explaining who I am to the owl? I suppose the owl spoke back to you?"

"Of course. You heard him, didn't you?"

"All I heard was a really annoying screech."

Adriel flew back down to Melissa's branch and whispered in her ear. "He can't understand me. He has too little faith."

"Adriel says you're too dumb to understand him."

"That's not what I said at all. Do not put false words into my beak."

"Gosh, you're no fun. Okay, he didn't say you're too dumb, but he does think you're a total moron." At this, the owl hooted loudly and flapped his wings vigorously. "Calm down o' majestic one, I'm just having a little fun," said Melissa. "Yeah, well, Seth, basically, you don't have enough faith to understand the owl, and if you ask me, some might call that slightly moronic."

"Hey, little sister, I bet you have never heard a turtle speak! Who's a moron now?"

Adriel objected. "Oh, the terrapene would not like to be called a turtle at all. Not at all. That upsets him greatly."

"Adriel the owl says that you shouldn't refer to a terrapene as a turtle. Like I said—dumb *and* moronic," said Melissa.

"It is important that you do not interpret my words incorrectly. Your brother is a very special young man, and this journey is just as important for him as it is for you," said Adriel.

"Oh, all right, whatever you say," said Melissa.

"What is he saying now?" asked Seth.

"Nothing important, but I will be more than happy to fill you in on the stuff that applies to you. I guess I was brought along as the interpreter."

"I don't get it. How come I can understand a talking turtle…I mean terrapene…but not an owl?"

"Don't ask me, brother. What exactly did the terrapene say to you anyway?"

"Not much, really. Come to think of it, he didn't really say anything except for me to climb until it was time to stop. Which I figure is probably now."

"Seriously? You just followed the orders of a hard-shelled reptile without so much as a single question why?"

"Look, I was amazed at the entire situation, and I didn't think I had anything to lose, so here I am. Now what?"

"How am I supposed to know?"

"I don't expect you to know, but I am pretty much figuring the owl has a clue."

"Oh, yeah, you're probably right. I'll ask him," said Melissa. Seth rolled his eyes and sat patiently on a branch just above Melissa and the owl.

"You both are on the same path, young ones, but even I cannot say what will become of the journey, just that you should continue."

Melissa looked up and repeated to Seth what the owl had just said. She then asked Adriel, "Surely, you must know what we're here for?"

"That is not important. The journey itself will reveal all you need to know. Shall we continue?"

"He wants to know if we want to continue," said Melissa.

"Of course we want to continue. I mean, don't you want to see what's next? We've come this far. Why not go all the way?"

"Very true. I don't know about you, but I've never heard of anyone hearing an animal speak, let alone having a total conversation with one. I'm down for whatever happens next," said Melissa.

Adriel rustled his feathers and spoke. "There are indeed recorded instances of animals speaking to humans."

"No, there aren't," said Melissa.

"Do you not think the Bible is an accurate source of history? The Bible records that a donkey spoke to a man named Balaam. One can challenge if the Bible is credible, and one that finds the Bible credible can challenge whether or not the donkey actually spoke, or if it was indeed Balaam's artistic interpretation of the events that day. When this journey is over, you too must ask the same questions. Test all things and hold onto that which is true.

Your conclusions on the matter are entirely your own, and you will indeed be none the wiser if you do not ponder the possibilities," said the owl.

"I see," said Melissa. "We are here, Seth, to ponder the possibility of God."

"There is one important catch," said the owl. "Only take this journey of recognition if you are prepared to accept the consequence of your choices after witnessing what some would say is God Himself."

"I guess that depends. What are the consequences?" asked Melissa.

"There is a reason the Creator of everything does not show Himself to his earthbound beings. God is to be respected and feared. No ordinary man has ever looked upon God and lived to tell the tale."

"Are you saying God's going to smote me if I look at him and decide I don't like what I see?" asked Melissa.

Seth chimed in. "You mean 'smite.' Let me answer that one, my white-feathered friend. Yes."

"He would have no need to smite you," said the owl. "Your thoughts alone would imprison and separate you from the light of the world for all of eternity. There are no second chances in this world beyond the tree, dear one. Once you actually see truth, with your own eyes, and know it is real with your own heart, there is only one choice that will lead to life, and one that will lead to death."

"What did he say?" asked Seth, impatiently.

"Basically, if we continue on and see God but still deny Him, then we will die." She spoke to Adriel. "So, do you mean 'die' like Abraham's son died when he went to sacrifice him before the Lord? You know, is this really just a big ol' test thingy?"

"Or does he mean die like Cain's brother Abel?" asked Seth.

"Neither," said the owl. "You seem to be somewhat familiar

with the Good Book. Do you know the story of Lot's wife?"

"Yeah, who doesn't? I mean we went to Sunday services with our grandmother sometimes. Lot's wife is the one that turned into a big pile of salt. That doesn't sound like a very nice thing for the Creator of the universe to do to a couple of teenagers," said Melissa.

"As said before, the choice is yours. The Lord does not condemn, but rather allows you free choice. May your pride subside, in all that you see and do on this journey, and you will make it back safely. But if you long for what was true to you before you entered this world, then God will be a gentleman, just as he was to Lot's wife. She became what she desired. She longed for what she left behind, and not for the truth that lay before her. The journey before you is not an easy one, but once taken, will begin a beautiful bounty that will never cease."

Melissa explained to her brother all that the owl had said. They discussed the pros and cons and if the whole proposition was even real. In the end, they were certain of the truthfulness of the owl, and that the proposal warranted further investigation.

Seth still had deeper concerns. These were supernatural events in unchartered territory. When he tried to speak, his throat became very dry, making it hard to ask any more questions without revealing how frightened he was. Rather than letting the fear completely overwhelm him, he forced himself to focus on the fact that he would never again have another chance to do anything remotely miraculous.

Melissa, perhaps less frightened of the opportunity before her, doubted the veracity of the owl's statements. She convinced herself that the owl exaggerated the possible dire consequences of the journey. If God truly existed out there somewhere, she thought, He would not let any harm come to Seth and her.

"We want to go on," Melissa told the owl.

"A simple decision this is not, young ones. In the other world you have a lifetime to seek and explore, but here, where things are, should we say, more immediate, there is no opportunity to ignore what is obvious. One embraces or rejects based on the truth that is."

"I don't understand. Why choose my brother and me to go through this if the consequences are so serious, as you seem to think they are? Wouldn't it make more sense for us to decide in our own time, like everyone else?"

"The Creator is mysterious. Not even I understand all that He is. He is. He does. That is enough for me. You are here and you have been chosen. However, you still have a choice. Continue on or turn back."

"Seth, what do you think? Basically we either turn back and go home, or continue on and risk eternal damnation."

"Or eternal enlightenment," Seth responded. "The way I see it, we can't turn this opportunity down. This is either some magical, crazy experience in our own minds, or perhaps we are being led by something greater than ourselves. I'm already a major skeptic. It stands to reason that if I leave now and there is a God, I might never know. Otherwise, why would God, if He is real, want me to go through such a test? Besides, I can't pass this up, my curiosity is beyond appeasement. This is the most exciting thing that's ever happened to me."

"If there is a God, He must be good, right? So surely He would not let me choose the wrong path...or would He? I'm so confused," said Melissa.

"You have a great gift, dear one, the gift of faith. Perhaps one of the greatest gifts of all. Don't you think it's about time to open that gift?" said the owl.

"I'm not sure what you even mean, but it sounds good." Melissa paused to think. "I'm in. Let's do it. Where do we go now?"

The owl hooted and laughed. "Just sit back and watch the universe come to us."

Slowly, the leaves of the vine rustled and a fierce wind rose up and circled around them. The branches they held began to vibrate gently. The sky darkened and the forest, or wherever they were now, became filled with the music of a thousand chimes. Both Seth and Melissa froze with fear, a fear that gradually morphed into reverence. They were in the midst of something more powerful than life itself.

Chapter 15

Tea and the Cross

Back in the world where miracles seemed a lot less common, Bethany and Azora had just finished bringing in the groceries. Bethany took the canned goods and other items out of the grocery bags while Azora placed them in the proper cabinets. This continued for a few minutes without much fanfare.

Bethany picked up the last remaining item, a box of breakfast tea. Azora loved a nice tall glass of tea. Even in the dead of winter, her tea had to be black, and it had to be cold, and she never wasted a drop. If she was unable to finish it, off to the refrigerator it would go until thirst struck again.

"Where do you keep your tea these days, Mom?"

"Let me show you." Azora pushed herself up off the floor where she had sat to put away the fifteen cans of nearly expired mixed fruit she got off the clearance rack. She walked over to the counter near the stove, opened a silver breadbox which had not held a loaf of bread for at least twenty years, and brought out a beautiful tin cross.

Azora opened a hinged door on the top of the cross. "Hand me some tea bags, will ya?" Bethany complied and Azora placed the tea bags inside the tin cross. She put five bags at the foot of the cross, five bags in the right arm, five bags in the left arm, five bags at the head of the cross, and another five in the middle.

"That can't be what that cross was made for," said Bethany.

"The cross was made for Jesus. The tea was made for us. Every time I open this cross, I'm reminded of three things."

"And what are those three things?"

"Blood, miracles, and salt. I don't think I own a blouse that hasn't been stained at least once by a drop of tea, just like the blood of Christ stained the cross. When I was a child it fascinated me to see the tea change clear water to the prettiest color of amber. Well, that reminds me of the first recorded miracle that Christ performed."

"Changing water to wine," Bethany said.

"That's right. And you know how I love the flavor of my tea. Christ said we are to be the salt, the flavor if you will, of the earth. So you see, blood, miracles, and salt."

"You are something else, Mom. How did you ever come to believe in God anyway?"

"I think that's a story to tell over a glass of tea. Put a pot on to boil and I'll get the ice and glasses. There's some mint growing right outside the door if you care to add any."

"No ice or mint for me. I'll take mine hot," said Bethany. Bethany added water to the teapot while Azora retrieved a cup for Bethany and a glass for herself. She filled her glass with as much ice as it would hold.

"You know, Beth, the absolute best modern invention in the world was the ice maker. You can forget about the television, the computer, or even the hand-propelled lawn mower. It's the icemaker that brings me the most joy. No more filling those ice trays or spilling water all over the floor. I never could get the ice to come out of those trays in one piece. Oh, how I despise ice trays."

Bethany smiled to herself as she turned up the heat under the teapot. She could not remember if her mom ever told her how she became such a diehard believer in the Bible, but she was sure the story would be an interesting one.

Bethany regretted, now that she was older and her own children were almost grown, that she had not paid more attention to her mother's stories. She wished she knew all the tales that her mother had shared over the years. Unfortunately, time would never give back what it was created to take away. Moments must be acknowledged or time will steal them forever.

Seconds before the teapot began to whistle, Azora turned off the gas burner. She gingerly poured the almost boiling water into Bethany's cup and then used the left over to fill a large pitcher, where it could steep and cool. "Why don't we sit outside underneath the willow, sweetheart? It's such a beautiful day," said Azora.

"That sounds great, Mom. You head out and I'll follow after the tea has steeped a bit longer."

"That's an excellent idea. Lord knows it'll take me a fair spell to get down there."

Her slower pace could not always be attributed to physical frailties, but rather to her sheer curiosity. Azora had a habit of poking and prodding every little thing her eyes caught sight of.

As she passed the patio, she paused to examine what appeared to be a long, skinny bug. Or was it a stick? She could not be sure because bending down far enough to nudge it with her finger would take more effort than it was worth.

As the tea steeped, Bethany placed her cup and her mother's glass on an old copper serving tray. She filled the glass with more ice until it bulged out over the top. The hot water would end up melting just enough of the ice to create the perfect shade of amber. She had learned the correct ratio of ice to hot tea from her mother, who preferred her tea a little weaker than most.

Tray in hand, she pushed the door open with her foot, carefully traversing the short trail to the willow tree, not spilling a drop. As Bethany placed the copper tray on the old wrought iron table, she was surprised to notice a contented look on her mother's face.

Azora never ceased to intrigue her daughter. How could a woman who grew up so poor, lost her husband so young, and depended on her son for shelter, seem so fulfilled? Oh, how Bethany resented her mother's resilience. If only she might catch her crying about something, anything, she might feel a bit of empathy.

For the most part, Bethany had always respected her mother, but she had not always appreciated her. After her father died, Bethany and her sister had been placed in foster care by Azora for a short time. Perhaps this would not have been so intolerable to Bethany if Azora had not chosen to keep the boys at home. Bethany had never questioned her mother about her reason for doing it. One day she would ask her. But not today.

Bethany attributed their strained relationship more to her mother's detached nature than anything else. She remembered friends being mad when their mothers would ground them or make them wait until they were sixteen to date boys. Bethany was never grounded and her mom never monitored her personal life that closely.

Azora also routinely embarrassed Bethany with her lack of social graces. She had a habit of showing up at relative's houses unannounced right before dinner or talking at length with strangers at the supermarket. Bethany supposed most of her issues revolved around her own insecurities. Insecurities that her mother helped to cultivate, no doubt.

"So, you want to know how I came to know the Lord?" asked Azora.

"Sure."

"I thought you would never ask. I mean, Lord knows I was hopin' you would be interested enough to bring up the subject yourself. And the time has finally arrived. Thank you, Jesus."

"All this talk about the children and church as well as some things Jimmy said earlier got my attention. I never thought science and God went together. It got me to thinking about you. I just always assumed you were born believing."

"Born believing? In a sense I guess there is some truth to that. I always had a feeling deep down that there was a God, and your grandparents were definitely of the Christian ilk. Jesus was my only early influence as far as religious teachers go. Being brought up in the church from day one and being taught all the Bible stories over and over again must have shaped me into who I am as a believer. But don't misunderstand me. I had all the same temptations and choices as the next person. My life, as you know, was never what anyone could call a bed of roses."

"But didn't you ever doubt?"

"I don't know. I'm sure I did but I can't really remember so far back. Perhaps a better way to look at it is that I always knew there was a God, but that didn't equate to a relationship with God. My relationship has grown stronger over the years. As a child, I took God for granted. Much like children simply assume that a meal is going to be on the table when they get hungry, I assumed that God would just be there. It wasn't important to have intimacy with Him or to really learn about Him or praise Him. As my understandin' of God developed, my love for Him grew."

"What about when people challenged your faith, didn't that cause you to think that maybe your way wasn't the only way?"

"Truth be told, honey, it was my own actions and desires that caused me to really contemplate other options."

"What do you mean?" asked Bethany.

"Well, I never really did like to give money to the church or people worse off than me. Never felt like I had enough to give. And the Bible is pretty clear that we should be cheerful givers. I was never cheerful about separating from what little money I seemed to have. I still grapple with giving money, yet I know everything I have is His and He gives me everything I have ever needed. But I struggle."

"How did that make you question the Bible?"

"I tried to find loopholes and reasons why I didn't have to give, and whenever I would come across related verses or heard a sermon that made me feel guilty, I would just reason to myself that that's the wrong interpretation, or it didn't apply to me because I was poor and a widow and had four children and on and on and on. God never asks us for more than we can bear, in all things. I was trying to conform God to my image and what I thought God should be—not who He said He was."

"So you can't name the place and time where you became an actual believer?" asked Bethany.

"No, I reckon I can't. I do think some people have that moment, that special place in time where the revelation of God hits them like a bolt of lightnin', but not me. You should talk to more believers and ask them the same questions. I bet every answer will be as different as the person tellin' it."

"I think I'll just do that, Mom."

"And what about you, do you believe in God?"

"I always thought I did. Now, I'm not so sure."

"Life is very short, dear. You could get squashed by a car tomorrow. There are no second chances. God has given you a lot of years to find Him and once you're in the grave, it's going to be too late. The Bible says that every man must be born again if he is to enter the kingdom of heaven."

"I just can't believe a loving God would ever condemn anyone to hell, Mom. I'm not sure I can believe in a God that would do that."

Azora did not say anything for a brief moment as she realized the conversation was headed down a volatile path. She tried hard to steer clear of raising her voice or becoming confrontational, but old habits die hard. She bit her lip, pressed her fingernails into her thigh and tried to keep quiet, but her resolve was short-lived.

"Well, first of all, you don't have to believe. Take it or leave it. But the Good Book says that God wishes that no man should perish. So hell is not a place God condemns you to but rather the place you choose to spend eternity. Look, hon, if you want to run around this world believin' in fairytales and denyin' God, that's your choice. I mean, why in hell would God make you spend eternity with Him if you didn't even want to spend ninety years down *here* with Him?"

Bethany, remembering why she seldom brought up controversial topics with her mother, paused briefly to contain herself. She stood, picked up her half empty cup of tea and proceeded to turn in the direction of the house. "You don't have to get snippy with me, Mother. I was only trying to have a conversation with you. And it was all going so well—until I disagreed with you, of course."

"You're right, Bethany. I'm sorry. You know I don't mean anything by it. I just get frustrated with silly ideas."

"So, my way of thinking is silly?"

"Oh, dear, I didn't mean it that way. Of course you are entitled to your ideas no matter how wrong they may be. Perhaps 'wrong' is not the best word choice…See what I mean, God is not finished with me yet!"

"Well, I should hope not," said Bethany.

"Please accept my apologies and sit back down, will you? Look at those beautiful dogwood blooms, would you? Have you ever seen so many?"

Bethany sat back down and took a sip of her tea. She did not say anything. The two of them looked at the flowers in the garden and on the trees. The breeze blew gently as two red birds flittered about on the ground looking for food or perhaps nesting material. Both she and Azora sat in uncomfortable silence.

Azora knew that she had just blown yet another chance to share something special with her daughter. Now that Bethany was finally open to talking to her mother, Azora realized she had to stop letting her emotions get the best of her. She thought she had learned to temper her tone, but she could see that she still had a long way to go.

As the moments passed, they began to relax. The conversation eventually resumed, albeit to more trivial matters than before.

"Mom, have you and Henry noticed all the dirt dauber nests under the eaves of the house? You really should have the gardener knock those down."

"Not in a million years, sweetheart. They may be a little unsightly, but those dirt daubers are very talented at catching black widow spiders and such."

Chapter 16

Whirlwind of Words

Seth and Melissa had climbed so far up the vine that the ground below could no longer be seen. Neither of them noticed how high they had traveled until the wind blew hard enough to make them lose their footing, forcing them to look down. Melissa felt very queasy, but her brother gave a reassuring nod, making her feel safe.

When Seth paused to grip the branches tighter, he saw strange objects circling around in the air. These floating pieces appeared to be symbols. He signaled for Melissa to look up, pointing to an area about fifty feet away from the branches.

To his astonishment, as Seth examined the swarming shapes in more detail, he noticed that they were distinct letters. He made out the letters *C, M,* several *E*'s, and a *T*. Then he saw *Y* and what appeared to be a *U*. In fact, the whole English alphabet was literally circling all around them.

As the wind blew stronger and more violent, it became very hard to distinguish individual letters. Instead, they just resembled streaks of light zooming across the darkening sky.

"What do we do now?" Seth yelled over the howling wind. The vine they were clinging to had become thinner and more fragile the higher up they traveled. It swayed back and forth. Melissa and Seth felt as though they were lost at sea in a boat being tossed about on ocean swells. They gripped the vine as tightly as possible, but they were not confident they could hold on much longer. Seth reached over and placed his hand on top of his sister's and pressed down hard. If she slipped, he would be ready to catch her.

They watched the owl fly up into the powerful wind. He stretched out his magnificent wings and slowly twisted in a spiral, like a powerful tornado. The owl seemed to be deflecting the storm away from the kids. Melissa and Seth were mesmerized by the owl's awesome display of agility and grace. His white wings appeared as large and strong as an airplane's, but they made Seth and Melissa feel as safe as baby chicks under a hen.

But most impressive of all were the owl's huge legs extending for what seemed to be a couple of yards. At the end of his legs, instead of gnarly claws, there were perfectly manicured talons. Bird feet, yes, but they were soft and warm rather than cold or reptilian, as one might expect. Adriel was truly the most beautiful animal either of them had ever seen.

His body fully outstretched, Adriel reached his legs into the swirling wind and took hold of a huge pinkish-brown object. Melissa and Seth could not make out what the owl had retrieved. Adriel pulled the odd looking object into the eye of the storm, flapping his wings to keep it steady. He flew close to his two companions, looking them directly in the eyes.

"This is our ride to the beginning of time, young ones. Go ahead and hop aboard, you will be perfectly safe, but we need to depart quickly, while still in the eye of the storm," said the owl.

"He wants us to get on that thing," Melissa repeated to Seth.

"Well, I don't know what it is, but it looks safer than where we are now," said Seth. He stepped onto the big floating taxi and immediately noticed a consistent vibration that tickled his feet and made him giggle. The sensation was exhilarating. He took another few steps and felt a low hum that warmed him to what seemed like the core of his being. His whole body felt alive like never before, yet comfortable and peaceful at the same time.

Melissa followed closely behind Seth, and she experienced the same sensations as her brother. She began to jump up and down, and she could not stop smiling and laughing. Their new ride felt like a big soft cushion filled with air from the heavens. Seth opened his arms as wide as they could go and slowly fell back into the balmy billowy perfection. Both Seth and Melissa suddenly knew what it was like to experience utter contentment.

Adriel, of course, was not surprised at their reaction. He also would have loved nothing more than to rest a while on the floating pillow, but he had work to do. Adriel flapped his wings and the soft mass with its young riders moved away from the branches and further into the center of the swirling wind. The closer they moved to the center, the calmer the atmosphere became. They seemed to be in the eye of a tornado, securely and perfectly positioned so that not even the hair on their heads moved.

Adriel continued to flap his powerful wings in a rhythmic meter in order to keep them away from the turbulent fringe. It was exhausting work for him, but the two teens drifting off to sleep below him would have never noticed. As they moved farther and farther away from the vine and the forest below, the noise of the swirling wind subsided. All became quiet and serene.

"Hey, Adriel, where are we?" asked Melissa, not wanting to

miss anything.

Adriel relaxed and flapped just hard enough to hold their position in the center. The swirling whirlwind they were in the middle of would get them the rest of the way to their final destination. "We, my dear, are traveling outside the known universe into another dimension. You are going to see something even I have never witnessed."

"Wow, this would be scary if I wasn't so incredibly comfortable," giggled Melissa.

"Ask him what we are sitting on. Better yet, ask him if I can take one home with me," said Seth.

"You mean you have not noticed?" asked the owl as he fiercely swiped his wing at the side of the swirling wall of wind. The change of current from his mighty stroke caused several objects to fall out of the whirlwind's orbit.

"You know what those look like to me, Seth?" asked Melissa.

"They look like letters. See that one is an *F* and that one to the right is a *P*," said Seth.

"The one above to the right of Adriel looks like a *T*, or an *L*. No, it's a *T*," Melissa said.

"Reach out and touch them, if you can," said the owl.

"He said to try and touch them." Melissa and Seth stood up and reached for the letters. Melissa scored first. She attempted to grab a *T*, but it bounced off her fingers. Even her slight touch caused the letter to release a low hum. It sounded like a musical instrument, the bottom string of a guitar perhaps.

Seth reached out for an *F*, but was only able to push it away. The *F* also made a beautiful humming noise, much higher pitched than the *T*, but just as sweet to the ears. The letters changed colors when touched and seemed to come alive. As the siblings walked around their own floating object they realized that it was no indistinguishable blob, but rather had a distinct shape all its own.

"We're riding on a circle," Melissa observed.

"No, I think it's a donut," said Seth.

"You are resting on one of the most important vowels of your language and you call it a donut? You are on an *O*," said the owl.

"Oh!" Melissa excitedly clapped her hands. "We are on the letter *O*. Crazy huh?"

"Weird, really," said Seth.

The owl responded while Melissa interpreted for her brother. "What is anything without language? How could we exist without communication? Even the simplest cell communicates to its counterparts. Language, words, letters, is what everything that ever was or is has in common. One of the most famous verses in the Testament of life—shall I quote: 'In the beginning was the Word, and the Word was with God, and the Word was God.' It goes on to say all things were made by God. And that's what our journey is all about...we are going to the very beginning of creation."

The owl continued to hold the *O* steady in the center of the whirlwind as they were carried to a place none of them had ever dreamed of going before. The surrounding air grew colder and colder, but fortunately, the letter they were traveling upon radiated warmth. The siblings felt as safe and cozy as baby kangaroos in their mother's pouch, but it was a feeling that would not last long.

After what seemed like minutes, but could have been hours, the owl stopped flapping his wings, and the tornado slowly peeled away from them. They saw the tornado form a straight line and shoot away, faster than the speed of light. They were left in a darkness that was comparable only to that of a black hole. Even the faint glow emanating from the letter they were riding on seemed to be suppressed, a tiny illumination fighting to stay alive. Apprehension swelled up in the young travelers for the first time since leaving the woods.

There were no stars in this place. No glow from the sun or the moon. Nothing. But perhaps it was the silence that disturbed them the most. Other than their own heartbeats, the only sound was their shallow, rapid breaths, which seemed to be unduly magnified in the absence of any other sound. There is a scientifically quantifiable limit to how cold it can get in the known universe, but the unnatural silence surrounding them was far colder in its chilling effect.

Despite the unease she felt, Melissa was the first to break the silence. "Freaky," she whispered.

"Scary," said Seth. "Where is this place? Are we in hell?"

The owl answered as Melissa interpreted, "We are in another realm. We are outside the known universe, before our universe began. We are nowhere but somewhere. I am so proud that you two were courageous enough to make this journey. Seemingly stronger individuals than you have failed in past attempts." Adriel obviously had more to say, but he choked on his words after he noticed a tiny spark in the far distance. He became too emotional to continue speaking.

Adriel suddenly felt the need be alone. He released the floating O, and ever so gently flapped his wings until he was a few yards above the other travelers. Before he got too far from her, Melissa thought she saw a tear forming in Adriel's eye. Then she too noticed the tiny spot of light.

The Great Owl, Melissa, and Seth all fixated on the light that now seemed to be growing in size. At that moment a drop of water fell upon Melissa's hand. She knew where it came from without even having to look up. The owl, who she regarded as the strongest and most powerful creature she had ever met, had shed a tear. She began to weep as well, knowing that they had just witnessed a very special event—the beginning of the universe itself.

After taking a few moments to compose himself, Adriel rejoined the siblings. "Your people call that spark the Big Bang," he said. "That name may change in time, but no matter what you shall call the beginning, the fact that there was a beginning will never change. In the beginning, God created the heavens and the earth. Before the spark, there was nothing—no time, matter, energy, or space. Many of your early scientists once scoffed at the notion there was a beginning. They thought the universe was eternal. Nothing could be farther from the truth. For reasons, only known to Him, you have been shown what it was like at the beginning."

Seth listened as Melissa translated the owl's words. "I remember what Jimmy told us at Grandma's. He said that in order to have a beginning you had to have a *beginner*," said Seth thoughtfully.

"But that spark was so tiny, just a bit of electricity. Where is earth? Where are all the planets and stars?" asked Melissa.

"All matter, space, energy and time is in there to grow and expand. You would not see the full formation for billions of years from now, my child. One should never rush genius. There was a verse left for you to read that says, 'He stretched out the heavens as a curtain, and spreadeth them out as a tent to dwell in.' The heavens are still expanding and your planet won't develop for almost ten billion more years from this point."

"Uh, are we going to have to wait here and watch all that?" asked Melissa.

Seth shrugged impatiently. "I don't get it," he said. "What does all this mean? I don't see God. I see science."

In the distance they noticed a huge wave of light heading directly towards them. Actually, the wave went in all directions. The powerful undulating force continued to come at them steady and fast. There was no possible way to discern how long it would take to encompass them or what would happen when it did. Seth jumped nervously to his feet and Melissa moved towards the direction of the Great Owl.

Quickly zooming past the three travelers, ahead of the actual wave itself, were words and phrases both familiar and unfamiliar. They all began reading as if the words were clues concerning what to do next. "...in the beginning God created, formless and empty, heavens and earth...night...moon...stars..." They also saw many words of another language. "bara, elohim, haaretz..."

The distraction caused them to miss the wave's initial impact which sent the three of them tossing violently into the midst of the squall. Melissa screamed. Seth swallowed hard and tried to find something to hold onto. Even the owl could not get his bearings in what amounted to a tsunami of air towering over and around them. Adriel, Melissa, and Seth were all rolling out of control into the very beginning of time.

Chapter 17

The Little Red Fox

Melissa woke with a pounding headache. She sat up and gently rubbed her eyes. While everything slowly came into focus, she began to recall what she thought had been a dream. She was surprised by her vivid imagination. Of course she had experienced many memorable dreams before, but none of them felt as real or as profound as this one—a trip to the beginning of time.

She proceeded to stand, pushing herself up with the help of a partially rotted stump. She hesitated briefly in order to get her bearings, but quickly became fixated on the fact that she had been lying on the cold, hard dirt for what could have been hours.

She worried that her head might have gotten injured. Thoughts began spinning around in her mind. Was she at home or still in the woods? Did she fall off her bike and hit that stump? Melissa felt around her scalp, searching for a cut or blood, but felt nothing out of the ordinary. She had a lot of questions, and the pounding in her head did not help bring any immediate answers.

After taking a deep breath, her composure slowly returned. It became obvious to her that she had never left the woods, or so she thought. She then remembered how she got there, and her attention shifted to finding her bike. She looked in every direction as far as her eyes could see, but no luck. In fact, not only could she not spot the bike, she could not identify anything that looked familiar.

The unrecognizable surroundings did not initially alarm Melissa because the slightest turn in the woods could make everything look entirely different. The situation was confusing, sure, but nothing to be overly concerned about. She walked down the most obvious path, the only path really, in search of anything that would tell her where in the woods she was.

While walking, Melissa became very unsettled by the details of her dream. What did it all mean? She was aware of the theories that dreams reflect inner needs and desires. Some people think dreams foretell the future or reveal forgotten events of the past. Melissa considered that her unconscious mind might have been contemplating things discussed earlier with Jimmy and her grandmother. Then came the nagging feeling that, perhaps, it was not a dream at all.

Dream or not, what could a talking owl and the Big Bang have in common? Melissa had become so completely wrapped up in her thoughts that she did not notice the small creature crouching on the trail directly in front of her. Had the animal not snarled, Melissa probably would have fallen over it. Instead, she froze in terror, unable to move an inch in any direction. This was not her day, she thought.

"What are you so scared of? I'm barely a fourth your size. But that's neither here nor there, really," said the animal.

"So, it wasn't a dream?" Melissa mumbled this more to

herself than to her newly acquired audience.

"Rarely does anyone travel with Adriel, the Great Owl, without making a choice. I mean, you spoke to the Great Owl, after all. You heard and understood the wisest creature in the entire world. Most in your shoes could not even understand the owl and those few that do always make a choice to believe or not to believe. But here you are now, cowering in utter fear of the little red fox, simple ol' me. Well, shame on you, little girl! Shame, shame, shame on you."

"I don't understand," said Melissa, quite confused.

"Of course you don't, otherwise you would be home already. It's about the heart, dear one. You can't fake it because the One that sent you here knows your heart better than you. You have seen, and yet you still do not believe. Now, you're further from home than you have ever been before, and you may never be getting back again," said the fox.

Melissa could not be sure if the fox had disdain for her, or sympathy. "What do you mean? Where is my brother? Is he here too?"

"Who? I know nothing of a brother, but, oh, brother, do I know that you're in a deep, deep mess of a pile of complications."

"What do I need to do to get home? I'm getting scared."

"Listen, I don't know what you saw or where you went, but apparently you're just like the rest of them in your world. You see, but you ignore. You call reality a dream. You witness the truth, but trivialize it. Look around. These trees are no longer living. The briars have all but choked the life right out of them. They are dead and lifeless, these once tall and majestic forms. Only their corpses remain to tell the story of what once might have been. This is not a nice place for little girls like you and me."

Melissa looked more closely at the tree branches towering

overhead. These were not the lush green woods in which she spent her summers roaming around. The fox was right. All the trees were covered in ivy and briars, dead as dead could be. A sense of despair enveloped Melissa like a thick, imposing fog.

Light was elusive and the shadowy overcast caused the forest floor to appear even more lifeless and gray than it actually was. The trees hung their decaying branches over Melissa and the fox as if they were prison guards welcoming their new inmates. There was no green grass or pretty colors to be found anywhere. Only big clusters of a thick grayish-yellow moss.

"If this place is so bad, why are you here?" asked Melissa.

"You really think I have a choice? I'm here because you're here. That, and I sort of messed up a little on my promise not to scavenge any more of my neighbors' burrows. Do you know how time consuming it is to dig a foxhole? Day after day of endless furrowing that does absolutely nothing for my nails! I was only going to borrow the one burrow until my kids were born and out on their own. I would have given it right back."

"Goodness. Where are your kids?"

"Well...I've never had any kids. Perhaps I did put the cart before the horse, but look, that's neither here nor there. What's critical is that you and I work together to figure things out. Then I can get back to looking for a respectable dog to father my future children, and you can get back to whatever it was you wanted to get back to." The little fox paused, admiring the scarf on Melissa's head. "Might I say that is a beautiful cloth you have around your fur?"

"What?" Melissa had completely forgotten about the gift from her mother. She remembered unwrapping it and not even saying "thank you." She viewed scarves as something old ladies wore, and the only reason she had it on today was so the wind would not mess up her hair on the ride to town. She had thought no one would see her wearing the old-fashioned head wrap in the woods.

Now, as she touched the soft silk, she felt incredibly sad. Regret about what an ungrateful daughter she had been washed over her like a bucket of ice water. She wondered if she would ever see her mom again. She held back tears, not wanting to seem weak in front of a stranger. The scarf she had held in such disregard only moments earlier had suddenly become her most cherished possession.

"So, it wasn't a dream," Melissa mumbled.

"I think we all know when we are dreaming and when we are not. Now you could ask if you are crazy, that would be more plausible. But I think you will find that you are neither crazy nor dreaming. But that's neither here nor there. Let's get moving, shall we?"

"So, you have been punished and that's why you were sent here? God punishes animals?"

"Not tit for tat exactly, and I'm not really being punished. God is good. God is just. Those two principles are known to all in the animal kingdom. Common sense really. It's you two-legged creations that screwed things up for us. The story of your kind's first man and woman has been passed down to all our generations. Ah, the wilderness was quite peaceful and harmonious before the apple thing happened. I hear tell that man and beast actually were friends before the tree of good and evil was infiltrated. But that's another story entirely, neither here nor there, so let's get going. Shall we?"

"Where are we going exactly?"

"I haven't the foggiest idea, but we can't get there if we don't leave here. So I say that direction is as good as any other." The fox pointed her tail to the north.

Melissa shook her head no. "I think that way looks much better. Let's go that way." Melissa pointed south.

"Very well. I'm sure the direction doesn't matter as much as the importance of taking one...a direction, that is," said the fox.

Without delay, the little red fox and the girl continued their journey south. The fox spryly hopped back and forth in front of and behind Melissa. Anyone else might have been annoyed at the fox, but Melissa found her charming and welcomed the company in such a lonely place. Fortunately, regardless of all the uncertainty, Melissa noticed that her headache had diminished greatly.

Chapter 18

The Wayside

Melissa spent the first hour of their walk in the woods of despair saying very little. Instead, she quietly contemplated her predicament. Was it a test, a punishment, or just an anomaly? Despite the fox's optimism, there were no guarantees that anything they did here would lead them back home.

All her doubt and confusion made Melissa very sleepy. Or perhaps the dreary surroundings were causing her drowsiness. If she could just find a cozy spot to rest a while, her mind might function better, she thought. A little sleep could not hurt. She stopped and sat down on a soft mossy mound just a few feet off the path.

"Oh, no, you mustn't rest here," said the fox. The fox knew that if sleep came upon Melissa in these woods, it could mean her certain death.

"I just want to take a little nap. All of this has been so overwhelming and confusing to me. Just a few winks and I'll be ready to march on," promised Melissa.

"Oh, this is bad. Really bad. If you fall asleep here you may never wake again. What to do, what to do."

Melissa paid the fox no attention as she stretched out on the comfortable mossy mound and closed her eyes.

The fox hoped that as long as one of them remained awake they would be safe, but she could not really be certain. She paced back and forth in a nervous display of disappointment and annoyance. "Should I let her be or should I pounce on her before she falls too deeply asleep? Oh, what to do, what to do? Perhaps I'll just scout the trail a few meters ahead and see what awaits us." The fox hesitantly trotted off, nervously peeking back at Melissa until the girl was no longer in sight.

While the fox scouted, Melissa fell into a restful slumber. It only took a few minutes before her feet were partially covered in the gray-yellow moss that she slept upon. The moss felt like a soft cotton blanket that was keeping her warm and safe.

Nothing could have been further from the truth, however. As the fox had warned, danger lurked everywhere in these dead woods. If Melissa did not wake soon, the moss would completely cover her, making escape impossible. The smothering moss, as it was known to the few living creatures in these parts, could completely consume any unsuspecting passerby.

To make matters even worse, two vultures had been following Melissa and the fox for quite some time. They could not have wished for more. As soon as the girl was unable to move, once the moss covered her like a heavy embroidered chain, they planned to sweep down and devour their prey.

Screech, the more dominant of the two vultures, consistently managed to be the first on the scene. He always got the choicest selections. Every vulture knows that eyes are the tastiest portion of the kill. Soft, chewy, and oh, so full of flavor are the eyes. Gawker, the skinny vulture with bald patches, refused to be outwitted yet again. She had a plan to outwit big, fat Screech and finally get her first set of eyeballs.

"Look there," said Screech. "The moss is already well past her ankles. All we need do is wait until it reaches her waist and then we can feast till morning," he snorted.

"To her waist? Why not to her neck? Would that not be the safest bet? We wouldn't want her to reach out with her arms and strike one of us, now would we?" said Gawker.

"She's just a mere girl and she already sleeps so soundly. Surely we can pluck out her eyes and her fingers before she has a chance to fight us off," said Screech confidently.

"Yes, just a young girl at that, but the fox might return at any time. Perhaps you should fly up and see where the red varmint is."

"Me? Why should I fly away to find the fox? Perhaps you should find the fox. The idea was yours."

"Yes, but you are much stronger than I, and if the girl is more capable than we give her credit for, I will need all my strength. A little flight before feasting will make *you* none the worse for wear, o' brave one." Gawker placed her raggedy wings together and gave a slight bow.

"I see your point," said a puffed up Screech. "I will find the fox. Besides, it will be quite a while yet before the moss has worked its way far enough to restrain her properly."

"Of course. Of course," said Gawker. Gawker, however, had other plans. As soon as Screech flew far enough away, she would swoop down and grasp the prize. She did not care if the girl got away blinded. She would be happy with just her eyes, even one would suffice.

Screech plucked a feather from Gawker's head and let it loose into the breeze. "I'll be back before this free feather floats past the lowest branch," said Screech as he lifted off. As soon as Gawker could hear his wings flap no more, she dropped to the floor below and scuttled over to where the girl lay. "Such a pretty little thing," she thought to herself. "I hope she has blue eyes. I've always wanted to taste blue."

Gawker flapped her wings and lifted off the ground high enough to position her wretched claws above her victim's head. She also needed to estimate the best momentum so that the force of the strike would plunge her claws deep enough to pluck out the young girl's eyes with one fell swoop. Unfortunately, she had never plunged her claws into an eye socket before. She did not know exactly how high or fast she should go.

She hovered back and forth, trying to determine the best method of attack. She did not dare puncture the actual eyeballs. The vulture wanted them whole so they would not lose a bit of their juicy flavor.

After much contemplation, she finally decided on a trajectory that seemed appropriate. She turned her head towards the victim and began a rapid descent. Unfortunately for Gawker, during all of her indecisiveness, a single feather fell off her tail and floated right beneath Melissa's nose.

A vulture's feather, especially from the likes of Gawker, packed a mighty punch. Gawker's feather smelled worse than the foulest of feathers. Never was there a filthier feather to be found. The aroma of decaying meat and dried blood permeated the air. The dreadful smelling irritant landed directly on Melissa's upper lip.

Gawker had already traveled halfway through her descent at the precise moment Melissa sneezed. The shocking noise surprised Gawker so much that the vulture screamed in horror. Melissa awoke to the big, ugly vulture coming straight towards her. She screamed even louder than Gawker. The skinny, patchy vulture became so disjointed that she missed her target entirely, and crash landed hard into the ground.

"Ouch," moaned Gawker. "I think my wing is broken."

"What in the world are you doing?" Melissa shouted at her.

Gawker managed to move her head to look at Melissa, her body remained motionless. After a moment she gathered her wits and responded, "Oh, dear, and they are blue. Oh, my."

"Blue? What are you talking about?"

"You must understand. I meant no harm. It's just that Screech always gets the eyes first, and I've never gotten any eyes, let alone blue ones," said Gawker sweetly.

Melissa gasped, clapping her hand to her mouth. "You were going to take my eyes? You were trying to eat me, weren't you?"

"Don't be so upset. It's nothing personal. It's just what we do. My job, if you will."

"Your job, as I understand it, is to clean the floor of dead and decaying rotting flesh. *Not* to take the eyes of the living," scolded Melissa.

"But it would not have been long before the moss got you. If we waited for you to die it would have been too late. The moss is not even a discerning consumer. I, on the other hand, would have delighted in your sweet delectables. I am, what you might call, a connoisseur," said the vulture in the most sincere of tones.

"That's disgusting. You're disgusting. You ugly vile creature! Aren't there rules and regulations regarding these things around here?"

"Well, sure there are. But we are certainly allowed to eat that which has fallen by the wayside, which you surely have. If you had listened to your guide, you would not have fallen prey to the moss."

Melissa peeled the moss from her legs and sat upright. "I certainly will not make the same mistake twice. Where is that fox anyway?"

"Oh, dear, they will be coming back shortly, won't they? Mind if I ask you a little favor?"

"You think I'm going to be nice to you after you tried to pluck the eyes out of my head? I think not."

"What if I help you through the dark woods? There are even more perils along the way, you know. I could tell you what's ahead and give you advice to make the journey safely."

"What would you want in return?"

"Just don't mention a word of this to the fox. My friend might hear you and he would just as well pluck *my* eyes out and eat them. We are going to pretend you woke on your own and I had nothing to do with this unfortunate...I mean—*fortunate* outcome."

"Well, as mean as your intentions were, I would not want you to suffer the same fate as you had intended for me. I promise not to breathe a word as long as you and your friend stay away from us."

"Oh, thank you, thank you, and thank you. Now listen closely, here is my advice to you. Once clear of this covering, you will be in a strange place with many delightful temptations. You must not consume anything of this land or you will surely lose yourself. If you are to make it through, you must prepare and equip yourself with three things."

"And what would those be?"

"To tell you the truth, I don't know what the first two things are. Just that you will need whatever they happen to be. These two things are very important things to have."

"How in the world is that supposed to be of any help?" asked Melissa.

Gawker shrugged submissively. "Knowledge is the key, so they say."

Melissa shook her head in frustration and asked, "And the third thing?"

"The third thing is harder to find but it lies within you, or so the wise ones tell. Ponder all that you have learned and will learn. Hold onto that which is true."

"What does that mean?"

"I don't know exactly. I'm just a vulture and I'm not looking to go anywhere but here. You, however, have other choices, other places, and more options. It cannot be easy this journey you are on, few of the good ones are, I hear tell. Thank you for your secrecy, and for that, I wish you well. I must get back to my branch now, before Screech returns."

Gawker straightened out her wing one last time, and flew up to the branch to await her friend's return. Full of contempt for the vulture, Melissa shook her head in disgust as she continued peeling the moss off her clothes. She began to walk in the same direction the fox had gone.

Chapter 19

Never-was Land

Seth desperately wanted to sit and rest, but the darkness made it impossible for him to see his own hand in front of his face or the ground beneath him. The prospect of some hungry animal attacking him as he sat motionless also made stopping a less than desirable option.

He kept a steady but somewhat stilted pace as his arms constantly flailed at the black unknown before him. He would rather his hands take the punishment just in case something might be prepared to smack him in the face as he moved forward.

His newfound blindness, whether or not due to loss of sight or lack of light, could not compare to the eerie silence. At some point, Seth realized his own footsteps were soundless. If it had not been for the pounding in his chest, which seemed freakishly loud, he would have thought his ears had lost their function along with his eyes.

Seth walked uninterrupted for what seemed exhaustingly

long to him, but could have been mere minutes. His fully extended arms had yet to encounter any obstacles in his path. Besides his pounding heart, the only other sound to be heard originated from his lungs. His heavy breathing resulted more from anxiety than physical exertion.

Yet, even with these intensely frustrating circumstances, the more time that passed, the more calm he became. With each uninterrupted step forward, his breathing slowed. He even relaxed his arms—but just a bit. His lack of panic surprised him. He had not allowed himself to become overly inquisitive at first, but with composure came clarity of thought. A barrage of questions quickly filled his mind.

"Turtle!" he yelled aloud just to hear the sound of his own voice, or perhaps hoping that the terrapene might indeed answer back. The talking turtle had stretched Seth's understanding of supernatural events far beyond that which most people could imagine or tolerate.

And riding on a big floating vowel carried by an owl to the beginning of time would have undoubtedly driven most normal people to the brink of insanity. But somehow, Seth had managed to maintain a grip on his mental stability, despite these recent events.

However, this place, filled with its unimaginable darkness and silence, might just get the best of him. How much more could he be expected to take?

"This is a joke!" he said in case someone might be listening. Yes, he had become quite irritated. He was ready for a revelation now, and he no longer feared the possible answer that it was a dream, a hallucination, or even a punishment. He simply needed to know the score—how he got there and why.

He focused on the very last thing that happened while being hurled off the letter O. He remembered trying to grasp Melissa's hand, but not even getting close enough to touch her. He recalled seeing the owl twist and turn until it completely vanished. The very next thing he knew, he was alone in the quiet darkness.

As Seth contemplated the prior events of the day it occurred to him that perhaps his actions were not as important as his thoughts. It has been said you are what you think. But what had he been thinking? He considered that it did not matter to him if there was a big bang and a beginner that started the universe. If there is a God who began it all," Seth thought, "who created *Him?*"

Seth struggled to remain open and objective to what he had witnessed with the owl and his sister. He could not help thinking that if he were the creator of everything, he would have done things differently. He realized the arrogance of the proposition, but still could not resist pondering the possibilities of what he would have done if *he* were God.

Seth mumbled to himself, "I wonder if this is hell." He figured that this place could indeed be his eternal damnation. "Well, what a fine piece of work this is. What in hell am I supposed to do now?" he asked. He had hope that perhaps a voice would break the silence and offer an answer.

Seth spent the next several minutes thinking about the qualities attributed to hell—based on the way hell had been described to him. He recalled a few Sunday sermons and determined that this place certainly did not resemble any of those sketches. No fire or brimstone here. No gnashing of teeth. No little devils running around. No pain. But then again, eternity is a long time. Perhaps after eons of wandering around in the darkness, one's mind could conjure up the worst of images. Seth began to worry.

Deep in his spirit, Seth hoped a lesson was waiting around the next dark corner, and that he would soon find himself safe on the other side with the lesson learned. Yet, what could the lesson be? What he would not do to have that terrapene with him now, for someone or something to help him, to show him the way out of this place.

"Well, the truth is," Seth yelled defiantly into the darkness, "if I had been the creator of the world, I wouldn't have wasted time with billions of years of planetary development. I mean, what's the benefit of being God if you can't just snap your fingers and get a planet?"

Seth snapped his fingers and he instantaneously felt the foundation change underneath him. He could not see how it changed, just that it had. He snapped his fingers again and said, "And I would create light." At that exact moment all was illuminated, and Seth found himself standing on a strange looking terrain; a blank canvas of neutral colors as far as the eye could see.

Seth smiled. "How cool this is going to be." He looked at the flat, ugly land around him and imagined improvements. He thought of all the beautiful things back home. Pine trees came to mind first. Then he thought of roses, mountains, clouds, birds, lakes, and oceans. He kept snapping his fingers until his thumb became raw and blistered. He switched to his left hand and in a relatively short amount of time he had made what appeared to be a somewhat earth-like planet.

"Hmmm, well that wasn't very creative of me, was it? It looks just like home. Maybe I should change a few things? First the sky. I think the sky should be green." He snapped his fingers, but the sky did not change color. He tried changing the pine trees to blue, but that did not work either. Despite all his attempts to create something original, nothing came out the way he imagined.

Maybe he needed to make a green sun to get a green sky. What would be in a green sun? Seth recalled his geophysical science classes. The professor taught that the sun basically contained certain gaseous elements that appeared to the naked eye to give off a yellowish emission. Seth had no idea what kind of gasses one would need to fabricate the type of light that would cause the sky to appear green.

Surely he could create some original life form, something that only he could come up with. His own personal masterpiece. He had never before experienced such determination to succeed. The ideas came like fastballs from a major league pitcher.

He imagined a big fat polar bearish animal with flippers for feet and orange fur. Seth snapped his fingers and to his amazement the odd looking creature appeared. Unfortunately, because its weight could not be supported by flimsy flippers, walking would be impossible. The furry orange bear just flopped over on its back, quickly giving up any attempts to stand upright. Seth, much like the bear, crumpled down to the ground in utter frustration.

"I can't believe this. I have the power to do everything and I can't do...anything! It's not fair! If you're going to give me the ability to play God, at least be reasonable! Ugh!"

After a few moments of stewing in defeat, Seth stood up and began defiantly snapping his fingers. He refused to give up just yet. He wanted to show, whoever might be watching, that he too could create from his imagination—on his own terms.

What seemed a miraculous opportunity had quickly become the most frustrating activity Seth had ever undertaken. He snapped and he snapped. He thought about three legged animals, birds with hands, and snakes made out of water. His imagination seemed to have no limits. But the fruits of his labor proved that imagination alone could not produce even one unique, viable creation.

Seth once again collapsed to the ground. All around him laid the disturbing results of his ineptitude. There were square elephants, too tall giraffes, and monkey type creatures that could not quite balance themselves well enough to sit—so they just rolled around bumping into each other like balls in an obstacle course.

There would have been many more outlandish monstrosities for the monkeys to bump into had Seth not had the compassion to snap them away. He could not bear to watch these poor creatures thrashing about in their miserable bodies. Seth had been given the ability to snap his fingers and make his wishes come true, like a magic Genie, but he woefully lacked the intellect to apply these supernatural powers effectively. All he could manage were crude representations of things created by something or someone else. The realization of his smallness eventually took its toll. Seth became dizzy, confused, and disoriented. He slowly sank to the ground and hoped his hands had enough strength remaining to steady his crumbling reality.

Hours passed. Seth felt hopeless as he lay on his side, staring blankly into space. The hot sun beat down on him and he vaguely became aware of the need for shade. He had no idea how to make a planet revolve around a sun. So he slowly inched his hand into position and snapped the sun away.

As soon as the sun vanished, everything else disappeared in a cataclysmic windstorm. There he lay, vacuous, just like his surroundings. He would need to do it all over again, in order to perhaps find a way back home. What he did instead was cross his arms, frown, and whimper like a little child separated from his parents. Seth had never been more miserable or lonely in his life. Hell, it seems, may just be the creation of one's own desires.

Chapter 20

The Land of Indulgences

Not much time had passed before Melissa met up with the fox again. Melissa had decided somewhere along their short journey to unofficially name her new friend "Fox." Her choice of an uncreative moniker did not phase the ever optimistic red-haired vixen one bit. Melissa could not be sure if Fox even knew that the name applied to all in her species, and she did not want to ask.

True to form, Fox came bounding back toward Melissa hopping and pouncing with as much energy as a bee in a honeysuckle patch. Melissa herself had felt a little forlorn, but Fox seemed to pick her spirits right up. Melissa liked this creature, despite the fact that she had not exactly been of much help thus far.

"I told you so. Told you so. Told you so, I did, I did," said Fox, while running circles around Melissa.

"Told me what?"

"We should have gone in the other direction. There is

nothing up ahead but a way not to go."

"What does that mean? What is it that you saw?"

"That's neither here nor there as it's not what I saw, but what I did not see that's important," said Fox.

"Quit trying to be clever and just speak plainly, please."

"Plainly, you say? There's a big wall that we cannot get over, unless you can fly. You can't fly, can you?"

"Of course I can't fly. A wall? What kind of wall?"

"Well, see for yourself. It's just right around the bend a bit."

They were confronted by a seemingly insurmountable hedge. When Melissa considered pushing her way through it, she quickly realized it was impossible. The hedge stood before them as thick and strong as masonry, with thorns sharp enough to cut someone to the bone. Melissa looked to the right and then to the left. The hedge appeared to have no end.

"I don't get it. Why would the trail lead to a dead end? It makes no sense," said Melissa.

"Perhaps to teach you a lesson, I'd say."

"Yes? And would you care to school me on that?"

"Isn't it obvious? One should perhaps listen to her four-legged friend when one's four-legged friend says to go in the other direction."

"Lesson learned. Next time we go the way you want to go." Melissa patted Fox on the head, and Fox rolled over to expose her belly, which Melissa happily rubbed. "There has to be a way through this hedge," Melissa said. "Look for an opening. A hole to crawl under. Or maybe there's a ladder somewhere near."

Fox trotted to the east looking here, there, and everywhere for holes, ladders, and openings. Far too often, however, she would get distracted by a falling leaf or a fluttering butterfly. Melissa took the western route and walked much slower as if looking for a secret lever to pull. But if a lever ever existed it had long since gotten buried within the thick growth.

Fox, not known for her persistence, gave up and found a comfortable spot to rest. She watched admiringly as Melissa darted back and forth, crawled on her knees, and stretched high on her toes in an intense effort to find a way through the barrier. Her tenacity impressed even the lone butterfly that perched high atop the hedge.

Back home, Fox had often been curious about humans. Even though her elders had taught her to never trust them, Fox very much liked Melissa and hoped they could be friends forever. Melissa's kindness made Fox feel safe, and the girl's hands were warm and soft when they rubbed her belly.

Melissa shouted in Fox's direction, "There's no need to look too far from here, Fox. If there is a way through, it would be somewhere near the end of the trail." Melissa intensified her search within a two-foot perimeter of the trail's end. She examined the ground. She looked up in the trees, on the hedge, and in the sky. She scratched around in the dirt, kicked the leaves away, and basically exhausted every possibility.

"I give up," Melissa said as she sat down next to Fox. "Thanks for all the help, by the way."

Fox stood and curtsied. "You're quite welcome, of course."

"I was being sarcastic."

"Of course you were, but that's neither here nor there."

Melissa scowled at her. "You're impossible."

"Shall we go...in the other direction now?" asked Fox.

"Sure, why not. What else are we going to do?"

The fox quickly headed down the path.

Melissa put her hands on the ground to help raise herself, but stopped when she felt something strange in the dirt. A flat stone sat directly underneath where the fox had been resting. Melissa brushed the dirt away to reveal an engraving. The words read, "Behold, a sower went out to sow..." The phrase seemed incomplete and was followed by three dots, as if the reader should complete it.

"Where have I heard that before?" Melissa asked.

By this time Fox had returned to see what all the fuss was about. "What is it?"

"It's what you were sitting on. Perhaps it's the clue we need to figure out how to get to the other side."

"Clue? It's just a rock."

"Can't you read? Don't you see the words engraved in the stone?"

"Read? Heavens no. I'm just a fox. I can see the signs on a tree scratched by a fellow fox or smell the sweet lingering scent of urine. But read? What do you take me for?"

"Well, you're talking. I guess I assumed you would also be able to read."

"Talking? I'm not talking, dear. I'm yapping with my tongue—yapping in tongues you might say. Occasionally, I'll whimper as well. But that's neither here nor there. So what does this clue tell us?"

"It says, 'Behold, a sower went out to sow dot dot dot.' You know, dot dot dot."

"Dot dot dot, you say? Is that some kind of code?"

"No, it means there's something more. There's another part of the phrase," answered Melissa.

"Behold, a sower went out to sow? I'm afraid I can't help you with that, friend. Foxes don't wear clothes, just our fur. Would it be alright if I called you *friend*?"

"Sow, I think that means to plant. And yes, friends should call one another *friend*." Melissa smiled.

"We're friends? Really? Oh, that's the best. Friend of a real live person is something I always wanted to be." Fox rubbed her nose and face all over Melissa's legs. "What kinds of things do people plant?"

"Vegetables."

"That's it! Vegetables. We'll plant beans next to the hedge and use the vines to climb up and over! You're a genius! My friend is a genius!" yapped Fox.

"You, my friend, are not. We don't have time to grow beans. I've heard this phrase before. It's something profound, a parable...something Jesus taught, I'm sure. If only I had listened to my grandmother more. Help me think."

The two of them thought long and hard while pacing back and forth in front of the great green wall. Melissa occasionally blurted out a phrase or a word and the fox quickly followed up behind her with a slight variation. When Melissa said "Behold, a sower went out to sow and what he sowed did not grow," Fox replied with "Behold, a sower went out to sow and what he sowed did not show." Melissa struggled mightily to hide her irritation.

They kept at it for quite some time. Melissa racked her brain, and she became hoarse from shouting out various phrases. Fox, fortunately for Melissa, gave up and took a nap on the stone. Melissa was out of ideas. She thought about the vulture that had almost eaten her. Perhaps the advice she had received from Gawker in exchange for her silence would help solve the parable. But after a few minutes of contemplation, Melissa realized that nothing the vulture had to say seemed to apply.

Then it occurred to her that a sower sows seeds. Birds eat seeds. Perhaps the vultures themselves were the clue. The vulture tried to eat her. "That's it!" she shouted. "Some seeds fell by the wayside, and the birds came along and devoured them."

Suddenly something miraculous happened. The stone with the writing lifted up out of the ground by at least a foot.

The moving stone startled Fox. She almost cleared the hedge when she sprang up. Melissa laughed so hard she had to wipe tears from her eyes. When Fox landed on her feet, she too laughed, and rolled on the ground, kicking her legs up in the air. After regaining their composure, the two of them stood back in amazement. They were obviously doing something right.

"We must be close," said Melissa. She remembered learning that parable in Sunday school. She was thankful, for the first time ever, that her grandmother made her go to church. She knew there were a few more elements to the parable, she just had to concentrate.

She began to recall the first part of the parable. "After the birds came the stones. And some of the seeds fell among the stones and there wasn't much dirt." Once again the stone moved up and another stone simultaneous sprang up, creating a step to the first.

Melissa continued to recite what she could remember. "So the seeds quickly sprang up because there was no dirt." Another step appeared as the others continued to rise. "And the sun scorched them and the seedlings withered away because they had no roots." More steps appeared. Melissa could not remember any more of the parable, but the steps had not yet reached the top of the hedge.

"What now?" asked Fox.

"Where else could the seeds have fallen?" While Melissa thought, Fox scaled the steps to see if she could see the other side. She could not quite see over it by jumping so she decided to give herself a little boost by gingerly pushing off the hedge.

"Owwwwwww," howled Fox.

"What happened?"

"The thorns stuck me. My paw, it hurts."

"That's it. Fox, you did it!"

"I did?" Fox jumped down off the steps. The excitement made her forget all about her painful paw.

"Yes, my little red fur ball, you did!" Melissa lovingly patted the fox's head. "The other seeds fell among the thorns and they choked the seedlings." Once those words had been recited, the steps rose all the way to the top of the hedge.

The two travelers were very proud of themselves for figuring out the secret code.

"Let's have a victory dance," exclaimed Melissa as she reached out for Fox's two front paws. They danced around the base of the steps and giggled like two best friends at a slumber party. Melissa curtsied and extended her arm for Fox to climb the stairs first. She happily obliged, hopping all the way to the top. Melissa quickly followed her.

What they saw over the hedge astounded them. On the other side of the dead forest lay a lush, colorful garden with all kinds of fruit trees and exotic plants. Gorgeous flowers covered the land as far as the eye could see. But as luck would have it, there were no steps leading down. Fox looked up at Melissa and whimpered.

"Don't worry my friend, there's one more important piece of the parable. I had a feeling this might happen, so I saved the best for last. Thank you, Grandma!" Melissa began to recite: "Some of the seeds fell upon good soil and they yielded bountiful crops."

Suddenly, the earth began to rumble, and right before their eyes stones miraculously rose out of the ground, creating a stairway into the garden below. Melissa and Fox hurried down the stairway, and Melissa immediately started to touch and smell everything within reach.

Fox turned to look at the steps from which they had descended. She noticed more engraving. She barked and yapped to get Melissa's attention, but to no avail. Melissa was racing around the garden, in a frenzy, overcome with excitement, and she never heard Fox. Fox hoped the message was nothing more than a friendly greeting to welcome visitors, but she had a feeling that the symbols might actually be some kind of warning. She decided she would give Melissa some time to explore the new land. Then she would inform the girl about the additional engraving, and they would go back to the stairway to read it.

Fox turned around to an amazing assortment of peach trees, blueberry bushes, and huge strawberries growing everywhere. There were mangos, melons of every variety, and the most beautiful robust berries. They were not the sickly looking fruits one usually finds at the local market. These remarkable specimens were large, without blemish, and stunningly colorful. All the aromatic smells and bright colors overpowered Fox's senses.

There were even things neither of them had seen before. Melissa could not resist the urge to grab the first fruit she laid eyes on. Once she had that perfect peach in her hands, she took a bite from it. Immediately, everything she had ever eaten before seemed as tasteless as a glass of water.

An hour later, Melissa resembled something out of a slimy rainbow swamp. Juices of at least a dozen different varieties of fruit seeped through her clothing, ran down her arms, dripped off her hands, and stuck to her feet. Dirt and leaves clung to her fingers as if secured by glue. But not even her sticky shoes slowed her down. She kept eating and moving from tree to tree, frantically. Her stomach had already begun to protrude, and she clearly was oblivious to how irrational she was behaving.

Melissa had just finished cramming a big soft purple thing that looked like a cross between a banana and a star fruit into her mouth when her nose detected a scent that stopped her cold. She stood frozen in her tracks, trying to determine where the smell came from. The sweet heavenly aroma captivated her like nothing she had encountered before.

"Do you smell that?" she asked Fox.

"What I smell is trouble. Yes, I smell trouble," Fox

answered.

"No. No. This is outrageous, this smell. I can't describe the perfumed delicacy that's overtaking me, but I'll find where it's coming from, if it's the last thing I do." Melissa was led by her nose in the direction of the sweet smelling mystery. Fox followed closely behind.

"Don't you want to eat? Aren't you hungry?" asked Melissa.

"First of all, we foxes don't eat things we don't trust are safe. Secondly, that's neither here nor there because I'm not the least bit hungry, and neither are you, really. No one is hungry here, have you not noticed?"

"Hungry smungry, who cares! How could anyone pass up these wonderful edibles? You would have to be a fool not to try everything," Melissa said. There was a crazed look in her eyes.

Fox glanced at the large peach in Melissa's hand. "It appears that you've not passed up anything, and you've gobbled up seconds of each. It could take a lifetime to try all the different varieties in this garden."

"Everything. Yes. We must try everything at least once, twice even. Oh my, but I am stuffed! I think I could burst. Perhaps I'll just rest a while and let my stomach settle. Afterwards, I'll finish looking for that wonderful delicacy that smells so good."

Melissa found a nice soft spot under a Mukoosow Tree, a tree that had gone extinct thousands of years before in her own world. There were a few seeds lying next to where she sat. They were large and interesting looking, oddly beautiful for such an ordinary thing as a seed. She tucked one of them into her pocket, just in case she ever did make it back home.

A gentle breeze blew on Melissa as she rested. The fresh air might as well have been administered by an anesthesiologist. Melissa thought of nothing, her mind had gone completely blank.

"Shouldn't we be on our way? Don't you have somewhere

to be?" asked Fox, nudging Melissa with her cold nose. But Melissa had already dozed off to sleep. After all, harvesting fruit all day is an exhausting task.

Fox figured a little nap could not hurt. She saw no other choice because Melissa was out cold. "This seems as safe a place as any to rest," Fox whispered to herself. But she really was not convinced. After nervously pacing back and forth for a few minutes, Fox gave in to her own fatigue and sat down, snuggling next to Melissa. She intended to stay awake and keep guard, but her eyelids were heavy, and try as she might, she could not keep them open. In no time at all both girls were sleeping peacefully underneath the Mukoosow tree.

Chapter 21

Madness

Right away the next morning, if indeed this strange land had mornings, Melissa set out in hopes of finding the mystery fruit that had plagued her senses. She did not wake Fox, choosing instead to venture out on her own. She quickly disappeared into the lush green orchard among the trees with their abundant, colorful temptations.

After waking, only moments later, Fox sniffed around for Melissa's scent. Sadly, the wind had already carried every trace of Melissa away. Although beautiful, the garden proved to be eerily lonesome without companionship. Fox had never been so forlorn.

She whimpered and rolled dramatically on the ground, but no one came to pat her on the head or rub her belly. She missed her newfound friend, but why did she feel such dread? Melissa had only been gone for a short while.

She might not have been the smartest fox in her clan, but she knew this garden intended no good for those that stumbled in uninvited. She would use this time away from Melissa to find out why the overpowering smells and tastes seemed to bewitch her friend.

It was obvious to Fox that Melissa's recent behavior indicated there were sinister forces at work. Fox was determined to not let her guard down for a second. She would use all of her clever skills and instincts to keep Melissa safe. She would pounce on any adversary that threatened them.

Far away, lost in the seductive embrace of the orchard, Melissa searched frantically for the source of the enchanting smell. The look in her eyes had become one of a madwoman. Nothing could deter her from finding the treasure. If the fruit tasted only half as delicious as it smelled, Melissa would gladly ransom her soul for just one bite.

At some point while stuffing her mouth, Melissa had convinced herself that they were in the Garden of Eden. She felt a sense of pride as if someone or something had finally rewarded her for being such a good person. Everything within reach had been put there just for her delight, or so she thought.

If that were true, however, why the difficulty in finding the one thing she really wanted the most? She stopped eating the boring, mundane fare before her and focused solely on the only sustenance that mattered. Her whole existence now centered on finding that one elusive prize that she knew only by its smell.

Her nose, not her brain, led the way. She must have been getting closer because the scent kept getting stronger. Whatever infiltrated her nostrils could not be much farther away than the breeze itself. Unfortunately for Melissa, the wind kept changing directions, causing her to run in circles.

Even though she labored to breathe, and her feet had gone numb, Melissa kept searching. She would not stop until her legs could not physically move anymore. Her mind and her body were in complete agreement—find the source of the smell *or die trying.*

After Melissa repeated the same circular path through the garden for the fifth time, Fox caught her scent. She contemplated following Melissa, but decided her energies were best spent finding a cure for whatever had infected the girl—if a cure even existed. Melissa had obviously been overtaken by the evil of this place, and nothing Fox could say or do would convince her to leave.

Their only chance of escape rested with Fox. She alone had to figure out the cause and the solution for Melissa's transformation. But what could she do? She was just a little fox, after all. Perhaps God expected too much from such a modest creature.

"Hello there," bellowed a voice from somewhere near the tree under which Fox had taken a momentary respite. The voice resonated so strongly that the ground beneath Fox rumbled, or so it seemed.

"Who goes there?" Fox's voice cracked.

"I was about to ask you the same thing," the voice said. It was an ancient voice, masculine and confident.

Fox cowered and hid her face with both paws. "I'm just a little fox, passing through."

"And your friend?"

"Yes, she is my friend." Fox moved her left paw so she could peek out. She continued, "Friend, indeed. She is the reason I am here. The young girl is trying to get back home, and I am here to help."

"No one leaves the Land of Indulgences, little fox," said the burly voice.

"May I ask who you are? Would you be so kind as to show your face?"

"I'm here, right beside you. You have been seeking shelter under my limbs. I am the oldest and grandest tree in the Land of Indulgences."

"A tree, are you?" Fox stood upright, slowly regaining her confidence. "I've never spoken to a tree before. Well, that's neither here nor there. I'd never spoken to a human before either. In fact, am I really speaking at all? Yapping is really all I do, but that's neither here nor there either, I suppose. What's your name, Mr. Tree?"

"My name has no language other than that which can be heard in the wind." As if on command, a breeze rustled the tree's limbs and made music with its leaves.

"That's the prettiest name I've ever heard. I wish I could say your name, but command of the wind I don't have. Say, if you are the grandest tree in these parts, why don't you have any fruit hanging from your branches?"

"You're a very clever fox, aren't you? My fruit bearing days are long over."

"What is this place, and which direction is the way out?"

"As I said before, no one leaves my land. Why would anyone want to leave? None can compare to my orchards which bear the sweetest delicacies in the entire realm. Even if one were able to leave, they would surely die of starvation. After tasting the divine, a body cannot digest anything else. All other nutrients are rubbish and not suitable for maggots compared to what my garden offers."

"But I haven't eaten anything here and I do want to go," pleaded Fox.

"And leave your friend? That's not very nice now, is it, little one? I hear foxes love fruit and berries. I have something you surely would find irresistible. Just a nibble and all would become clear to you. One mouth watering bite and you and your friend would never long for any other food again."

"Yes, you must have heard that most foxes will eat a juicy berry here and there, but my mother could never get me to eat fruit when I was a pup. In the stream it would go. Mom was none the wiser."

"Such a bad little fox you were. But perhaps you should taste my berries and see what you have been missing." The wind blew and the scent of berries came wafting all around Fox. She stuck her nose up in the air and even stood high on her hind feet. She could not resist the temptation to walk towards the exquisite fragrance. Fortunately for Fox, she lacked the skills to walk on two legs and quickly stumbled. The fall knocked some sense back into her.

"Why are you so concerned about me eating from your garden? I thought you said there was no way to leave? So why would it matter if I ate the berries or not?" asked Fox.

"Well, I am nothing if not a proper host. Eat and be merry, I say."

"You don't have any real power at all, do you?"

"Careful. One should not disrespect her host."

"You don't look very grand to me. No fruit? In the real world you would have been cut down and thrown into the fire long ago. What use is a fruitless fruit tree?"

The tree began to shake wildly, prompting Fox to dart out from underneath his limbs.

"Why, you can't even chase me, your roots are so old and deep."

"How dare you speak to me with such vile disrespect!"

"Perhaps I could respect you if indeed you were worthy. What makes you any better than the other trees here?"

"I have the wisdom of the ages. No other tree can compare."

"Well, that's good to hear because you certainly lack the fruit of the day."

"How dare you mock me!"

"I mean, really. What's wisdom worth these days? You can't

eat wisdom, you can't smell wisdom, and you certainly can't see wisdom. I'm not even convinced you're wise at all."

"Hush, little red. Wisdom is what could find you a way out of here, that's what wisdom is good for. If you had any, you would already be gone!"

The fox laughed while frolicking all around the tree. "Prove it," Fox taunted him.

"I will do nothing of the sort. I needn't prove anything to such a simpleton as you. Besides, if I told you the secret, you would leave, now wouldn't you?"

"Well, like you said, oh wise one, since my friend has eaten the fruit, she cannot leave. I would never abandon her, of that you can be sure. She is my only companion and my first human friend."

"How do I know you are not trying to trick me?" asked the tree.

"You're the smart one, aren't you? Surely you don't think such a simpleton as me could outwit a mighty giant like you?"

"I do deserve your respect, and if you are going to stay here, I suppose it would not hurt to share my wisdom in order to gain a convert."

"Sounds like a deal. The wisdom of the ages in exchange for a convert."

"I will only tell you this once, so listen well," said the tree. "Before anyone enters this land, a parable must be completed. 'Behold, a sower went out to sow...'"

"Yes, yes, I do remember those symbols on the rock. The girl read them to me. I myself don't know how to read," said Fox.

"In order to have raised the steps, she must have known the parable."

"She shouted a bunch of words and phrases her grandmother taught her."

"The ability to recite does not mean one understands."

"But the steps rose."

"Yes, of course. They are merely performing the task for which they were created. In ages past, wary travelers who knew the parable also knew its meaning. Times have changed, it seems."

"What does the parable mean?" asked Fox.

"It has been told that the parable is as old as the land my roots now cover. An allegedly wise prophet taught that those who understand and heeded his words would be planted in good soil to prosper, while all others would wither into oblivion, or some such gibberish."

"Who is this wise prophet?"

"Look around, furry child. See how prosperous this land has become. Have you ever seen such rich and fertile soil? Does this look like oblivion to you?"

"Are you the prophet?"

"Nonsense. The prophet intended to keep the so-called wise ones free from this bountiful land. He assumed only the wise would know the answer and once on the other side, the warning would be heeded," said the tree.

"Warning?" asked Fox.

"Of sorts. But it's of no consequence to you now. Lucky for you, your friend did not notice the useless doodle."

"But what does the warning say?"

"I shall not repeat the words, but the writing is on the wall from where you entered, should one insist on wasting the time to read it."

The fox did not fully understand the parable or the implications of the warning, but she knew in her heart that the tree could not be trusted. No well-meaning host would trap someone against her will. She must find Melissa and get her to the wall to read the writing. Perhaps they would find a way out after all.

"One last thing, oh wise tree. I think I am ready to try your treats after all. Where might I find your most aromatic offering?"

"Ah, you have finally come to your senses. It was only a matter of time, now wasn't it?" said the tree.

"Yes, sir, indeed. If you can't beat them, eat them, I always say."

The tree laughed and rustled his leaves. "You will find the most aromatic fruit to be the Glouscenshire. The Glouscenshire is very hard to find and many starve to death trying. You, however, seem to have somehow avoided indulging in any of my offerings, so perhaps I can share the location of the Glouscenshire with you. Now hear me well, you must swear an oath never to tell anyone else where this tree grows."

The shrewd tree knew that Fox would not be able to resist the Glouscenshire. One bite would insure the fox's devotion to the old tree forevermore. There would be no chance of disenchantment or escape. The girl and the fox would have no choice but to fully surrender to the Land of Indulgences.

"You have my word, and the word of a fox is just as good as the word of a moth in a cocoon."

"What is friendship without trust, I say. You will find the Glouscenshire underneath the weeping willow with the limb which points towards the Lake of Entitlement."

"Where shall I find this weeping willow?"

"There is but one. She weeps because she never bore fruit. I allowed her to stay in the garden to keep me company in my old age. You will find her not more than two thousand paces to the east of the spot on which you are now standing. The tree which bears the sacred fruit is hidden by her weeping branches."

"Thank you for your trust. You are indeed the most knowledgeable tree in these parts." The fox excitedly pounced and pranced towards the direction of the weeping willow. She had a plan to save Melissa. She had hope.

"I'll be seeing you again soon, little red," rustled the tree.

Chapter 22

Willow

Fox's finely tuned tracking skills brought her to the weeping willow in no time at all. The beautiful tree rested all alone on a sloping mound overlooking the Lake of Entitlement. The lake paled in comparison to the graceful presence of the weeping willow. In fact, the so-called lake looked bone dry. Crusty edges were the only indication it once held water.

Fox wondered why anyone would refer to this as a lake. A complete absence of trees as far as the eye could see further defined the desolate landscape north of the weeping willow. Fox imagined that there must be thirsty trees on the other side of the lake. Perhaps these trees had drained all the water.

"But where do they get water now?" Fox mumbled to herself.

"When it rains, it pours," said the weeping willow.

"Do all the trees here talk?" asked Fox.

"The ones that have something to say," answered the weeping willow.

Fox could not help but admire the weeping willow's beauty. Her branches were thin and fragile and flowed all the way to the ground like a waterfall of leaves. The branches almost, but not quite, touched the soil beneath them.

"Why do they call you the weeping willow?" Fox gently nuzzled a few of the willow branches. "You have nothing to be sad about. Look how beautiful you are."

"Ah, such a lovely creature are you. And quite beautiful yourself, might I add. I adore your crimson tail and such a cute and noble furry face is yours."

"Crimson? Wow, thanks. I don't know what that means, but it sure sounds pretty. But that's neither here nor there. Do you know why I came?" asked the fox.

"Yes, of course," responded Willow. "News travels quickly around here. A rumor is just a breeze away." The weeping willow's voice sounded as smooth as silk. Those few that had the privilege of hearing her speak described her cadence as one of a mother singing a lullaby.

"You seem awful nice, not at all like the big nasty tree in the middle of the orchard."

"Hush, little one. The wind has ears and you mustn't speak poorly of the old wise one. Come, come under my canopy and seek refuge from the sun."

"Oh, no worries, I'm not the least bit hot," said Fox.

"But you will be soon. Come, it's really quite peaceful underneath my branches."

"Alright then." Fox obliged Willow and worked her way inside the overhanging limbs. She had no idea of the tree's enormity until she began to push past all the branches. They were thick and many, tickling Fox's ribs and belly as she brushed by them. She could not help but giggle.

Once inside she became utterly speechless as she took a few moments to look around. Soothing light bounced from leaf to leaf illuminating a path for Fox. The rich amber dirt felt soft and cool to her paws as she followed a trail of roots towards the center of the tree. Beautiful white mushrooms seemed to be smiling as they pointed her in the right direction. Once in the main chamber, next to the trunk, she could see even more paths leading in many different directions.

It felt peaceful and safe under the weeping willow's branches. The atmosphere was joyful. Fox could imagine many happy gatherings with friends and family under this tree. There were leaves on every limb making music. Not loud music that demanded attention or distracted from conversation, but soothing undertones flowing like a babbling brook.

"We can speak freely in here," said Willow. "No one can hear us and the breeze cannot readily penetrate my musical branches. You are special, my crimson one."

"Special? I've never been called special before. How am I special?"

"No soul has ever been in the Land of Indulgences as long as you without having been overcome by gluttony."

"Well, I really am here to help my friend, but I'm afraid she has succumbed to what you are talking about—that gluttony thing."

"Yes. She has been almost completely consumed. It won't be much longer until she too merges with the land," answered Willow.

"What do you mean by that?"

"A mind consumed with gluttony will not stop until the entire vessel is destroyed. Your friend is losing her mind. She will eventually become that which she consumes. Her very bones will become the nourishment for my kind. That's what the Land of Indulgences demands of everyone."

"What does that mean?" Fox whimpered.

"She will seek out the hidden fruit, but never find it. There are choices all around, but none will satisfy her hunger except that which she cannot have. The irony is that she will starve to death. Her body will then be consumed by the land, and she will end up as nothing more than fertilizer for the very fruit she so desperately desired."

"But we must warn her. We must stop her," cried Fox.

"Only she can stop herself. However, you have all the answers you need to help her, and I think, the plan to make it work. Just be careful when taking the Glouscenshire. That is what you came here for, I know. You think you are strong, and you have indeed proven stronger than any other, but no one has taken the fruit off the tree before. The self-professed wise one would not have led you here if he thought you could resist the Glouscenshire's power."

"Where is this thing called the Glouscenshire?"

"Look for my dead branch that points towards the north. There is only one, and the tree that carries the Glouscenshire will reside directly beneath."

"You never answered my other question. Why would someone as beautiful and peaceful as you be called a weeping willow?"

"I have many names, my crimson one. There is a rumor amongst those around here that I am the bringer of water and fertility, but that is not true. I have no special powers except perhaps to bring forth stories and images from one's own imagination."

"But I have very little imagination, and I see you as the most beautiful tree ever."

"That's because your spirit is innocent and you easily see beauty in others," responded Willow. "I am, however, proud of my species' ancestral contribution. On the riverbanks of Babylon those that came before me held the musical lyres, a comfort to those remembering Zion. My heritage is rich and so my history shall continue with you and your friend. Remember me for the branch I shall give to you when you need it most. Now run along, you haven't much time."

The fox looked up and around at all the branches and the beauty surrounding her. She whimpered a sweet goodbye and went off in search of the dead branch pointing to the North. She could not see much from under the tree so she had to run out in the open.

She slowly backed away from the weeping willow until she spotted the dead branch. She now knew exactly where to find the evil fruit. She quickly ran around to the right spot and darted back underneath the weeping willow. The tree that held the infamous Glouscenshire stood before Fox as if challenging a duel.

"What a pathetic looking little tree," Fox said. But Willow did not respond. Perhaps Fox was too far away from the trunk for Willow to hear. Only one fruit hung on the tree. The singular ornament was bright red and squishy looking. Fox thought the fruit might burst at any moment. How in the world could she pick the fruit without half of the juice dripping into her mouth? She had to think.

As Fox began to pace back and forth nervously, she noticed a branch of the weeping willow slowly creeping down around the Glouscenshire fruit. The branch, thin and limber, wrapped itself around the fruit several times. In a matter of seconds, the fruit had been contained in a little carrying pouch.

Fox bit the branch off inches above the fruit. She carefully held on as she darted outside and headed back towards the orchard. There was no time to waste. It would not be long before Melissa would be past the point of return. If time had not run out for her already.

Chapter 23

The Land of Indulgences Part II

Many hours passed before Fox found Melissa lying on the ground. At first she thought the girl was asleep, exhausted from her search for the elusive Glouscenshire, but then she noticed that Melissa's eyes were wide open. Fox realized that her friend seemed to be in some sort of trance. Or had Melissa already gone completely mad?

Fox prayed she still had time to rescue Melissa from the evil that captivated her. With the willow branch that held the Glouscenshire firmly in her mouth, Fox circled around her friend. She swung the fruit as if it were a thurible, much like a priest swinging incense.

The aroma that had pushed Melissa to the brink of insanity emanated from the fruit now in Fox's possession. As soon as the scent from the Glouscenshire filled her nostrils, Melissa stood at attention. She wanted that fruit more than life itself.

"Well, hello, Fox," said Melissa. "Where have you been all this time? I've been looking for you. I've missed you. What's that you have in your mouth there?"

"That's for me to know and for you to find out," said Fox, who did not dare get too close to the crazy-eyed girl standing before her.

"Aren't you going to share?" asked Melissa.

"Share? That was surely my intention. But, we mustn't eat out here in the open. Follow me and we shall partake of this lovely fruit under cover."

"I'm so tired. I need to eat first, to get my strength back."

"We're not going that far. Follow me." Fox rushed off in the direction of the great hedge from where they had entered. Melissa followed closely behind, appearing to have regained all her strength. She kept Fox's pace without faltering.

The smell of the Glouscenshire, so the rumor went, could revive the recently deceased. Fox could not be sure her plan would work, but time would not allow for any other option. If she failed to bring Melissa out of her catatonic state, all would be lost. Fox wanted to get back home, but without Melissa, that might not be a possibility. Their two fates were tightly interwoven.

Fox was more than just some imaginary friend on a mythical journey with a human girl. Fox was a warm-blooded creature doing God's work. She had a family, friends, and a life beyond this experience. Her unfailing loyalty, unknown even to herself, had been why God chose her to be Melissa's companion. But loyalty to her newfound friend did not keep Fox from thinking about the possibilities of her own future.

Since she was young, Fox had dreamed of the day when she would have a den all her own. In fact, one particularly handsome dog (that is what male foxes are sometimes called) had been sniffing around for several months. If she did not get back soon, some other vixen might stick her nose where it did not belong. But even the hope of love and family would not allow her to abandon Melissa in the girl's time of need. Fox's loyalty could not be questioned.

Melissa, following closely behind Fox, seemed to be coming slowly to her senses. She had not eaten anything in the garden for several hours, and though the effects of the intoxicating fruit were wearing off, nothing short of a miracle would keep her from devouring the Glouscenshire once she caught up to Fox. She was still very much in jeopardy of losing her soul to the Land of Indulgences forever. Fortunately, four legs were faster than two.

Melissa managed a few lucid thoughts while chasing after Fox. She thought of her brother and wondered if he had made it back home, or if he might be waiting somewhere down the trail. She felt a tinge of guilt for not trying to find him and instead had chosen to chase after her own desires. Even though Melissa and Seth had not always gotten along, he was still her big brother, and she knew he would always protect her, and would spare nothing to keep her out of harm's way. Had this place actually caused her to forget about everything that really mattered?

Melissa's thoughts of her brother quickly vanished when Fox stopped running. Fox stood just a few feet away on the same stairs that had brought them into the Land of Indulgences. She growled as Melissa attempted to move closer. The girl slowly backed away, never taking her eyes off the Glouscenshire.

Fox set the fruit down just long enough to yap. "There is something written on the last step that you were supposed to have read before entering into the garden. What does it say?"

"This is silly," said Melissa. "Give me the fruit. I am famished."

"I haven't heard you mention anyone but yourself since we got here. Everything out of your mouth is about you. What you want. What *you* need. I haven't heard you even mention your family back home, or your brother who might be risking his life right at this moment to save you. Worse yet, what if you are the one that's supposed to save him?"

"That's preposterous. All this talk is a waste of time. My brother can handle himself. How could I possibly help him? I am hungry and I want that fruit. You promised me the fruit!"

"After you read what's written on these steps, and after you have interpreted the meaning for me, if you still want the fruit, I shall give you the devil's bounty. Now tell me what the writing says—and the meaning."

"That's it? And then you will give me what I want? You promise?"

The fox's normally joyful face showed concern and vulnerability. "I promise."

"Here goes." Melissa read the words aloud. "'Man shall not live by bread alone, but by every word of God.' That's it. Let's eat."

"Not so fast. What does it mean?"

"It means that if you love God you must starve to death because that's what I'm doing right now."

"Really? Look at your belly. Stuffed with all you have been shoving in your mouth since we got here. Your body is not starving. But your brain is famished! You have willingly left everything you have known behind in order to fill your mouth with what you so desperately and unashamedly desire. You have become nothing more than a blind, gluttonous fool!"

"Okay! You're right. The verse means that food alone will not lead to life. We also need God's words and His wisdom to make it to the other side. To survive. Maybe the verse is a warning about this place. How dare you call me a gluttonous fool. I could stop eating and leave this place anytime I want to."

"Really? Prove it!" Fox tossed the fruit a few feet away from Melissa.

When the Glouscenshire hit the ground with a mushy thud, Fox saw the horrifying truth for the very first time. The fruit instantly turned into maggots. Hundreds of small, yellowish worms swarmed in a ball. But that did not stop Melissa from quickly scooping up the vile deception with her bare hands. Not seeing its true form, she peeled back the willow branch. Her mouth watered and she swallowed in anticipation.

She slowly brought the cluster of maggots closer to her mouth. She savored the thought of her first bite. Just as she was about to devour the undulating ball of worms, she glanced at Fox who had slumped down into a hopeless sprawl.

She never would have believed that the happiest, most cheerful animal in the world could become so sad. She looked back at what her hands held and she began to weep. She cried uncontrollably, sobbing louder than a newborn baby.

"Oh, forgive me, Fox. What have I done? What am I doing? Am I willing to forsake everyone and everything for this? But I can't resist. Please, dear God, if you are real, if you are true, I promise that I will read your Word. I will discover who you are, if you let me. If you break this spell that is upon me, I will find out who you are. Please, dear God, if you love me, please help me now."

As Melissa sat on her knees holding the fruit before her, sobbing uncontrollably, she saw the beautiful sweet smelling Glouscenshire turn into what it had always been, a vile disgusting ball of putrid maggots. The pudgy worms began to swarm all over her hands and up her arms. Melissa screamed.

She jumped to her feet and shook her limbs wildly in an attempt to free herself of the deception. One by one she picked off the remaining worms that had managed to cling to her clothes. When she had gotten the last of them, she paused to thank God. She then looked up to find Fox. Suddenly, she began to throw up everything she had eaten.

Melissa paused to take a couple of deep breaths, then wiped her face with the sleeve of her shirt. "Come on, Fox. We have to get out of here. We have to run as fast as we can." Melissa ran up the steps towards Fox, but Fox put her two front paws up to block Melissa.

"No. We go through the garden. We must continue the way you chose to go. Together we will make it through this horrible place. We will run and God will be on our side. If He is with us, who can be against us? Come, we must do this quickly," said Fox.

"Wait." Melissa untied the scarf around her neck and took it over to Fox. "I want you to have something. This was from someone very special to me and I don't deserve it. You, on the other hand, are the most deserving lady I have ever met. You had faith in me. You always believed I would make the right choice." Melissa tied the scarf around Fox's neck and tried to hold back a few sniffles—she did not want to cry. "It looks lovely on you," she said.

"No one has ever given me anything so beautiful before. Thank you. I will cherish this gift always. Come, we must hurry." Fox swiftly ran past Melissa. Melissa watched Fox, but hesitated for a moment because she wanted to go back the way they came. The wind began to pick up and all the trees moved back and forth. Melissa wiped her tears (because she did cry, after all) and followed quickly after Fox.

Fox and Melissa ran as fast as they could, but the wind continued to increase in strength. Just as they entered the thickest area of the orchard the wind became so strong that the two of them were unable to gain any ground at all.

Melissa pushed one foot in front of the other with her whole body leaning in front of her. If the wind were to suddenly stop blowing, she would fall forward, flat on her face. Fox could not make much progress either. Even with her four powerful legs and sleek body, the wind made it nearly impossible for her to move.

Fox thought about the weeping willow and the safety that her branches had provided. If they could just get to Willow she would be able to give them refuge, and help them make a plan to get across to the other side of the Lake of Entitlement. But the wind had other ideas, and was growing stronger and louder as each moment passed. Not only were they not making progress, they were being pushed backwards, towards the old fruitless tree in the middle of the orchard.

Just as all hope seemed lost, something miraculous happened. Willow branches came out of nowhere and quickly wrapped around Fox. Some of the limbs also wrapped around Melissa. But the girl began to panic, and she attempted to pull free of the rope-like entanglement. Fox shouted something that she could not hear over the howling wind. Then she saw Fox shaking her head frantically—indicating for her not to fight off the branches, that they were friendly. Even though the wind had begun to push even harder than before, Melissa stopped struggling. She trusted Fox and so she would trust the branches as well.

One by one the branches intertwined until they were securely fastened around the two weary travelers. The willow branches had combined their strength to form a bond as strong as a metal chain. Melissa and Fox suddenly began to make forward progress despite the powerful wind's effort to push them backwards. They could feel the strength of the limbs around them, pulling them forward with every step.

With the help of their newfound friend and her branches, Melissa and Fox soon found themselves under the strong and graceful arms of the weeping willow tree. Melissa sighed as she dropped to her knees with exhaustion. Under Willow, she immediately felt secure, like a baby chick under her mother's feathery breast.

"Melissa meet Willow. Willow this is Melissa," said Fox.

"I'm so honored to meet you, Miss Melissa. You have brought hope to all who live in this place," said Willow.

"Who me?" asked Melissa.

"Yes. You are the first to make it this far, and you and Fox are the first to resist the power of the Glouscenshire, a feat that will be remembered for all the ages to come. You will never know how narrow your escape was. We have all been watching and listening."

"We?" asked Fox.

"Yes, all the trees here. You have given them hope that perhaps there is something more, something better than what they know. In fact, the Lake of Entitlement has been dry for thousands of years, but the springs are once again feeding water into her belly. The living waters, they are sometimes called, have been awakened by your bravery and perseverance. It won't be long before the lake is full again."

"Thank you, but I am surely not worthy of such honor. Fox is the one that deserves all the credit," said Melissa.

The weeping willow rustled her leaves and laughed. "Yes, Miss Melissa, the crimson one is an amazing creature. But this is your journey, and it is just beginning. You have a promise to fulfill and a mission to accomplish. Your life has purpose now, dear, even if you don't quite fully understand what that purpose is just yet."

"Can't you tell me?" asked Melissa.

The weeping willow laughed again and her leaves made music. "Shhh," said Willow to her leaves. "In due time, little ones." Willow then addressed Melissa. "I have no doubt that you will discover it on your own, and with the help of your brother."

"How do you know about my brother?"

"He was supposed to come here with you, so the winds told. But alas, it was not to be. Rumors perhaps, but I am worried nonetheless. You must find him and finish this journey together. He will be behind you—in more ways than one. But your faith and the things you are yet to learn will benefit him— and the rest of your world—for all eternity."

"I don't understand. How do you know so much about me?" asked Melissa.

"Miss Melissa, I am old and my roots are deep, my branches touch the sky and my leaves absorb the light. There is not much I do not know. But I cannot know everything, so let's do the best we can to help you make it out of here safely."

"But aren't we safe now?" asked Melissa, getting the words out with some difficulty.

"You are safe as long as I am sheltering you, but you must leave my branches and find your way out of this orchard. The old tree will not let you go easily, but if you follow my directions you have a very good chance. Now, listen carefully..."

As Willow laid out the plan Fox and Melissa were to follow, Melissa sat down on the soft dirt underneath Willow's branches and placed her head against the tree's strong trunk. Slowly, the branches of the weeping willow began to creep underneath Melissa, forming a hammock. And as the leaves played a soft hymn, the branches lifted Melissa off the ground and gently swung her back and forth as she listened closely to Willow's instructions.

Melissa's mind turned to thoughts of home and the willow tree where her grandmother had recited Bible stories to Seth and her. Her grandmother often told stories about Jonah and the Whale, David and Goliath, the walls of Jericho, and so many others. Melissa loved hearing how Esther saved the Israelites from certain death. It showed her that girls could be heroes too.

Melissa was amazed at how many of the stories were coming

back to her and how, for some reason, they no longer seemed like fairytales, but rather stories to be honored—stories that taught life lessons. They were stories to live by, and stories to learn from.

An hour had passed when Willow informed Melissa and Fox that it was time for them to leave. "Don't deviate from the plan if at all possible," she said. "I wish I could tell you what's waiting for you on the other side of the Lake of Entitlement, but not even my roots go that far, and the wind has not blown from that direction for as long as I have been. I wish you well, my friends. God speed. Go. You must go."

Chapter 24

The Lake of Entitlement

Fox and Melissa headed north under the cover of darkness towards the Lake of Entitlement. Willow had warned them that they must conceal their scent should the wind begin to blow, so they had rubbed dirt into their clothing and wrapped branches of the willow tree around each other. Fox resembled some sort of swamp creature. Melissa hated to think of what she looked like.

The wind, Willow said, always blew, but depending on the direction of the breeze, it might not necessarily be against them. They walked quietly and methodically towards their hopeful escape.

Although Willow had prepared them as best as she could, not even she knew the obstacles they would face. They were instructed to speak only when necessary, until they cleared the lake. Keeping her mouth shut, usually a hard task for Melissa, had become much easier in this strange and dangerous world.

Only once did Melissa feel a breeze, and a very slight one at that, but the flowing air chilled her to the bone as goose bumps raced down her arms. She could not imagine ever liking the wind again. Concentrating on Willow's instructions helped keep the fear from paralyzing her.

Fox whimpered uncontrollably when the breeze ruffled her fur. The usually bold and carefree vixen froze in her tracks. Melissa, who had somehow managed to convince herself that this particular breeze only had good intentions, bent down and gave Fox a reassuring hug. Fox's shaking stopped as Melissa stroked her fur, and they were able to keep moving forward.

With their newfound confidence and a quickened pace, it did not take long to reach the shore line. "I thought you said the lake was dry," whispered Melissa.

"It was dry, but Willow said the springs started flowing again. Remember? I guess they flowed faster than she thought. Anyway, that's neither here nor there. Full or not, we still must get across. Do you have the stone?" asked Fox.

"Of course. The stone is safe and sound right here." Melissa reached into her pocket and pulled out a fairly average looking rock. The smooth rock had a dull, reddish brown color. Willow said this would be the most important stone they would ever possess, and that if trusted with its task would provide them a way across the lake.

Trusted with its task? How could Melissa trust an inanimate rock if she had no idea of its purpose? She trusted rocks to break glass and bruise someone's head, but beyond that she had no clue as to what a rock like this could be used for.

But Melissa knew she could trust Willow, and if Willow said this rock would help them out of the Land of Indulgences, she believed it surely would. After all, Willow had saved them from the old tree, and that awful, nasty wind.

Willow had sternly warned Melissa and Fox not to attempt going around the lake or they would be discovered, and if that happened, not even she could help them. So evidently, this rock held the only key to their escape. Melissa lifted the rock to her face, said a quick prayer, and then threw the precious stone into the lake, just as Willow had instructed.

A few moments passed but nothing happened. "How long do you suppose we are supposed to wait?" Fox asked.

"I don't even know what we are waiting for. Maybe it already happened. I don't know."

"Maybe *what* already happened?" asked Fox.

"Whatever was supposed to happen," answered Melissa.

"What was supposed to happen?" asked Fox again.

"If I knew that, I wouldn't be standing in front of this lake feeling so helpless," said a frustrated Melissa.

"I see. Well, do you think we should do something?"

"Like what?"

"Willow said you had to have faith. Do you have faith?"

"I don't know. How does one know if they have faith?" asked Melissa.

"You just know," answered Fox.

"Do you have faith?"

"Sure, all foxes have faith."

"But how do you know for sure."

"Well, we don't question it for starters!"

"Then why didn't Willow give *you* the stone?"

"I guessed it was because I don't have pockets," said Fox.

Melissa's head hung low as she plopped down on the shoreline. She crossed her arms and waited. Fox nuzzled up next to her and looked across the water with hopeful eyes. Both of them sat quietly together, waiting for something to happen. Fox occasionally looked over her shoulder, and then back at Melissa, and then back at the water again.

Melissa refused to make eye contact with Fox. Fox's repetitive glances caused Melissa to consider that her own lack of faith might have put the two of them in grave danger. They waited and waited, but nothing happened. Neither of them admitted to considering the alternative, however. If Willow said not to go around the lake, they would simply keep waiting. If Willow said the stone would work, then the stone would work.

"Do you hear that?" asked Fox.

"I don't hear anything."

"My hearing is superior. Keep listening and you will hear it also."

"Should we run?" asked Melissa.

"I don't think so," said Fox.

"Look. The water is moving."

"That's not the water. There's something *in* the water," exclaimed Fox.

"Oh, my goodness, could it be? Fox, I think those are rocks coming out of the water."

"Yes. Yes, they are indeed. And they are humming."

"Rocks don't hum."

"These rocks hum. Listen closer," said Fox.

Melissa and Fox listened and watched as one by one the rocks marched ashore. They were making some kind of rhythmic noise.

"Brum chi chi chi, brum chi chi chi, click ta, click ta, click click click ta ta ta, brum chi chi chi, brum chi chi chi, click ta, click ta..."

Melissa could not tell if the sound came from the water splashing and trickling off the rocks or from the fact that they were bumping and scraping each other. Whatever the cause, the rocks were rhythmic and harmonious, and undeniably charming and playful. The music and movement of the rocks reminded Melissa of an Irish step-dance she once saw at her school.

In only a matter of minutes, there must have been hundreds

or perhaps thousands of stones circling around the shore near Melissa and Fox. If Melissa had not known better, she would have sworn they were doing a choreographed dance to go along with their merry music.

"Look, Melissa. They're dancing for us. How cute is that?"

"They're not dancing..." Before Melissa could finish her sentence, Fox got on her hind feet and began prancing around with the stones. Melissa found herself in the middle of a celebration of sorts. Fox, and what must have been a thousand rocks, danced joyously before her.

She had to admit that this jaw-dropping, supernatural spectacle was an incredible sight to behold. As she watched their whimsical dance, or whatever it was that the rocks were doing, Melissa stood up to get a better look at the lake. Out of the water, about every foot or so, arose a pile of stepping stones. All the little rocks were piling on top of one another, creating a path across the water, a way for Melissa and Fox to escape. It was happening not a moment too soon because the wind had started to blow.

The wind had actually begun stirring minutes earlier, but in all the excitement no one had noticed. All the noise must have exposed their whereabouts to the old tree. As much fun as Fox and the rocks were having, it was now a matter of life and death that they stop everything and focus on getting across the lake as quickly as possible.

"Wow," Melissa said quietly to herself. "I guess I do have faith after all." She waved her arms to get Fox's attention. "Let's go, Fox. We need to hurry. The wind has found us."

Melissa ventured onto the lake first. With every step she took, the stones sounded as if they were giggling. Melissa wished she could be having as much fun as the rocks, but she feared being blown into the water. She focused intensely on each step, quickly continuing forward, as Fox followed closely behind.

The wind increased in strength the further out they got, and it came at them from every direction, determined to blow them into the turbulent water. Melissa put her head down and jumped from stone to stone. Fox struggled to fit all four legs onto one small group of stones at the same time. Melissa was slowing the fox's natural gait, making it nearly impossible for her to jump without having to stop and wait on Melissa to move forward.

Melissa motioned for Fox to lead the way as she crouched low to the water. Fox would need to jump over Melissa because one group of stones could not support both of them. Of course Fox's jumping abilities were one of her greatest assets, even in the worst of weather.

The maneuver should have worked without a hitch. But just as Fox leapt into the air, a strong gust of wind came from nowhere and pushed her into the murky water below. Melissa tried desperately to grab Fox, but the current had already taken her out of arm's reach.

The large waves forced Fox's head under the water. No matter how hard she paddled she could not get back to the stone path. The current wasted no time in carrying her farther and farther away. Fox gulped for air as her head bobbed up and down. Melissa screamed for Fox to get close enough so she could grab her, but neither of them could manage the waves or the fierce wind.

"You must go on without me," Fox yapped as loud as she could in-between waves. "You must go on without me." Fox tried to get air, but swallowed a mouth full of water instead. "I'm a good swimmer," she managed to shout. "I'll meet you on the other side."

"I won't leave without you!" screamed Melissa.

"Go. I will see you on the other side. I'll never leave you, my friend. Run!" She barely managed to choke out her last words before a huge wave took her under.

Melissa crouched down on the rocks, helpless and heartbroken, as the relentless current dragged her only friend in the world out of reach. Fox could barely keep her head above water as she paddled with her four legs as fast and hard as she had ever done before. In a matter of seconds, Fox had completely vanished from Melissa's sight.

Melissa stood up and ran a few more steps. She could not help but think about how Fox had saved her from her own demons. She stopped in her tracks and turned around. She would not be able to live with herself if something had happened to Fox.

Melissa, struggling to maintain her balance on the rocks, ran back to where she had last seen her. Melissa had always been a strong swimmer. She had to save her friend. Fox would have done no less for her. Without another thought she dove into the water.

There seemed to be multiple currents going in several different directions at the same time. Melissa could only guess which way Fox might have gone. Melissa could not even be certain that a fox could survive in water for this long.

Melissa dove under for a look, but the murkiness made it impossible to see past her own hands. She waited for a lull in the waves in order to look above the water, but she could see nothing, not even the shoreline. She did not know what to do next. Nothing in her life back home could have prepared her for such a life or death situation. Fox was gone.

Melissa could only hope that Fox figured out the currents and made it to shore. The feeling in her heart, however, left little room for hope or faith. Melissa feared she would never see the little red fox again.

"Oh, God, I can't see the shore anymore." Melissa's strokes became erratic. Instead of strong thoughtful strokes, her arms chopped wildly at the water in a futile attempt to gain speed. Her panic caused disorientation and confusion, the battle for survival did not look promising.

Melissa prayed, "Please, God, help me get to shore. Please bring me back to my brother, help us both to live another day to learn about you. I beg you, God. Please give me enough energy to find the shore."

Melissa attempted floating on her back in order to conserve energy, but the waves crashed over her. She kept swallowing water and gasping for air. The panic did not subside. Desperation overtook her. "I can't do this, God. I'm not going to make it. If you are real, I apologize for every bad thing I've ever done. Please, let me be with you."

Chapter 25

Missing

"I've called everyone—neighbors and even strangers. No one has heard or seen anything. It's been almost two days and nothing. My husband flew back from his business trip and he's at our house contacting school friends and looking through our children's personal belongings for anything that might help tell us...if they were planning something. My Mom has been all over town talking to anyone who will listen. Jimmy has gotten a bunch of people to scour the woods. I don't know what else to do. And if you, the police, can't do anything, what hope is there?"

It was difficult for Bethany to remain polite to the deputy on the other end of the phone as her irritation and panic increased. "Listen, I've heard all this before. They did not run away. Why would a college kid need to run away? He can leave anytime he wants, and my daughter would never go more than five miles from her wardrobe and black nail polish. Yes, black. What's that supposed to mean? No, she is not into the occult. And, so what if she was. Would that mean you wouldn't be as concerned?"

The front door opened, and Azora staggered in with Jimmy following closely behind.

"I have to go now. Please call me the minute you hear anything." Bethany hung up the phone, and quickly joined the two-member search party in the living room.

"Please, tell me you know something more than the police do," pleaded Bethany.

"I'm sorry, Bethany. There are still people looking in the woods and all around town, but no, we haven't found anything," said Jimmy.

Azora slowly lowered her tired body into the equally worn out recliner. Her physical and emotional exhaustion could not be hidden by her wide-brimmed flap hat. Bethany sat nervously on the sofa while Jimmy stood awkwardly near the front door.

"What are we supposed to do now?" Bethany asked.

"Pray," answered Azora.

"Seriously? That's your answer? Pray? Well, I don't know about you, but I have already prayed and here we sit worse off than yesterday. The police say the first 24 hours are the most important. We are well beyond that now."

"We have to think positively. We *will* find them," Jimmy said.

"How do you know that? Did God tell you that?" asked Bethany.

"Of course not, but there's no gain in thinking the worst. Maybe Azora is right. We should all pray."

Bethany stood up. "You will excuse me if I don't join you. I've got more important things to do. Like make phone calls and..." Bethany could not hold back her tears any longer. Jimmy walked over and put his arm around her.

"Thank you for all that you are doing, Jimmy. Please excuse me. I need a few moments alone." Bethany went into the back bedroom, fell onto the bed, and placed a pillow over her head to soften the sounds of her weeping.

Jimmy did not quite know whether to stay or leave. He also had no clue about what to say, but he gave it a shot anyway. "God hears the prayers of the righteous, Azora. You just keep praying. Okay?"

"Thanks, Jimmy. I know you're right and I believe everything is going to turn out just fine, even if I can't help feelin' a little powerless right now."

"For a believer, there is nothing more powerful than prayer. You are the prayer warrior in this family and God hears you. Don't stop praying."

"Yes, but all things accordin' to His will. What if this *is* His will?" asked Azora.

"We don't know God's will, but we do have examples where God was petitioned to respond to the hearts of His people. You have a heart for God, and everything will work out for good for those who love the Lord," said Jimmy.

"I wish I could be as confident as you are."

"Just rely on the truth of His word, not your own confidence."

"Will you pray with me before you go, Jimmy?"

"Of course I will."

Jimmy knelt down next to Azora. He took her hand in his and gave it a reassuring squeeze. They both bowed their heads, but neither said anything for a long while. When they finally did pray, they spoke not only for the children, but also for Bethany, and ultimately, for God's will to be done. After a short while Jimmy stopped praying, but only after he noticed Azora had nodded off to sleep.

He quietly let himself out of the house. As he gently closed the door behind him, he noticed a large bug clinging to the bricks next to the door. He placed his hand in front of the insect and gave a slight nudge to encourage it to crawl onto his hand. The insect obliged, albeit with cautious hesitation. Had it been just any ol' Diapheromera Femorata, that is what the book learners call them, and not Sticky, it probably would have scurried off under the eaves.

Jimmy lifted the bug up to his face for a closer inspection. "Aren't you a beautiful specimen. I don't think I've seen one of your kind for…Gosh, I don't remember how long. What is it we used to call you guys? Oh, yeah, Walking Sticks." Jimmy placed a finger from his other hand in front of the bug's face. Sticky did not appreciate the added scrutiny and reared up in defense.

"That's okay, little guy. I'm not going to hurt you." Jimmy placed his hand back on the brick where he first saw Sticky. Although Sticky found the human to be warm and texturally interesting, he did not care for the odd odor and so quickly crawled back onto familiar ground.

"Walking…the old road to town. Maybe they stashed Melissa's bike and walked the old road into town. Thank you, Mr. Walking Stick, you just made me think of another place to look." Sticky was proud of himself for completing his latest task. He straightened his antennae as if to acknowledge the human's brilliant idea. He then let out a huge yawn as he turned towards his favorite napping spot under the window.

Sticky paused to look back at Jimmy one last time. "That was kind of fun, taking a ride on a human's hand. Wouldn't it be great if all of them were so kind? What fun we could have together." He turned back around and crawled towards his dark crevice under the eaves. Along the way he hummed the lullaby his mother always sang to help him sleep.

Chapter 26

The Salt Lands

Melissa awoke shivering on the shores of the Lake of Entitlement. Her soaked clothes hung heavy on her body, making it difficult for her to move. She was too exhausted to lift her head. She tried to open her eyes, but the bright sun caused her to squint as she looked toward the sky. She felt someone's hand brushing the hair from her face. When she turned to see who was trying to comfort her, she began to cough up what seemed like a bucket of water.

After expelling most of the liquid from her lungs, she looked up to see a face slowly come into focus. It was Seth smiling down at her, and as he wrapped his arms around Melissa, she realized that she had never been happier to see her brother. She hoped she would remember this feeling for the rest of her life.

"I thought I lost you there for a second," Seth said.

"Well, would you look at this, it's Santa's little helper! Where did you come from? Are we home? Where are we?" asked Melissa in-between coughs.

"I don't have a clue. I was hoping you could tell me."

"How did you get here?" asked Melissa.

"I don't really know that either. The place I was at before here was...Well, let's just say it was not a nice place. It was awful, Melissa. I never want to go back there again."

"I haven't exactly been having a picnic either." Melissa giggled as it suddenly occurred to her what she had just said.

"What's so funny?"

"Well, I sort of *was* having a picnic. A picnic from hell."

"What do you mean?"

"I'm sure we will have plenty of time to fill each other in on all the details, but first we need to get home." Melissa slowly got to her feet.

"How do you know that home even exists anymore?"

"I just know, that's all. Do you have anything dry I can wear?" Melissa suddenly froze. "Oh, no, have you seen Fox? I totally forgot about Fox." Her forehead was wrinkled with worry.

"Fox? Who's Fox?"

"Fox is, well...a fox. She's my friend. Umm, we both fell in the lake and..." Melissa choked on her words as she quickly ran to the water's edge looking for Fox. She felt sick to her stomach. She ran up and down the shoreline, but found no sign of her friend.

She looked anxiously out into the lake. She spotted something floating in the water and started to go after it. Seth put a hand on her shoulder. "I'll get it. You stay here." After stripping down to his boxer shorts, he waded out to retrieve the floating debris. "It looks like a piece of clothing," he yelled.

Not able to wait for him to get back to shore, Melissa met him half way. She took the material out of his hands and held it up to her cheek. She struggled to hold back tears as she scanned the water, desperately trying to remain hopeful.

"Did that belong to your friend?" asked Seth.

"Yes. She was such a kindhearted soul. She saved my life, Seth."

"I'm sure she made it back to shore. Foxes can swim pretty well."

"No, she didn't make it. She would never leave this behind. I gave her this scarf and she would never have let it out of her sight."

"She may not have even noticed it came off. This isn't proof that she didn't make it to shore."

"No. She would have waited for me. She would have been here. I know her."

"Don't try to convince yourself of the worst case scenario. You don't know anything for sure. She might be fine. Maybe she had to go and she couldn't wait for you."

"I hope you're right, Seth. Since when did you become the optimist?" asked Melissa.

Seth helped Melissa back to dry land, not saying another word. He could sense her heavy burden, and knew that nothing he could say would be of any comfort. Melissa found a soft patch of sand and sat down, feeling defeated. Seth used his shirt to dry off and then quickly got dressed. He wanted to get his bearings as soon as possible.

After haphazardly tying his shoelaces, Seth rushed a few yards to the top of the ridge. He felt both amazed and confused as he viewed a flat endless sea of white. There were no hills, mountains, plants, or anything other than the white ground that eventually met a blue sky at the horizon line.

He walked a bit further down the ridge onto the strange crystallized surface. He could not ascertain the composition of the substance by merely standing on it. The white surface had the texture of dried mud, but sounded more like crushed ice beneath his feet.

He knelt down and attempted to scrape up a sample with his fingers. Not only did the ground feel like rough sand paper, but a chisel and hammer would be necessary to pry the stuff loose. Since tools were in short supply, Seth leaned over and gave the ground a lick with his tongue.

"Salt! It's all salt. This can't be good." Seth stood up and headed back to share the news with his sister, but she had already ventured over the hill and was only a few yards away.

"It's salt," Seth yelled to Melissa.

"Salt? This can't be good."

"That's exactly what I said."

"Funny," said Melissa as she caught up to him.

"What?"

"That's the first time in a long time we've agreed on something."

"Shall we?" asked Seth as he extended his arm out to Melissa.

"Yes, I think we shall."

They marched arm in arm onto the salt lands. Neither spoke for a long while. For miles and miles, as far as the eye could see, a flat, hard, bed of sodium chloride stood before them. The same thought occurred to Melissa and Seth as they walked in silence. Which direction should they go? Every direction looked the same—white! Was this another test or just an elaborate dream? Perhaps someone or something would come and help them, or even better, they would wake up safely in their beds.

"What did you do with your scarf?" asked Seth, finally breaking the silence.

"I left it tied around a rock, just in case Fox made it after all. She'll know that I survived too."

"You should see yourself in a mirror," said Seth.

"Do I look that bad?"

"No, you look beautiful, actually. All that black dye is out of your hair, and your fingernails...they're normal. And there's a look on your face that I've never seen before."

"How? What do you mean?"

"I don't know how to describe it exactly," said Seth.

"Try."

"You look grounded. Wise, you might say. Sorta peaceful, I guess."

"Yeah, that is odd. That's everything I'm not," joked Melissa.

"Maybe you are those things now. How do I look?"

"The same."

"Gee, thanks."

"What? You want me to lie? Look, Seth, I don't have all the answers to why this is happening to us, but I made some promises back there."

"Promises? To whom?"

"To God."

"Oh, brother. You think this is all God's doing? Well, if it is, I don't like God very much."

"I don't know, Seth, but do you have any other reasonable explanation? Just hear me out and don't interrupt. I made a promise to at least give the possibility of God a chance. I promised that if whoever this God is got me out of that place I was in, I would read and study His word. I intend on doing that."

"Where would you begin? Do you know how many religious books there are in the world?"

"No, but I'll keep reading them until they prove themselves false or until I can find the one that tells the truth. It seems to me that all the religious books of the world could be wrong, but they can't all be right. In fact only one, if any, could be right. From what I have seen and read so far, every religion has something contradictory to say about the other. Do you think it's a coincidence all this happened to us at Grandma's house while we were just discussing all that religious and science stuff with Jimmy? There has to be some kind of cosmic connection."

"I don't know," said Seth.

"Look, I made a promise for you, too. I asked God to reunite us. Everything I asked for and sincerely prayed about was granted to me, Seth. You don't even know how you got here."

"So, God's the same as a magic Genie now? All we have to do is ask and we receive?" Seth looked up and shouted, "God, please zap me and Melissa back home please. See. Nothing. Still here. No God. No Genie."

"Oh, brother! You are hopeless. Would it really be too much for you to dedicate a year or so to finding out if this God of the Bible is real or not?"

"A whole year? That's a long time. How do you think you can prove anything one way or the other?"

"I don't know the answer to that. But I promised I would seek Him out and I know, if there is such a God, He will reveal himself. We owe it to ourselves and the Creator, if there is one, to try and figure out the truth."

"So what do we do?" asked Seth.

"I was thinking. Why would we be shown the beginning of time? Was that for me or you, or both of us? I personally don't care how God created the universe, but obviously you do. What I care about is finding out who God says He is, and if He is even real. You, on the other hand need to reconcile this faith and science thing. That sounds like a pretty good team to me. I remember Jimmy saying something about a dual revelation. Well maybe this duo, you and me, can figure some stuff out together. I'll help you with what God says, and you help me with what God did, and we'll see if that jives with what we know about science."

Seth did not have an immediate response, and so the two continued walking in silence while Seth thoughtfully considered what Melissa had said. As much as his ego would like to be contrary, he concluded she might be on to something. What harm could there be in trying her suggestion.

Seth always talked about his great love for learning, but his sister had made him suddenly realize that he had been too close-minded to consider beliefs that were different from his own. What could it hurt to learn about this other idea? He would either continue to believe that everything was random. Or that there *is* a God.

"You and me, a team?" asked Seth.

"Yeah, I know, that alone would mean there's a God. Right?" They both laughed.

"You keep saying Him. What makes you think God is male?" asked Seth.

"I don't know. I'm not sure it even matters. Just easier, I guess. If God turns out to be feminine in nature, we'll add that to our list of discoveries."

"Alright, I'm on board. Let's do it. I'll give a year towards the pursuit of finding God."

"You promise to give your best effort, no matter what? To do it with all of your heart, mind, and soul?"

"I promise, with all of my heart, mind, and soul," said Seth.

Melissa put her hands in front of Seth to stop him from walking. "Okay. Let's start with a prayer."

"How can I pray if I don't know who or what I'm praying to? If in a year—supposing we get out of this place—I find out there is a God, then I can pray to Him or Her or It."

"Humor me. I can't tell you why, but I know we need to pray. I'll say the words, just give me your best game face. Try to mean this, Seth. Really, open yourself up to the possibilities."

"Okay, okay."

Melissa took Seth's hands and held them as she prayed aloud. "Dear Creator God. I ask you to bless this journey Seth and I are on. I pray you lead us to the answers we need or whatever it is you want us to know. We promise to give our time and energy to finding out who you are, and all we ask in return is that you help us and reveal yourself to us. Amen."

"You sound like you already believe," said Seth.

"I do. Now I just need to find out what I believe. I'm excited, Seth. I can't explain how I feel, but my life, our lives, are about to change. A change that is going to be even more profound than this mind-blowing experience we are going through right now."

"I hope you're right. In the meantime, I'm thinking we should have brought some water out of that lake with us. The air is getting hotter and dryer. If we don't find some shade and water soon, I'm afraid we are going to wither away."

"We didn't have anything to put water in anyway. Do you have any idea what the time might be?"

"Does time even exist here?" asked Seth.

"I guess there's no chance of the sun going down in a place without time. Dear God, please bring us shade or water or both," said Melissa.

"Here, take my shirt." Seth ripped his shirt in half and tied the fabric over Melissa's head so that it covered her forehead and her neck. "This should help a little bit."

"Thanks, but what about you?" Melissa asked

Seth wrapped the other half of his shirt around his head. "I've got it covered," he said, winking at his sister.

They continued walking for hours with nothing in sight. No trees, water, or any indication of civilization. Nothing.

Even though they were not completely dehydrated, the thought of water consumed them. Sweat poured off Seth, soaking his clothes. Melissa prayed for a mirage. She figured if the end came soon, at least she could die in an imaginary paradise. But on they walked with no mirages, no water, and no shade.

To Melissa's surprise, her brother reached out to God. He asked for a breeze, but none came. Melissa, who thought she could never like the wind again, would have welcomed even the most unfriendly breeze to cool her skin. Why did they ever leave the lake, she thought? Maybe they should have stayed and waited for Fox.

"I can't go on any more. I'm too tired and I'm so thirsty. Maybe we should stay here and try to dig for water," said Melissa.

"With what? We don't have anything to dig with, and we don't even know if there's water beneath this stuff. What am I talking about? If there was water beneath us it would be too salty to drink."

"So, we agree to stop and rest a while?" asked Melissa.

"No, we have to keep moving. If we stop, we don't stand a chance."

Melissa managed to convince her feet to move forward by pretending that her legs were running a race against each other. Her left foot taunted the right. "Go ahead and stop righty, but if you do, I win." Her right foot took another step and again the left foot taunted. "Is that the best you can do? Ha-ha. Alas, you are going to lose the race and I am going to win. I am going to take a bigger step and watch you fall behind." The left foot, true to its word, took a humongous step forward.

Melissa, close to losing all perception, focused on nothing but the salt twelve inches directly in front of her. This worked well until Melissa's left foot, very much on purpose she supposed, crossed over and tripped the right, forcing Melissa to tumble down onto the hard, coarse ground.

Seth bent down to help his sister. "Here, take my hand. You can lean on me."

"I can't go any farther. I would if I could. You know that."

Seth joined Melissa on the ground. Melissa put her head on his shoulder and cried.

"You're wasting precious water doing that, you know," said Seth.

"I'm a girl and I can cry if I want to. You would cry too if you weren't always acting like such a boy all the time! Crying doesn't mean I'm weak. It just means...I'm expressive, that's all," said Melissa.

The two sat and rested while Seth contemplated their options. But no matter how hard he racked his brain, the same conclusion kept coming to him. He had seen enough movies and heard enough stories about people lost in the desert or in the cold. Without the possibility of shelter, their only option would be to continue on. To march, to push forward, to...pray.

As Melissa rested her weary feet, Seth, very much to himself, said his first earnest prayer. If asked, he would deny ever having said it. However, the annals of time would prove otherwise. Not only did the prayer get said, it got heard, and most importantly, it got answered.

Chapter 27

The Woman with Emerald Eyes

While seated, Seth scanned the horizon in front of them, but he did not see anything he had not seen the last three times he lifted his head to look. Just as Seth was about to give up hope, he felt something rub against his back. He looked over his shoulder but did not see anything.

"Was that you?" he asked Melissa.

"Was what me?"

"Did you just move your arm over my hip?"

"No. I can't move a muscle," said Melissa.

"I could have sworn I felt something. We have got to get up and keep moving, Melissa. You can lean on me."

Melissa did not respond so Seth remained on the ground with his legs crossed as he contemplated what to do next. He obviously was in no shape to carry his sister, and even if he could it would not be far enough to make much difference. As he thought about the next move, he felt something jump over his right shoulder.

"What was that? Did you see that?" asked Seth.

"I can't see anything. I have snow blindness, or salt blindness, I guess. I think your brain is playing tricks on you. The heat was bound to get to us sooner or later."

Seth, ignoring his sister, jumped quickly to his feet to locate the culprit. All he could see was white, however. Obviously, nothing could hide here. Anything with the smallest amount of color would stand out like a sore thumb.

Maybe Melissa had it right. He had begun to lose his mind. Or they were both going blind from the bright reflection off the salt. All the more reason to press on, he thought.

"Get up. We have to go now. Take my hand." Melissa complied and Seth lifted her off the ground. She leaned on him and they trudged forward once again. They did not get more than a few feet before Seth felt something hit his chest. He could feel claws sink into his flesh. Seth fell back on the ground and screamed. He grabbed at his chest and rolled around on the salt as if he were on fire.

"What is wrong with you, Seth? Get a grip. Snap out of it!" Melissa dropped to her knees and crawled over to Seth. "There's nothing physically happening to you. Don't let your mind play games. Focus."

"It felt so real. Like some wild beast tore into my chest with sharp claws."

"If something attacked you, there should be marks."

Seth stood up and saw that there were two distinct scratches, neither of which was bleeding. He was relieved to know he had not imagined it.

"See, I'm not crazy! Something is out here," Seth said. "Perhaps it's following us."

"You probably did that with your own fingernails when you were rolling around on the ground screaming like a wild banshee," said Melissa.

If nothing else, all the excitement gave them renewed energy to continue walking. But they got no farther than a few yards when Seth began to cry out in pain again.

"Get it off me. Get it off. It's on my back. Get it off!" shouted Seth.

Melissa chased after Seth in hopes of calming him down, but then she suddenly stopped, pointed her finger at him, and began laughing.

"What are you laughing at? Help me! Get this monster off me."

"Oh, my goodness, it's so cute." Melissa walked up to Seth and pulled the beast off his back. He turned around to see Melissa holding what appeared to be a long-haired house cat that just happened to be white as snow, or in this case, salt. "Is this the beast that you were referring to?" asked Melissa.

"Funny. Let that creature stick its claws into you and we'll see how you like it!"

Melissa held the cat up in the air for a quick inspection. The cat appeared normal in every respect except that his eyes matched his white coat. She had never seen a cat with such odd eyes before. In fact, the only pigment on this cat appeared to be the teeniest hint of pink on his nose. His pads were white. His eyes were white. Even his lips were white.

"Does it talk?" asked Seth.

"Not yet," answered Melissa.

"Ask it something."

Melissa held the cat up to her face and spoke. "Do you know where we could get some water and shelter?" She waited unsuccessfully for a response. "Do you perhaps know the way back to my world, beautiful boy?" But the cat did not utter a sound. Melissa stroked his coat and the cat began to purr, but he could not or would not answer her questions.

"He had to come from somewhere near. Look at how soft

and fluffy his fur is. He looks very well-fed. That means his home must be close. Put the little monster down and we'll follow him," said Seth.

"How do you plan to follow him? You couldn't even see him when he was attached to your chest. He blends in perfectly with the ground."

"Okay. So how do you propose we find out where he lives?" asked Seth.

"We need a leash or something," suggested Melissa.

"Great idea. Let's use our shoelaces. We'll tie them together and make a leash."

"What if he won't walk on a leash?" asked Melissa.

"We'll cross that bridge when we come to it." Seth immediately undid his shoelaces. "Well, aren't you going to take yours off too?"

"Do you want me to set the cat down? He might run away. You go first and then you hold him when it's my turn."

"I'm not holding that thing," said Seth.

"Seth, he's a harmless furry love machine. He's purring like a tractor."

"Love machine, yeah, right. Then why is my chest pouring out blood where it sank its death weapons into me?"

"Oh, please, he barely scratched you. And he's not an it, he's a he," said Melissa.

"Whatever. Hand it over." Seth held the cat by the nape of the neck with his arms fully extended. The cat did not protest, but rather dangled peacefully. Once Melissa undid her shoelaces, she traded them for the cat.

Seth took all four laces and tied them together. He then looped the makeshift leash around the cat's head and secured it with a knot. After double checking Seth's work, Melissa gingerly placed the white feline on the ground.

"Okay, Mr. Kitty, show us where you live," said Melissa. The cat did not move an inch, but rather sat sprawled on the ground as if paralyzed.

"Give it a push," Seth said.

"You can't push a cat. Don't you know anything?"

"Here, give me the leash." Seth took the leash and walked forward. The cat did not move. Seth tugged on the laces, but the cat dug his claws deeper into the salt. "This isn't getting us anywhere," said Seth.

"We have no choice but to take the leash off and hopefully we can follow him," suggested Melissa.

"I guess you're right. I can't stand another minute of this heat, and we've got to find some water soon." Seth knelt down to put his shoelaces back on. The cat instantly jumped on Seth's shoulder.

"I think he likes you," Melissa said as she tied her shoe.

"Great. Why couldn't he like you more? Let's just keep going. His home must be close by."

The siblings walked with renewed vigor. The prospect of finding out where the cat lived had given them hope of finding water and shade. The cat comfortably and contentedly sat atop Seth's broad shoulders, and the three of them moved forward at a fairly brisk pace.

"Ow!" Seth exclaimed.

"What now?"

"The cat just hauled off and slapped me in the face with his paw."

"Hmm, maybe he's trying to tell you something."

"I don't decipher paw slaps. Do you?" asked Seth.

Melissa shrugged her shoulders and they continued walking. The cat once again took his paw and slapped Seth on the right cheek.

"Ow! That's it! You take this foul creature off my shoulders right now."

"Where did he strike you?" she asked.

"On the right cheek."

"Both times?"

"Yes."

"When I used to ride horses we would pull the reins to the right for the horse to go right, and left for the horse to go left. Maybe we should go more towards the right."

"What are you implying here? That the cat is the jockey and I'm the horse?"

"I don't know. Let's find out." Melissa instructed Seth to go to the left, and when he did the cat struck Seth on the right cheek again. When they went straight, Seth got hit with a paw to the right once more. But when they went right, the cat purred.

Although they were pleased to discover that they were more than likely headed in the right direction, Seth was not too happy with his new position as a sulky, also known as a one person horse carriage. "You are not to mention a word of this to anyone," demanded Seth.

"I'll try my best," laughed Melissa.

A few more slaps of the paw and the three of them found themselves in front of what could only be compared to an igloo. Salt blocks substituting for ice, of course. Seth and Melissa were not too concerned about the structure's building material. They would have willingly taken refuge in a cardboard outhouse. They did not bother to knock or announce themselves. Without giving it a second thought, they dashed inside, out of the heat.

The cat jumped off Seth and quickly disappeared into one of the adjoining rooms. In a matter of seconds, a beautiful woman wearing a long white robe entered carrying a pitcher of what they hoped was water. She was perhaps in her sixties, and appeared to be perfect in every way.

Her flawless skin was glowing, and her emerald green eyes were so stunning that it mesmerized anyone who looked upon them. The white walls of the room appeared almost pink due to the reflection of her radiant red hair.

"Welcome, friends. My name is Harmony." Her introduction took the siblings by surprise. Neither of them had ever heard such an enchanting voice before. They were left speechless. Stringed instruments seemed to underscore every word that escaped her mouth. A soft, sweet, reassuring lullaby might describe her way of speaking, yet she did not sing, and no music played.

"We so seldom get visitors here, so this is a most welcomed treat. Please have a seat and rest. I have some cold water for you. My chamber maids will bring you clean clothes and food. Please, by all means, relax and enjoy my hospitality. When you are refreshed, I shall return and we will get to know each other a little better."

"Can you tell us where we are?" asked Seth.

Harmony placed a finger on Seth's lips. "Shhh. There is no need to talk until you have replenished yourselves. There is plenty of time to explain everything after you have rested. Please, take advantage of my hospitality. Become one with these lovely surroundings."

Harmony turned and left from the same place she entered. Not a second passed before two pretty young maidens, also wearing white robes, joined Seth and Melissa. While they were obviously younger than Harmony, they could not match her beauty. They said nothing as they placed two white robes on a table. From a pitcher, they filled two glasses with water, and then left the room.

"I think we're in some sort of spa, Melissa. And I have a feeling it's going to cost a fortune."

Melissa did not miss a beat as she grabbed a glass of water and drank. She swallowed three glasses before responding to Seth, who did his best to finish off the pitcher. "Let's worry about the bill later. What do you suppose they want us to do with these?" Melissa held up one of the robes. As if on cue, another beautiful young woman entered, took Melissa by the arm, and gently led her to a door.

Melissa peeked in and saw what could only be described as a massage table. To the right were partially open curtains revealing a large white cast iron tub with a plush towel hanging on the wall. Simultaneously, another woman led Seth into an identical room with all the same accoutrements.

Seth stuck his head out the door and yelled to his sister. "Yup, it's a spa and I'm not asking any more questions. I'll pay anything. Just put it on my bill."

Seth closed the door and immediately noticed the tub filled with water. He found the temperature to be ideal; not too hot and not too cold. He undressed and submerged himself into the warm, sparkling blue water. He could not remember the last time he had a bath, showers were his usual practice, but that might all change after the way this felt.

Melissa, much like Seth, was too exhausted to ask any questions. She lazily expelled a sigh of relief as she submerged her body into the warm, aromatic water. Oddly, the water smelled faintly like bubble gum. A nice smell, Melissa thought. She felt the salt and sweat drift away as if the water had magical powers. She relaxed and thought about how fortunate they were that the cat had found them when he did.

Chapter 28

A Clue Back Home

No one had ever gotten kidnapped in Garland County, so when the Sheriff got the call concerning two missing youths, he did not assume the worst. Odds were that the teens would turn up when they ran out of money. Besides, there was not much his small department could do if someone did not want to be found. Other than sending out a few deputies to knock on doors and putting out an APB, all they could do was wait and see.

Jimmy refused to take such a lighthearted approach. He feared that Seth and Melissa might have stumbled into one of the many caves in the area. There were old mines too. As far as he knew, no one had ever gotten trapped in one before, but that did not negate the possibility. If they were not found today, he would put together a search party himself.

Although he had only just met this family, he felt a need to help them. Like so many of their generation, Melissa and Seth seemed to be faithless. It was as if they were not only lost in the physical world, but also the spiritual world as well. And while he knew he could neither guarantee their safe return or their spiritual well being, Jimmy would put forth his best effort to honor his God's second greatest commandment—to love your neighbor as yourself.

Jimmy parked his dad's faded black 1956 Ford F-150 near the entrance to the old road. He remembered the location, now obscured with vines, because his dad commented about it every time they passed it. Jimmy's dad often pined for the days of old. If he had his way, everyone would still be using horse and buggies to get around.

Although old and rusted in places, Jimmy loved his dad's truck because it made a statement against modern consumerism. Old was the new cool in Jimmy's mind.

At first he would not use it for work. He thought a 1956 truck too fragile and rare to haul lawn mowers and rubbish. That all changed when his dad, during one of their last rides together, slapped the dashboard and said, "Don't you dare let this truck sit in the barn waiting for the day you fix her up. You'll never fix her up unless you get to know her first." Jimmy loved his truck, and he loved knowing it had belonged to his dad first. Yup, in this small town Jimmy fit right in, and God willing, he would never leave.

His dad's nostalgic ways had definitely rubbed off on Jimmy in other ways as well. Like his father, Jimmy despised most modern technology, especially cell phones. He only kept one for emergencies, and refused to use it for anything else. Today, however, he appreciated having a phone in his pocket, and he hoped he would be using it to report good news very soon.

Jimmy had been walking down the old road for about ten minutes before spotting a bicycle partially obscured by undergrowth. He could not be certain who the bike belonged to, but it looked very similar to the one Azora had described.

Furthermore, the old road led directly to town, Melissa's intended destination.

No one but Jimmy considered that Melissa would have taken her bike on such a dilapidated road. The police said that it would be nearly impossible for her to traverse such rough terrain on a bicycle and that she would have quickly turned around. This was the reason they chose not to search the area.

Jimmy checked his phone for a signal. Surprisingly, he had reception. He looked up Azora's number and dialed. "Hi, Bethany? This is Jimmy. I think you and Azora should meet me at the side of the road on the way to town. Just look for my pickup truck. I don't want to get your hopes up, but I may have found a clue. If I'm not at the truck when you get there, just wait, I won't be long."

He hung up the phone, but before putting it back in his pocket he used it to take a few pictures of the bike. He did not want to tamper with potential evidence because the police might need to take fingerprints or something. First, however, they would need to know if the bicycle belonged to Melissa and the pictures would help with that.

Before returning to meet the women, Jimmy decided to walk a little farther down the path. He noticed that a bike would still be easy to maneuver for several hundred yards. Melissa would not have abandoned her bike at this point on the road. She would have either continued on or turned back altogether.

There were no obvious signs of a struggle near the bike. But what signs would a struggle produce? Pieces of ripped clothing or broken twigs? Jimmy was smart, but he was no detective. If the bike belonged to Melissa, they would immediately inform the Sheriff and proceed from there. He did not notice any other clues so he decided to head back. But not before stopping to say a prayer.

Chapter 29

Choosing a Door

After soaking in their tubs, Seth and Melissa got dressed and were then ushered into what appeared to be some type of waiting room. The ambient lighting illuminated the room with a soft amber color that felt somewhat clinical. A single light beamed down on each chair as if its occupants were to be specimens on display.

The chairs floated off the ground and adjusted automatically to fit each guest perfectly. When Seth thought about moving to get more comfortable, the chair anticipated his need and puffed up in just the right place, making any adjustments unnecessary. He imagined a mind-reading cloud would not feel any more relaxing.

There were no walls, or at least none that could be seen beyond the shadows of the minimal lighting. Natural stone covered the floor, but oddly enough, it felt like soft carpet when walked upon. Other than the two floating chairs, the room lacked anything a normal room would have, that is if floating chairs could be considered normal. No table, sofa, or television. Nothing practical whatsoever.

What stuck out rather hauntingly in the room were the many doors lined up in a row. Even though the doors had hinges and knobs, they appeared to be floating freely, unattached to any walls, yet they were motionless. All the doors were the same intense color of red. Melissa and Seth had to squint when looking at them, they were so bright. But strangely, there appeared to be no light source illuminating them.

The glowing red doors were spaced approximately two feet apart. Each one prominently featured a window about six inches wide and six inches tall that was covered by a small latched door with black iron handles. A faint outline of light could be seen emanating through the cracks of some of these little windows.

Seth and Melissa started to discuss where all the doors might lead, but Melissa soon fell asleep. They both were exhausted after all, and the chairs were heavenly. Seth concluded, all by himself, that each door led to something very important. This explained why nothing else had been placed in the room. Anything of relevance probably resided in the other rooms behind the doors.

He realized the heavy fatigue that had taken over his mind and body was not from spending hours in the heat with no water, but from all the strange places and supernatural challenges that were being forced upon him. One moment dehydration threatened his life, and the very next he was offered a soak in a tub full of water, and his first-ever massage. Yes, his mind and body had reached their limits.

He could not wrap his head around any of the recent mind-boggling events. Yet he had no problem partaking in the finer aspects of the experience. The way he figured, if he and his sister did not make it home soon, this might be the last comfortable place they ever visited. Besides, who in their right mind would turn down a massage and a warm bath after nearly dying in a desert of salt?

As he relaxed in the floating chair, Seth thought about Melissa's newfound confidence and how he did not know his sister anymore. This new Melissa was displaying courage and compassion, she appeared hopeful, and had far more self-control than she ever had before. Seth thought that she might even welcome the next part of this adventure, should there be one.

But he also had an uncomfortable sense that maybe, just maybe, his sister did not even exist anymore. How could he be sure that this girl next to him was real? He still had not convinced himself of the authenticity of anything in this world. Before he could fully contemplate the possibility of an imposter impersonating Melissa, Harmony entered the room.

"I trust you enjoyed the little luxuries I provided you." Harmony's voice startled them. Melissa woke abruptly, and Seth looked around to see where Harmony had come from. She seemed to appear out of nowhere. From behind the floating chairs, perhaps? Seth quickly decided not to waste time dwelling on the trivial aspects of quantum physics, but rather concentrate on that which he might have a chance of understanding.

Harmony obviously had something on her mind. Perhaps she wanted to share the dinner menu with them. Seth could not remember the last time he had eaten and just the thought of food made him hungry. "Yes, thank you. Your hospitality has almost made nearly dying worth it," said Seth.

"I'm so glad to hear your praises. You know, the things I have to offer only get better the longer you stay."

"Stay? Who said we were staying?" asked Melissa.

"Aren't you?" asked Harmony.

"We want to go home," Melissa responded.

"Home? Of course, Melissa. Everyone yearns to go home. But who is to say where home is, really? Here, in my world, there are many paths to home. All you need do is choose."

"I don't understand," said Seth.

"You didn't think you could go back to your old home, did you?" Harmony laughed softly. "Come now, why would you want to go back when forward is the only choice that will make you truly happy."

"Are you saying you aren't going to let us go home?" asked Melissa suspiciously.

"Not anything of the sort. I'm asking that we all put our thinking caps on, that's all, Melissa. I do think your brother Seth has his thinking cap on. Don't you, Seth?"

"Sure. I guess. I mean, I'd like to think I always have my thinking cap on, Harmony."

"You are so bright, young man. So wise are you," said Harmony with a flirtatious smile.

"Thank you, Harmony," said Seth.

Melissa mocked Seth under her breath. "Thank you, Harmony."

"What was that, Miss? Speak up, will you? Mumbling is a sure sign of insecurity and confusion. Are you confused, poor girl? No worries. I am here to help," said Harmony.

"Yes, I am confused, Harmony. But if you show me the door that leads out of here, I'll be more than glad to be confused someplace else."

"Is that how one shows gratitude for all the hospitality I have shown? Really, Melissa, not very becoming, is it?"

Melissa crossed her arms and refused to say another word. She glanced over at Seth who had not only become enamored with Harmony, but actually believed the praises she was heaping on him.

"So, may I ask what you mean, Harmony? About going

forward?" said Seth.

"Yes, handsome one. In my house there are many options from which to choose. And the choice is always yours and yours alone."

"Can we choose to go home? We really would like to go back home," said Seth.

"I'm glad to tell you that your old home doesn't exist anymore, at least not for you. One can't go back when forward is available. The good news is that a better place is waiting for you. That's my gospel truth. A place where you can be your own person, make your own rules."

Melissa interrupted. "You mean be our own God?"

"Miss, don't interrupt. I am what is. And you are what is. And Seth is what is. That's all. That's the gospel truth."

"The gospel according to whom?" asked Melissa.

"All will be revealed in time. You just need to have faith," Harmony assured her.

"Melissa, that's what you've been talking about for the last day, having faith. Maybe this is where we need to be. It's much better than everywhere else we've been so far," said Seth.

"Spoken like a true prophet, Seth," added Harmony.

"Better than home, Seth? Have you lost your cotton pickin' mind? So all someone has to do is rub your belly and whisper sweet nothings into your ear and you roll over like a dog and believe everything they say?" asked Melissa.

"Miss, I would never expect you to take my word alone. You are welcome to experience your new home for yourself. Just pick a door, any door, and I promise you, you will be home. Home, after all, is where the heart is, and that's where your heart will be," said Harmony.

"Okay, Harmony," said Melissa, beginning to raise her voice. "Let's say I go through one of your doors there, I don't like what's inside, and I want to leave. *Is that allowed?*"

"Why would one want to leave their home? When you enter, you will never want to leave," answered Harmony.

"So, why are you here, Harmony? Why aren't you in one of those rooms or doors or whatever they are? Why are you even here? Who are you anyway?" asked Melissa.

"I could ask the same thing of you, Miss. Couldn't we, Seth?"

"What are you talking about?" asked Seth.

"Why don't you tell her what you were thinking, Seth? Go ahead. There is no judgment here."

"Yeah, Seth. Why don't you tell me, your sister, what you are thinking?"

"Me? I'm not thinking anything. Really." He shrugged his shoulders nervously.

"Come now, Seth. You were questioning if that's really your sister, weren't you? How can one really know who the other is, really?"

"Is that true, Seth? Is that what you were thinking?"

"No, Melissa. Not exactly. But maybe she's right. I mean, how can we really know what's real or who's who here?"

"Precisely. One must simply have faith that we are who we say we are, and that what we say is true," added Harmony.

"Seth. You of all people know that you don't just have blind faith in something. You don't believe in blind faith. Anything that is true and real would not require a blind faith. What you are asking us to do is walk through a door blindly, and I refuse to do that. Harmony, prove to me that what you say is true. Prove it!"

"Silly girl. How would one prove anything true or false? Have I not been the best of hostesses? Have I not shown you kindness?"

"I know how you could prove what you say is true and show your faith at the same time," said Melissa.

"I'm listening," said Harmony.

"You pick a door and go through it."

Harmony laughed and shook her head while trying to conceal her frustration. For the first time Melissa had struck a blow that revealed Harmony's vulnerability. The three of them remained in awkward silence for a few moments as Harmony regained her composure.

Confusion overtook Seth, but he knew his sister brought up a valid point. If things were so wonderful and safe on the other side of those doors, why would Harmony hesitate to enter one herself?

Melissa quickly scanned the room, trying to figure a way out. But she could not remember the door through which they came. She had been so relaxed and distracted that it never occurred to her to make mental notes. Finally, Harmony broke the silence.

"I am insulted to the highest degree. My whole character has been attacked simply because I have shown you kindness and offered you a home in paradise! I do not know what to do with the two of you."

"Why must you do anything with us?" asked Seth. "Is it so much to ask that you just let us go back the same way we came? My sister and I don't want a new home. We want our old home."

Harmony motioned for Seth to join her where she was standing by one of the doors. Seth complied, hesitantly. She waved her hand and the latched panel covering the small window in the door opened. Seth could not help but look through the glass to the other side. Harmony wasted no time in seizing the moment. "This could be your new home."

The view through the window immediately mesmerized Seth. To Melissa, he looked drugged and paralyzed. She knew they did not have much time left. She had to figure a way out, and do it quickly.

Melissa continued to scan the room. Out of the corner of her eye she noticed something quickly brush underneath one of the doors. Then it slowly dawned on her that she had just seen the tail of a cat, a white cat. She thought she saw it protrude out of the seventh door from the left, the one directly to the right of Harmony and Seth.

Seth placed his hand on the handle of the sixth door. Melissa felt that if he walked through that door she would never see him again. "Dear God, please give me the strength to do this." She had a plan to escape, but if she miscalculated, it might be the end for both of them.

Melissa, in stealth mode, made her way towards the seventh and eighth doors. Harmony, preoccupied with Seth, momentarily lost track of Melissa. Or either she did not care, thinking Melissa too stupid to escape on her own.

While pretending to open the eighth door, Melissa's moment of truth arrived. She saw a few white hairs sticking out from under the seventh door, confirming her earlier observation. She moved to the left and quickly opened the seventh door, while bending down to scoop up the white cat. Everything happened so fast that she felt as though she was outside of her own body—looking down.

"I'm sorry, cat, but I have no other choice. If your master is telling the truth, you will be just fine," said Melissa as she simultaneously opened the eighth door. She held the cat by the nape of the neck over the threshold, careful not to peer into the room herself. The cat squealed loudly, getting the attention of Harmony who turned towards Melissa with a look that could have melted iron.

"You wouldn't dare."

"Why not? I would never hurt a poor little helpless cat, any more than you would hurt one of us," answered Melissa.

"Let go of him. Now!" Harmony dug her nails into Seth's

shoulder.

"Or what? You listen to me now, Harmony. Take my brother's hand off that door handle and place him in front of the seventh door."

Harmony huffed with frustration, but did exactly what Melissa demanded, not once taking her eyes off her prized kitty. She gently took Seth's hand and removed it from the door, one finger at a time. She then guided him slowly in front of the seventh door, next to Melissa. Seth, still in some type of trance, maintained his gaze on the sixth door.

"Now, you go sit in the farthest chair over there. Quickly, or the cat goes to *paradise!*" said Melissa.

Harmony again complied, containing her rage as she calmly sat down, never taking her steely gaze off Melissa or the cat.

Melissa, acting solely on impulse, used her hip to bump Seth through the seventh door. She managed to position herself so that her lower body resided within the seventh door while her arms stretched over the threshold of the eighth door, where the dangling cat hung precariously from her tight grip. The last thing Melissa saw before falling backwards to safety was Harmony rushing towards her, screeching like a witch being burned at the stake.

Melissa landed on the ground hard, caboose first. In all the excitement, Melissa dropped the cat just before the seventh door slammed shut behind her. She could not be sure exactly where the cat had ended up. However, if Harmony's screams, which sounded like the devil himself, were any indication, it was not paradise.

Chapter 30

Pillars

Melissa took a moment to look around before giving a sigh of relief. She had a strong sense that they had narrowly escaped the clutches of an evil far greater than the most sinister criminal in her world. The seventh door had led them to their freedom, but they were once again in the desert of salt. They were back where they had started, feeling just as hot, just as dry, and just as desperate.

"What have you done, Melissa? Do you have any idea what you have done?" The veins on Seth's neck flared and his face reddened.

"I saved your stupid, gullible life. That's what I've done. You are pathetic. All this time you have been arguing for proof and science, but the minute someone shows you something pretty, comfortable, and easy, you throw reason out the door. Literally."

"I had proof. I saw it with my own eyes. On the other side of that door was everything a person could possibly want. The perfect paradise, right beyond that door, Melissa, and you took it all away from me!"

"I took away a lie ignited by your own desires. A lie nurtured by the devil himself. Now snap out of it, and get up off the ground. We've got to move quickly. I have a feeling home is near, Seth, our real home."

Seth, taken aback by Melissa's unprecedented resolve, had no choice but to heed her command. He knew her words were true, even if he would not admit it. He shook off the illusionary haze of paradise found, and much like a scolded puppy, stood quietly next to his sister, waiting for orders on what to do next.

Melissa had no way of knowing the direction that might lead towards home, but the confidence she exuded said otherwise. So Seth did not hesitate to follow as his sister hastily marched north, opposite the Land of Indulgences, the Lake of Entitlement, and the igloo made of salt.

After a safe distance had been placed between themselves and Harmony, the siblings slowed to a more relaxed pace. Other than the occasional pillar of salt, their surroundings appeared to be quite benign.

Seth, still slightly hung over from the effects of Harmony's charms, interrupted the calm to challenge Melissa's decision one last time. "What if that woman spoke the unfortunate truth that home is not waiting for us. What if one of those doors was our last best hope to salvage this nightmare we are in? A lie in paradise is better than the truth out here."

"I refuse to believe that. I also can't believe you would forsake everything for an imposter. I would rather die out here looking for the truth than go back there for a convenient lie. Have you considered that once you entered your little room of paradise that everything would change into something horrible?"

"I don't know. I just feel so desperate, I guess. Hopeless.

Even scared, maybe," answered Seth.

"Let me ask you something. Why wouldn't she go in? Did you think about that? She was terrified I was going to throw her cat through one of those doors. Terrified! You're the one that taught me to question and to seek verification and proof. You gave me your promise to seek out the truth with all your heart and mind."

"I'm sorry, maybe you're right, but that place was insanely beautiful, if only you had seen it with your own eyes, Melissa."

"You want to go back? You want to turn around and go back or do you want to remember who you are and the promise you made? We've been given a second chance here. Actually, I've been given a bunch of second chances lately. Are you a person of your word, or a helpless creature without the choice to do what's right?"

"It's hard. The world Harmony showed me gave me a feeling of euphoria...it was like a drug. I saw it all through the window. Had you looked, you would understand."

"You should never have looked in the first place. And I'm warning you. You better make a stand never to look back again. As hard as it is, don't look back. I'm not sure I can help you next time. Promise me. I need you. I want to go home, and I can't get there alone. Seth, promise me," pleaded Melissa.

"Okay. Okay. You're right. My little sister is right. I never thought I would see the day when I would be the one following behind you. Let's get out of here. Come on. Let's go."

Seth and Melissa ran as fast as their feet would carry them, dodging one pillar of salt after another. When Melissa finally ran out of breath, she slowed down and leaned on one of the salt structures. Seeing it up close, she realized there was something peculiar about the form her shoulder rested against.

"Hey, Seth, what do these things remind you of?"

"I don't know. They remind me of mounds of salt. Maybe

this used to be a salty ocean and it dried up."

"I hope I'm wrong, but look." Melissa took her feet and legs and placed them together as close as they would go. She then bent her torso slightly forward and raised her right arm a little to the south and her left arm to the north as if she were running. Her motionless body looked eerily similar to the salt pillars.

"What does it remind you of now?" asked Melissa.

"It can't be. These things we have been passing by...They're people?"

"They used to be people, I think. Other than being salt they all have one thing in common."

"They're looking back towards where they came from," answered Seth. "We need to get as far away from this place as possible. Run!"

They ran as fast as they could, without once looking back. Eventually the salt statues declined in numbers. The distance between each lonely, frozen figure increased until only one remained. Melissa shuttered as she passed it, but she also felt hopeful. They pushed each other to keep moving north, towards what they hoped would be home.

Melissa's mind raced faster than her feet. She felt as though she were running on air, gliding on autopilot. Seth, with his own renewed sense of optimism, had a runner's high and it felt refreshing. He had no idea where his newfound strength came from, but he did not consider stopping to question it. Seth reached over and grabbed Melissa's hand, and together they ran.

"We are going to make it home, Melissa. I don't know how, but we are going home. And when we get there, I promise to find out if there is a Creator. I promise to study and learn about the universe, about the stars in the sky, about the manuscripts of antiquity, archeology, prophecy, science, and anything else that might possibly lead us to the creator of it all."

Seth stopped running. All the talking had left him breathless. He put his hands on his knees and gulped for air. Melissa welcomed the break. She dropped to her knees and wiped the sweat from her brow.

To Melissa's horror, the break turned out to be short-lived. She looked up to see a huge funnel cloud racing towards them. Her fear had left her speechless, but she managed to get Seth's attention by pointing at the oncoming disaster.

They were completely vulnerable out in the open. Melissa huddled as low to the ground as possible, and Seth joined her by shielding her body with his own. Before they knew it, the wind had completely engulfed them. They held onto one another tightly. Everything went completely dark. Although they could still hear the wind, they could not feel it on their skin. Instead, they felt a soft, warm shield of protection.

In spite of the storm and against all odds, Melissa and Seth were out of danger. They had been embraced by Adriel, the beautiful white owl who once again had taken them under his wings. They knew no harm would come to them now. Melissa hugged her brother tightly and whispered, "Don't ever forget your promise." Seth smiled and returned her embrace. They were finally safe. They were together, and they were going home.

Chapter 31

In the Woods Again

Jimmy must have spent a good five minutes praying. He prayed for the safe return of the kids, but mostly he prayed for God's will to be done. Jimmy had no way of knowing what the future held for this family, but he had committed himself to doing everything possible to help them.

He stood up, brushed the dark, loose dirt from his jeans, looked around one last time, and walked back towards his pickup. Bethany and Azora were probably already there anxiously waiting for him. He wished he had better news, but if the bike belonged to Melissa, it could be the clue to help them find out what had happened.

Jimmy had just passed the large oak under which he had prayed when he heard a loud cracking noise. He could not believe his eyes as he looked up. There, hanging not ten feet above him, were four dangling legs. After closer examination, and a little squinting, Jimmy realized that these legs belonged to two of the most wanted teens in Garland County.

At first, Jimmy felt a huge sense of relief. But his initial feelings quickly turned into confusion. His mind raced as he tried to figure out what had happened. Where had the two of them been all this time, and why in the world were they sitting in a tree? He tried to clear his mind in order to focus on the most important question of the moment. Were Seth and Melissa safe and healthy?

"Hey. Hey. Can you two hear me? Hey, up there!" He picked up a pine cone and tossed it into the tree. The human ornaments failed to respond. Not so much as a twitch. Jimmy wondered if they were in fact sleeping. Jimmy continued calling out their names as he looked for the best route to climb the tree.

He could not recall ever having seen limbs as large and strong as the ones on this old oak. The gnarly bark gave his hands plenty to grasp as he pulled himself up to the first limb. This lucky tree must have somehow escaped the deforestation during the industrial revolution, which meant it had to be well over three centuries old.

After scaling a few more branches, Jimmy was soon eye to eye with the siblings. To his surprise they appeared to be asleep while sitting in a tree! Jimmy did not want to startle them so much that they would fall, so he gently nudged Seth until he got a response.

"Who are you?" Seth rubbed his eyes. "Jimmy? What are you doing here? Wait, where are we? Melissa?"

"What's going on?" asked Melissa groggily. "Is that you Jimmy?" She looked around to get her bearings. "Are we in a tree?"

"I would say so. What are you two doing up here?"

Melissa looked up, down, and around. She seemed lost and confused. The realization of her position in the tree caused a moment of dizziness, so she latched tightly onto the nearest limb. She soon realized that she could not have fallen out of the tree, even if someone had pushed her. Her body had been lodged securely between several branches. Her rear end sat on a large limb that must have been nearly two feet wide. Another branch came across her chest much like a seatbelt in a car, and a smaller limb pushed snugly against her lower back.

"I saw this animal down there and I climbed up in the tree to get away from it. I just remember being scared to death," said Melissa.

"What kind of animal?" asked Jimmy.

"I don't know. It was a mean looking wolf or something." Melissa glanced at her brother and then back at Jimmy. "Did you guys come out here to look for me? That's so sweet. My nights and shining armors."

"You mean knights in shining armor, dip-wad." Seth shook his head and rolled his eyes.

"We have been looking for the two of you all night and day. Are you going to tell me that you have been in this tree hiding from an animal for all that time?"

"I don't remember any animal," said Seth. "I just remember climbing up here for a better view, but that was just a few moments ago."

"I don't know what's going on, but you two had better come down from here quick. It's safe, no animals," said Jimmy.

Jimmy led the way as they climbed down out of the magnificent oak. He lent a hand to steady Melissa who acted as though she needed a little more help than she actually did. Seth offered to help her as well, but she promptly ignored her brother and grabbed for Jimmy instead. Once Jimmy stepped on solid ground, Melissa quite literally jumped in his arms.

"Thank you so much, Jimmy. I don't think I would have ever gotten out of that tree had you not come to my rescue." Jimmy awkwardly placed Melissa on her own two feet.

"Look, you two," said Jimmy, "half the town has been out looking for you. Your mom and grandmother are absolutely sick with worry. If this is some kind of joke or something, you have seriously overestimated everyone's sense of humor."

Seth and Melissa looked at each other not knowing what to say or do. They appeared just as confused as Jimmy. Seth first thought that Jimmy must have been playing some kind of joke, but no one could act that convincingly.

The seriousness of Jimmy's tone made Melissa rethink her carefree attitude. She did not want to say anything that might upset him even more. Maybe she and Seth were gone longer than they should have been. Maybe they fell asleep...in the tree. Nothing made sense to any of them.

Melissa gave her best attempt at an explanation. "I'm sorry, Jimmy. Like I said, the last thing I remember is jumping off my bike and running away from that animal. I thought the tree would be the safest place to go. That's the last thing I remember. I'm not lying and I'm not..." She began to cry from sheer confusion and frustration.

Melissa tried with all her might to stop her adolescent behavior. The harder she tried to stop, however, the heavier the tears flowed. Her sobs were uncontrollable, but they had the pleasant side effect of causing Jimmy to act more sympathetic.

Jimmy placed his arms around Melissa and consoled her. "That makes perfect sense to me. The only option you had was to climb up in that tree. That was very smart. Maybe the animal—a wolf was it? Maybe it was hungry and wouldn't leave in hopes you would drop some food or something."

Jimmy playfully punched Seth in the shoulder. "I mean, you didn't know that it probably wasn't going to eat you. Whatever it was, it probably just wanted to find food, that's all."

Seth did not say a word. He really had no idea what had transpired over the last day or so. And because he did not want to sound crazy, he thought it was best to keep his mouth shut until he could make sense of things. Fortunately, Melissa's crying had stopped any more questions. At least for now.

As the three of them began to walk, Jimmy was faced with dealing with a secret he had been keeping since he was 17 years old. His two day disappearance—and sudden reappearance—with no recollection of where he had been. He wondered if his own strange, supernatural experience was being repeated. But this time with Seth and Melissa. He had not allowed himself to consider the possibility earlier, when he was searching for them, but he had no choice now. Perhaps if he shared his own story with the two frightened teens, he thought, it might help them.

Jimmy put his arms around Melissa and Seth. "Listen, you two, I've never really talked about this with anyone before. But something similar happened to me when I was about y'all's age. I didn't have any memories of what happened to me at first either. But slowly over time things started coming back to me. When I was ready, I remembered. I promise you both everything is going to be okay."

"What are you talking about?" asked Seth.

"Look, just know that I am here if either of you need to talk about what happened to you."

"But I don't remember anything," said Melissa.

Jimmy studied both of their faces and decided not to press any further. "That's fine. But if, by chance, things start coming to mind...anything, I'm here for you both."

They walked through the woods towards the truck. Jimmy had motioned for Seth to get Melissa's bike, which he pushed alongside them. No one spoke again until they were near the paved road, and then Melissa quietly thanked Jimmy for finding her.

Seth moved to the other side of Melissa so he could put his free arm around her shoulders. He had no need to say anything.

They were together and they were safe.

"We're safely home," Seth mumbled quietly to himself.

"What was that, Seth?" asked Jimmy.

"Nothing, just talking to myself. Hey, Jimmy..."

"Yes, Seth."

"You know a lot about God and the Bible, right?"

"A lot, yes, not everything, but I'm working on learning more."

"I think I understand what you were saying about the big bang and the age of the universe. I want to know more about that, but I also want to know about the manuscript evidence. Is there any proof that what we know as the Bible wasn't just mistranslated so many times that it's not even close to the original?"

"You want to talk about this now?" asked Jimmy.

"No, not now. But sometime soon. I want to know your reasons for believing in God. I want to know the truth, if there is such a thing."

"Okay. The truth is a good place to begin."

Melissa could see the sun hitting Jimmy's truck. The glare shone through the vines that covered the trail entrance. She quickened her pace, running full steam towards her mother and grandmother. She could not explain the urgent need she had to embrace her family. Seth too quickened his stride. He ended up sprinting towards his mom, and almost knocked her over with his embrace.

Jimmy stayed back in order to allow the family to reunite. They cried and shouted with joy. The reunion was as happy as any he had ever seen. The women wept while Seth tried hard to hold back his own tears. That joyous moment, where the new road meets the old, would never be forgotten.

Jimmy looked back at the trail and suddenly had the feeling that something in the woods was whispering to him. He was surprised to spot a couple of beautiful red foxes. He had never before seen a pair together in the woods, and watched in amazement as the two wild animals sat unafraid, staring back at him, just a few feet away.

Jimmy could have sworn that the female actually wanted to come closer. Her body leaned forward as if to approach him. She was displaying submissive behavior usually only associated with domesticated animals.

Melissa, not noticing the foxes, tapped Jimmy on the shoulder. "Are you ready to head back? It's almost dinner time and I'm sure there's enough food for everyone."

Jimmy motioned for Melissa to be quiet as he pointed towards the foxes. He whispered, "Look over there."

"Oh, my God. Wolves! What should we do?" Melissa took a step back, but stopped when she realized that there was another opportunity to hold onto Jimmy, which she did with both arms.

"There's no need to be frightened. They're not wolves, and they're usually more afraid of us than we are of them. It's a male and a female fox. Foxes mate for life, you know."

"I think I heard that somewhere before. I can't for the life of me think where. Foxes? They're so beautiful. Will they come any closer?" Melissa bent down and clapped her hands together as if calling a dog.

"No. I don't think you want to do that. They are wild, after all. Wait a minute, aren't you the one that just spent the night in a tree in order to avoid an animal?"

"You're right. I don't know what just got into me. But they do seem harmless. Plus I feel safe with you here." Melissa looked up into the sky. "Do you think animals go to heaven?"

"I don't know. I would like to think so."

"Well, maybe someday we'll all be up there together, people and animals playing together and getting along. Who knows, maybe we can even talk to animals in heaven. Wouldn't that be nice?"

Chapter 32

The Oath

Melissa had no idea why she had awakened at such an ungodly hour that morning, especially since she had nothing to do other than pack a few things before the family headed back home. She found herself in her grandmother's bathroom, with her back leaning against the sink, trying to remember what had happened during the last forty-eight hours.

Everyone else still clung to sleep while Melissa, lost in thought, absentmindedly straightened the orange towels. She had always found her grandmother's taste in decorating odd, but also comforting. Something about the orange hand towels, which were probably from the 1960's, made her feel safe. If towels could last through fifty years of washings and still remain vibrant, perhaps she had a chance to at least make it through adolescence.

Melissa slowly turned to face the sink. After twisting the handle for cold water, she methodically bent down and splashed her face with the icy liquid. The feeling of her pores tightening exhilarated her. She instantly felt alive and clean at the same time. It did not occur to her that she had never before splashed her face with frigid water, or that it would forevermore become a morning ritual.

She put a towel over her face and held it firmly in place until she felt dry. Then, quite by accident, she caught her image in the mirror. She could not stop staring. After they were reunited yesterday, her mother had gone on and on about how different Melissa looked, but until this moment, Melissa had not realized what her mother was talking about.

Melissa's blonde hair had returned, completely on its own. Her once spotty complexion now appeared flawless. The women in her family all had pretty smooth skin, but nothing like this.

"Maybe I just forgot what I looked like without makeup," Melissa said to her reflection in the mirror. She tried to remember the last time she had dyed her hair, but Seth began beating on the bathroom door, derailing her thoughts.

"Hurry up in there! I've gotta go!" Seth crossed his legs and bounced up and down.

"Alright, alright. I'm coming out." The second Melissa opened the door Seth rushed past her like a race horse at the starting line.

"Aren't you even going to wait until I'm out of the bathroom?"

"Yes," said Seth. "But please hurry. I really have to go bad."

"Alright, already. It's all yours! Such a gentleman." She shook her head.

"Sorry. Sometimes ya just gotta go."

"Whatever." Melissa walked out, closing the door behind her. Instead of going back to bed, which is what any normal teenager would have done, she leaned against the wall next to the bathroom. She and Seth had not spoken about what happened to them, at least not in private. There were things to talk about, and this seemed like as good a time as any.

Melissa had begun to recall bits and pieces from the time of their disappearance, but she had no way of knowing if the memories were from a dream or from actual events. Perhaps if Seth had the same memories they could begin to piece together the truth.

The rest of the family inquired about what had happened, but they treaded lightly. Melissa felt like she had just returned home after having been institutionalized. Everyone wanted to know about the asylum, but no one dared trigger a relapse.

Her grandmother's attentiveness and overly cautious attitude bugged Melissa. Azora usually blurted out anything that was on her mind, no matter how inappropriate, but now she was acting out of character. She was passing out baked goods as if they were at a bed and breakfast, and being extremely nice.

Bethany responded similarly. She had hugged both of her kids more times in the last twelve hours than she did during their entire childhood. Yes, indeed, if things were going to get back to normal, Melissa and Seth had to have a discussion, and soon.

Seth finished in the bathroom by drying his hands with the same damp towel his sister had left on the countertop. Since he was a child, Seth had meticulously maintained all things involving personal hygiene to near perfection. There could be no hair in the shower, he always wiped down the toilet seat, but most importantly, towels were only to be used once.

Yet, there he stood, wiping his hands on a damp, dirty towel. He realized that he would never be the same person again as he hung the towel back on its rod. Something had happened to him in the woods, something meaningful perhaps, but also possibly horrifying.

Seth could not shake the anxious feeling that had enveloped

him since he got back to his grandmother's house. He had never before felt anxious. His friends and family considered him to be quite stoic and secure, never nervous or unsure. What happened in those woods?

As Seth exited the bathroom, Melissa grabbed his arm. She attempted to whisper something in his ear, but Seth screamed and jumped back into the bathroom. After taking a second to regain her composure, Melissa peeked in to find Seth sitting on the toilet seat panting like a wide-eyed raccoon staring at a mountain lion. Yes, the normally stoic Seth had changed.

"What is wrong with you?" Melissa asked.

"With me? What's wrong with *you*? Are you trying to give me a heart attack?"

"Really? That scared you? I'm sorry. Since when did you become so edgy? I was just going to tell you something."

"How about telling me like a normal person, instead of jumping me in a dark hallway like some sort of ninja warrior?"

"Look, I think we need to talk before Mom and Grandma wake up and start asking a bunch of questions. We're lucky if you didn't wake everyone in the house just now with your girly scream."

"Whatever. I didn't get much sleep last night, that's all."

"Well, put some clothes on and meet me under the willow tree. I want to make sure no one overhears us talking," whispered Melissa.

"What's the big secret?"

"Just meet me outside."

"Fine. I'll throw on a shirt. Give me a second." Seth went into the office to finish dressing. Melissa stopped to check if anyone else was rustling around. It seemed that Seth's outburst had not awakened their mother or grandmother.

Melissa tiptoed over to the living room and retrieved a pair of sandals. She quietly moved across the room to the back door, carrying her shoes. She slowly turned the knob and stepped outside, leaving the door slightly ajar for Seth, who would hopefully be following closely behind.

Melissa slid her feet into the sandals and walked down the porch steps. The sun, creeping above the horizon, offered just enough light to illuminate the path through the garden to the willow tree. The fresh air smelled of damp grass clippings and earth. The chill of spring nipped the air, but the excitement from her early morning covert operation kept Melissa warm.

Seth, being practical, and perhaps slightly vindictive, thought he would pack after getting dressed. Melissa could wait. Essentially, that just meant picking out what he would need on the trip home and putting the rest into his duffle bag. Packing now would give him a few additional minutes to finish his schoolwork before they left.

He took extra time for folding, including things already worn. For some reason, unknown even to himself, Seth always folded his dirty clothes. He did not concern himself with Melissa's irritation at having to wait because that's what she deserved for referring to him as "girly." After taking much longer than necessary, Seth zipped up his bag and headed to the garden to meet his sister.

Seth admired the sun in all its morning glory as he casually strolled toward the willow tree. His anxiousness began to ease until Melissa snuck up behind him and tapped him on the shoulder. She doubted that anyone in the house had failed to hear him scream this time.

"Wow, Seth. I've not heard a squeal like that since Uncle Henry chased the pig out of his garden. You are so jumpy!"

"Just leave me alone. What do you want anyway?"

"Shh, don't talk so loud. I was just headed to the house to see what was taking you so long. Follow me." Seth obliged and walked behind Melissa. She sat down on the bench underneath the willow tree. "Sit." Melissa waved her hand over the open seat.

Seth sat, folded his arms, and stared intently at Melissa. "Fine. So what do you want me to say? I apparently don't know anything more than you do."

"Well, yesterday I would agree. I was in a daze. But this morning I woke up with a lot of memories that seemed real. But they also could have been from a dream."

"Okay, and so what," he said.

"I was hoping you could help."

"If you can't tell your own dreams from reality, how do you expect me to tell the difference? They're your dreams and your reality."

"Yes, unless they were your reality too."

"What do you mean?"

"If they were just dreams, it's highly unlikely you would have had the same ones, but if you have the same memories, maybe they weren't dreams," explained Melissa.

"Sure, I get it. But I told you that I don't remember anything, dream or otherwise."

Melissa pulled something out of her pocket and held it in the palm of her hand in front of Seth. "Do you know what this is?"

"It looks like a big nut or something."

"I think it's something more like a seed. But I've never seen anything like it, have you?" Seth took the object and examined it closely. He rolled it around in his palm, held it up to the light, and then smelled it.

"Interesting. It has a faint smell of something sweet. Smells delicious, actually. But how am I supposed to know what it is? I'm not a plant expert or anything. There must be a million species of plant life, and I probably couldn't identify one percent of it. Where did you get it from?" asked Seth.

"That's just it. I don't remember getting it from anywhere. I found it in my pocket when we got home yesterday. I didn't think much of it until this morning. You may only know one percent of the world's species, but I'm pretty sure we know most of the species in these woods. At least I thought I did."

"So what are you getting at?"

Melissa put the seed back into her pocket and looked up at the sky through the willow branches. She hemmed and hawed a bit before finally asking another question. "Do you remember being in an orchard or a forest of some sort?"

"Sure, stupid. We were in the cotton pickin' woods."

"No! Not our woods. I remember being in an orchard or an exotic place with lots of flowers and stuff. Do you?"

"Can't help you. Sorry. Nope. Don't recall anything like that," assured Seth.

"Seth. I know you remember something. There is something in your head that relates to what happened to us. You didn't just go brain dead. Think. Please think. This is important to me."

"I don't know what you want me to say."

"What are you afraid of? I'm your sister. Nothing you say will go beyond these branches. I swear an oath to the secret keychain of the hog." Melissa pulled out all the stops. The keychain of the hog had not been mentioned for at least five years.

When the siblings were younger they found a keychain with a lone key attached. They swore complete secrecy, never to tell anyone about the key. They never found what it opened, but the key provided many hours of bonding and exciting exploration. The keychain of the hog was a time they both remembered fondly.

"I'm not afraid of anything! Quit making this more than what it is," he said.

"That's great. Just great. You want to stick your head in the sand and sweep this under the rug? Go right ahead, but don't blame me when you find yourself in a psychiatrist's office spilling your guts about how your third wife left you because you jump out of your skin every time someone comes around a corner. Or that you're unable to share your feelings because you became a paranoid wreck after a springtime visit to your grandmother's house."

Melissa stood and quickly turned away from Seth. She refused to let him see her vulnerability, but if she did not move fast, he would surely notice the tears about to spill from her eyes. She stiffened her spine and attempted to appear confident as she began to walk back to the house.

She wanted more than anything to run back to bed and bury her head under the covers, but her pride would not give Seth the satisfaction. Emotion overwhelmed her, however, and her confident steps became awkward and less sure.

Seth did not need to see his sister's face to know tears were about to fall. She would always be the little girl whom he protected every chance he got.

"Wait!" Seth swallowed hard.

Melissa stopped in her tracks, and wiped her eyes before turning around. "What?"

"I do remember something." Seth had never seen anyone's face light up the way his sister's did when he said those four words. But the hope in her eyes caused him to pause. He did not want to let her down, but he could not be sure if what he had to say would live up to her expectations. "Last night I woke up, and at first I thought I had awakened from a dream, but it was more like a memory than a dream. And you were there with me."

"I was? What were we doing?" she asked.

"I don't know. It was more of a feeling than anything. The whole world was spinning, as if we were in the middle of a tornado, but safe from the storm. I felt exhausted and tired..."

"And very thirsty…"

"Yes, unquenchable thirst. But then we were wrapped up in something soft…"

"And white. Like feathers."

"Yes, how did you know?"

"I think whatever happened was real, Seth. How could we both be dreaming the same thing? What else do you remember?"

"Just bits and pieces really. Some other things that are harder to put into words, but there was one thing I remember very clearly," he said.

"What?" Time froze for Melissa and nothing existed at that moment except Seth and her.

"An oath," he said. "A promise…to read the word of God and to study…"

"…with all of my heart, mind, and soul," said Melissa, finishing the phrase with him.

The two of them stood for a moment. Neither said a word. Melissa reached for a branch of the willow tree and slowly began wrapping it around her finger. Seth gently shooed away what appeared to be a wasp.

Melissa broke the silence first. "I always knew there was a God, you know."

"I'm still not convinced," said Seth.

"But you made an oath."

"Yes, I did, and I plan on keeping it. We are both going to keep the oath. But you are not to breathe a word of this to anyone. You hear me? This is keychain of the hog priority, Sister."

"So, what do we do?"

He thought for a moment, and then answered, "We're going to read. Anything and everything we can get our hands on."

"I can't stand reading."

"You're going to start with the Bible, since you already seem to believe in it. I'm going to read about the other pervasive belief systems, and we will meet again on my next school break to discuss what we've learned."

"It might not be a bad idea to attend some different churches also."

"Good thought. It's a start anyway. We'll figure out the rest as we go along. Logic tells me that if there is a God out there, then we will find Him."

"Or maybe He will find us."

"Maybe He already has." Seth smiled as he put his arm over Melissa's shoulders. "Come on, let's make breakfast for the old folks."

"What should we make?" she asked.

"Let's just cut up some fruit."

"No! No fruit! How about breakfast burritos."

"And toast with muscadine jelly," added Seth.

Melissa and Seth continued to banter back and forth as they headed toward the house. This would be the last walk they would ever take together as kids. They were fast becoming young adults. These two siblings and their oath to work together to find the ultimate truth of the universe would not soon part.

Chapter 33

Till Next Time

The breakfast prepared by Melissa and Seth, although not as tasty as Azora's biscuits and gravy, made quite an impression on the adults. Other than a slight bit of friction regarding Melissa's peculiar insistence that there be no fruit on the table, the kids worked together in perfect harmony. Azora and Bethany made no comment on the unusual teamwork.

After breakfast, the guests slowly gathered their belongings for the journey home. The obvious lack of discussion of the previous days' events did not go unnoticed by anyone.

Jimmy arrived just in time to say goodbye and help with everyone's bags. That is, all of the bags except Melissa's. When Melissa caught a glimpse of Jimmy walking up to the front door she looked down at her comfortable, but much worn traveling pants, and gasped. She grabbed her case, ran into the back bedroom, and furiously looked for something more flattering in which to bid him adieu.

While Melissa was furiously scrambling to find something

else to wear, Seth checked the oil in the car. His dad had taught him to always perform a routine checklist before any trip of a hundred miles or more. Azora could not help but notice how responsible her young grandson had become.

"I hear they have imitation oil now," said Azora.

"It's called synthetic oil, Grandma."

"Is that what you put in this engine, synthetic oil? I wouldn't trust none of that stuff if I was you." Azora pulled something out of Seth's front shirt pocket. "Well, lookie here. What are you doin' with a leaf in your pocket?"

"I dunno, the wind must have blown it in there."

"They say that's good luck, to find a leaf in your pocket."

"I don't think I believe in luck anymore, Grandma."

"So, what do you believe in?"

"Something more. Maybe destiny, or a higher power. I'm not exactly sure."

"I have faith you'll find the way if you put your mind to it," said Azora.

Jimmy and the family waited outside by the car for at least ten minutes before Melissa emerged huffing and puffing, dragging an overstuffed bag. The extra time she took to change clothes had obviously paid off because the sight of her caused Jimmy to do a double take. This did not go unnoticed by Azora and Bethany.

Bethany thanked her lucky stars that they lived far enough away to make it nearly impossible for any real romance to blossom. Besides, she knew Jimmy could see through a schoolgirl crush with his eyes closed. If not, she would make sure to intervene if necessary. Bethany did not want her daughter getting distracted from making good grades.

Azora, on the other hand, could not help but show a little more concern. She would not stand for her granddaughter falling for a cult leader. Jimmy had not yet convinced her of his authenticity. She had not noticed how charismatic Jimmy could be until she saw the way Melissa looked at him. Seeing him through the eyes of a teenager gave her a whole new perspective on the gardener.

Jimmy, much like Azora, had also gained a new perspective. He was caught off guard with how much Melissa had changed in only a few short days. "May I bake your tag, I mean, take your bag, Melissa?" asked Jimmy.

"I would be much obliged if you did, Jimmy. You are so thoughtful and strong."

Seth, sitting in the driver's seat, pressed on the horn. Melissa glared in Seth's direction. "So unlike the other men around here."

"I guess y'all better be off," said Azora as she stepped between Jimmy and Melissa. "Or you'll be drivin' in the dark and that's not too safe these days. Off you go." Azora patted Melissa on the behind.

"Grandma, stop it. I'm not three years old." Melissa turned to smile at Jimmy who was already at the back of the car loading her luggage. Bethany hugged her mother, giving Melissa the perfect opportunity to saunter over to Jimmy. Seth, not missing a beat, honked the horn again.

"Mom, thank you so much for everything," said Bethany. "I can't tell you how much this trip meant to me. Even with the scare we had, or perhaps because of the scare, I feel closer to you than ever before. I don't know why we haven't always had such lovely talks."

"Why, what on earth do you mean? We always have lovely talks, dear."

"We do?"

"Well, of course we do. I always look forward to your visits," said Azora.

"I hope you mean that because I think the kids want to come

back for the holidays."

"Thanksgiving or Christmas?"

"Both, I think. I know. It's strange. But you heard them at breakfast. They're already talking about the next visit. I don't know if you are aware of this, but young adults don't usually want to spend so much time with their grandparents—away from their friends."

"Maybe it has something to do with that Jimmy," Azora said wryly.

"I don't think so, Mom, at least not on Seth's part." They both laughed.

"Well, whatever the case may be, we don't let them out of our sight next time," said Azora.

"Agreed!" They both hugged again, holding each other a little longer than they usually did.

Bethany opened the passenger side door and sat. She closed the door, rolled down the window, and shouted at her daughter. "Come on, Melissa. Say your farewells and get in the car. We're already an hour behind schedule."

"Old people, always in such a hurry," said Melissa. "I think it's because they know their time with the living is so limited." Melissa laughed nervously as Jimmy raised an eyebrow.

"It's been great getting to know you. I hope I'll see you again when you come back," said Jimmy.

"Of course you will, silly. Seth and I have tons of questions to ask you about God and all. In fact, I'll find you on the internet and we can chat about the Bible and stuff."

"That would be fine, except I don't use the internet for social stuff. Mostly just for research."

"Really? That's silly. I mean, it's a great way to witness to unbelievers."

"You think so?"

"Oh, sure. Don't worry, just give me your contact info and

I'll teach you all about it. You're gonna love it. You'll get so many converts."

"Melissa, you know I love Jesus, but I'm also just a normal guy."

"Of course you are. So what's your number?"

"Here, just take my card." Melissa snatched the card from his hand and giggled. She then gave him a hug that lasted a little longer than a friendly hug should.

"Bye now," she said.

"Till next time." Jimmy opened the rear door for Melissa and then firmly closed it behind her. Seth backed out of the driveway and before he could get the car into first gear, Melissa screamed.

"Stop!"

"What now?" asked Seth.

"I forgot to give Grandma something." Melissa quickly jumped out of the car and ran over to Azora who had moved under the hickory tree in order to escape the sun. Jimmy, already in his truck, honked and waved goodbye as he drove away. Melissa waved in return and then reached into her pocket to retrieve the object she and Seth had discussed a few hours earlier.

"I want you to have this, Grandma," said Melissa.

"What on earth is it?" asked Azora.

"I thought you might know. I found it. I think it's some sort of seed or something." Azora examined the object closely, shook it, and squinted her eyes for a better look. She had never seen any seed quite like this, but a seed it indeed appeared to be. Something between an avocado pit and a walnut, but closer in size to the latter, she thought. There was something peculiar about this thing that left Azora transfixed.

"Grandma? Grandma?" Melissa had to practically shout to get her attention.

"Yes, child. What?"

"Do you know what it is?"

"I'll tell you what. Why don't we plant this the next time you come to visit? We can set it out in a bucket in the greenhouse. If it's a tree, I have the perfect spot for it. If it's a flower, we'll let you decide where to plant it. Deal?"

"How exciting. I can't wait to see what happens."

"I can't either, sweetheart. You know how I love to watch things grow from seed," said Azora.

The car horn blew and reminded them both that people were waiting. Melissa hugged her grandmother one last time and quickly ran back to the car. As soon as she slammed the door shut, Seth stepped on the gas, his hand gesturing goodbye.

Azora leaned against the giant hickory tree and waved one final farewell. She looked down the road until they turned the corner and could no longer be seen.

Dauber, Sticky, and the other critters in the woods watched Azora linger under the hickory tree for quite some time. When the last bit of dust stirred up by the car found its way back to the quiet road, she slowly walked back to the now empty house, her head lowered and her shoulders slumped.

In an attempt to help their neighbor feel a little less forlorn, Dauber and Sticky requested the assistance of a few friends. So the lightning bugs glowed a little bit brighter that night, and the frogs croaked in perfect harmony. Thanks to her faith and God's amazing creatures, Azora felt a sense of peace that surpassed all understanding. She missed her loved ones, but she knew that someday soon they would all be together again.

ABOUT THE AUTHOR

J. Suthern Hicks was born in Little Rock, Arkansas. Shortly after his birth he moved with his parents to Thailand where his father was stationed in the United States Army. Thai became his first language, and when he returned to Arkansas at age five, he quickly learned to speak English—with a southern accent. He currently resides in Los Angeles, California where he has written several plays, including the acclaimed "Turtle Tears," which received accolades in 1995 from the Los Angeles Times, and Critics' Choice from the LA Weekly. His academic article, "Television theme songs: A content analysis," was published in "Popular Music and Society" while he was still a graduate student. In January 2013, the band "Seven Years" recorded a collection of his songs which are now on iTunes. Mr. Hicks' children's book, "Charlie and Chocolate's Purrfect Prayer," was published in 2014.

Made in the USA
San Bernardino, CA
17 April 2016